Praise for *Writing Landscape*

"An object lesson in attentive l[...]
intense ... a small book, but a [...]

"A really inspirational read ... a [...] the
hand and puts your fingers in the sand and soil ... a call
to meditation." —Alistair Braidwood, *Scots Whay Hae*

Praise for *Doubling Back*

"Cracknell wonderfully explores the strange durability
of the paths that we make in our lives, in our dreams
and after our deaths." —Robert Macfarlane, author of
Underland and *The Old Ways*

"Cracknell has a rare gift for conjuring experience."
—*The Great Outdoors Magazine*

"A winning combination of memoir, travelogue and
literary meditation." —*Daily Mail*

"With Cracknell's writing, you don't so much see the
landscape as feel it." —*Scotsman*

"Not so much a book to inspire you to do her walks,
but to challenge you to enjoy your own walks more.
Refreshing, lovely, fun: good walking and good writing."
—Sara Maitland, author of *From the Forest* and *A Book
of Silence*

"Like a multicoloured tapestry, memory and imagination
are beautifully evoked by the varied landscapes where
Linda Cracknell walked ... a joy to read." —Raja
Shehadeh, author of *Palestinian Walks: Forays into a
Vanishing Landscape*

Also by Linda Cracknell

Short Story Collections
Life Drawing
The Searching Glance

Novels
Call of the Undertow
The Other Side of Stone

Non-Fiction
Writing Landscape: Taking Note, Making Notes
Doubling Back: Paths trodden in memory
A Wilder Vein (Editor)

For Sally

Sea Marked

Throwing a Line
to a Coastal Past

with thanks for reading

Linda Cracknell

Linda Cracknell

Saraband

Published by Saraband
3 Clairmont Gardens
Glasgow, G3 7LW
www.saraband.net

ISBN: 9781916812505

Printed and bound in Great Britain by Clays Ltd, Elcograf S.p.A.

10 9 8 7 6 5 4 3 2 1

MIX
Paper | Supporting
responsible forestry
FSC® C018072

We are grateful to Creative Scotland and the National Lottery
Fund for financial support enabling the publication of this book.

ALBA | CHRUTHACHAIL

LOTTERY FUNDED

For Emily, Tom and Livi

'Consider them both, the sea and land; and do you
not find a strange analogy to something in yourself?
... God keep thee! Push not off from that isle,
thou canst never return.'

Herman Melville, *Moby Dick,* Chapter 58

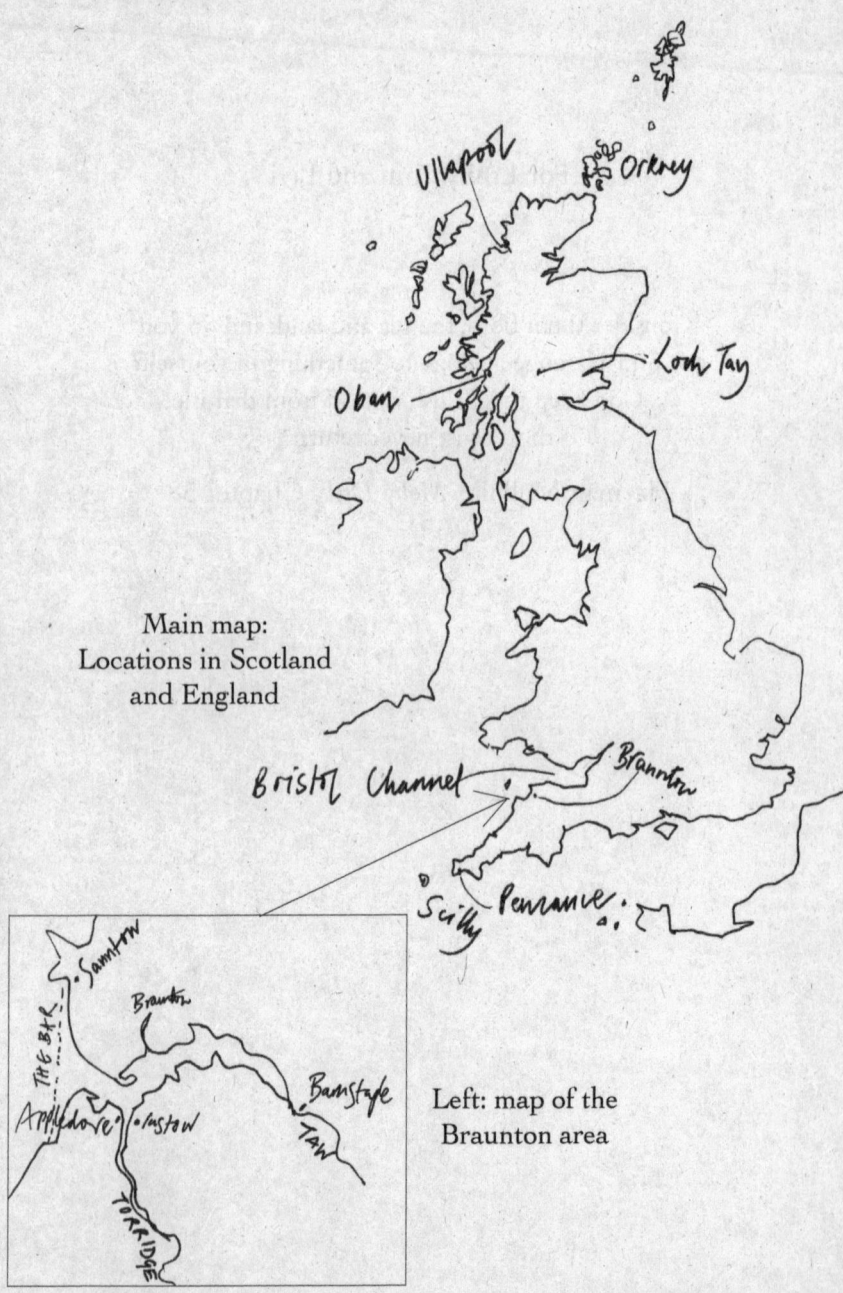

Main map:
Locations in Scotland
and England

Left: map of the
Braunton area

Contents

Diagram of a Ketch

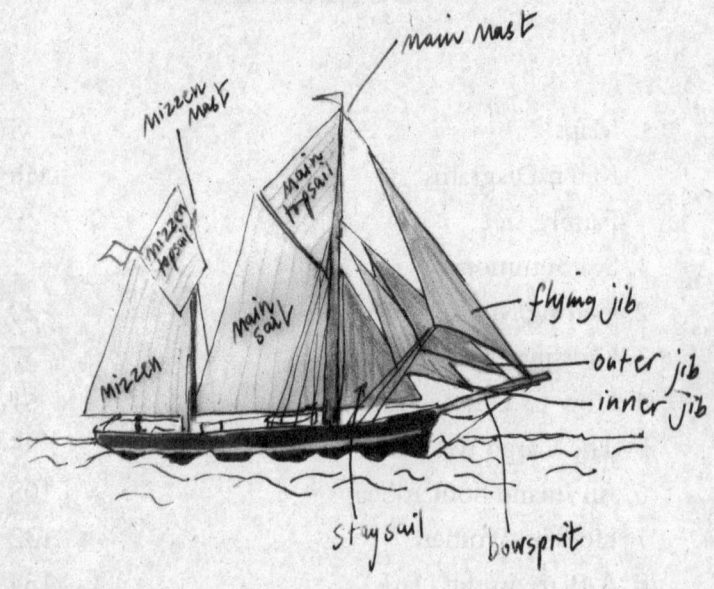

main mast

mizzen mast

mizzen topsail

main topsail

mizzen

main sail

flying jib

outer jib

inner jib

staysail

bowsprit

Sketch of a Skiff

St Ayles Skiff

Three Braunton Ketches

Pirate

- Built: Stromness, Orkney 1888
- Owners: Francis Drake senior and junior, Robert Drake, Holly Berry, J Hartnoll, Annie Lock Drake, William Drake
- Broken up in 1928

Emma Louise

- Built: Barnstaple 1883
- Named after Emma Louise Chichester/Drake
- First owner: Francis Drake, Samuel Berry
- Hulked in 1953

Bessie Ellen

- Built Plymouth 1907
- Named after first owner's daughters
- First owner: John Squire Chichester
- Still sailing

Francis Hacche Drake — M — Mary Gould

Francis Gould Drake — M — Mary Gorrill

Thomas How — M — Mary Ann Hartnoll

Francis Drake — M — Emma Louise Chichester

Josiah Roach — M — Agnes How

5 others   Francis   Robert Drake — M — Annie Lock Roach

Francis   Dorothy 'Granny' — M — Ernest Michael

Richard Cracknell — M — mother: Jennifer or 'Jill'

sister   brother   Linda

Sea Summons

I'd forgotten about my mother's sailing trip, when around 5pm my phone rang and a voice burst down the line with no greeting: 'I've just had the most fantastic Christmas present!'

It took me a moment to realise who it was because the excitable tone was unfamiliar and I wasn't used to her phoning me. Then the explosion of my own response – the prickle in my eyes – took me by surprise. 'You did?'

'Fantastic!' Each syllable stretched to its extreme.

It was a rare moment. Emotional territory was inferred but not usually communicated between us. This occasion seemed to sweep away barriers and a great welling caught me off guard; a mixture of relief and joy. At eighty-four years of age my mother had embraced an adventure foisted on her by her children.

It turned out that the weather had been good, winds helpful. They were able to have all eight sails up; a full rig. And my mother had taken the helm. Yes, she had! It came back to her, she said, from her days sailing on the Norfolk Broads as a young woman with my father and an Oxford professor of entomology obliquely connected to the Cracknell family.

'Perhaps you never forget it,' she said. 'The knack.'

I'd noticed the half-day trip in *Bessie Ellen's* itinerary for Easter, leaving from Newlyn, which was a fifteen-minute walk from our mother's home in Penzance. She would be aboard a historic small ship with a family connection.

I proposed it as a joint Christmas present from the three of us. My sister was dubious.

'Do you really think she'd do it? She doesn't really go anywhere any more,' she reminded me on the phone, 'so on a ship?'

My mother was still living independently but it seemed to be a long time since she'd ventured beyond the bounds of Penzance.

I tried my brother. 'Great idea,' he said.

So together we took a chance and booked her aboard quickly, before the places filled. I corresponded briefly with Nikki Alford, the skipper-owner. I wasn't sure my mother would be able to climb a two-metre vertical ladder, a capability which clients were asked to guarantee.

'No problem on this trip,' Nikki said. 'We'll be tying up alongside the pier, so she'll just be able to come across on the boardwalk.'

On vellum paper I printed the pierhead painting of the ship in full sail with a brief history of her building in Plymouth, her launch there in 1907 and her current status as one of the last West Country trading ketches still sailing from a former fleet of nearly seven hundred. Underneath I wrote: 'We have booked you on a trip on *Bessie Ellen* around Mount's Bay 1st April 2016.' I felt proud. It was unusual for me to take the initiative as the youngest of three, forever the 'baby' and the least diligent in attention to our mother.

'Oh, how super, thank you,' she had said, reacting as ever with a sense of surprised appreciation. And later: 'I shall look forward to that.'

As the time drew near I wondered whether she would actually make it. There were a few (unusual) phone calls. Which pier exactly would the ship be at in Newlyn? What should she wear? Perhaps she should take a taxi.

She had been a great walker and outdoor painter, never happier than when wandering over the headlands of West Penwith amongst flower-filled hedges with binoculars, sketchpad, paints and a small canvas-seated stool. She still took an intelligent interest in many things, but recently there was a sense of her having retired from the outdoor life beyond pottering in her own tiny terraced garden. There, she managed to grow flamboyant Echium and Datura in the subtropical climate of West Cornwall despite the occasional lash of salt spray that swept over high buildings from the promenade to reach her a two-minute walk inland. She now accessed the wider world through TV, newspapers and numerous books, from the cradle of her sofa.

I pictured her as anxiety built, agonising over one of the infamous lists she tended to do weeks in advance of going away. It's a habit that both my sister and I have noted in ourselves; a growing resistance to the distraction from our routine which makes departures into a major challenge.

I became sure she wouldn't go. She'd catch a cold and not feel up to it or the weather forecast would impose a struggle between her and Newlyn harbour. I felt bad that I had suggested it, handing her a challenge she would rather not have had.

As I was only eighteen months old when my father died, I had never felt at the centre of my mother's gaze. I'd come at the tail end of our family life and seemed to remain trailing behind. Although fair-minded and non-judgemental, my mother rarely had the opportunity to participate in any approving family rituals of my adulthood as I didn't marry or have children. I've had different careers, travelled and had a number of partners. When I began writing in the late 1990s, she applauded my publishing successes and was kind in her responses to me when occasionally I disclosed more personal aspects of my life. But she rarely asked questions or offered views.

In 1990 I'd moved from Devon to Scotland because of a love affair with land and mountains. Over half my lifetime later I still call Scotland 'home'. Envious of those who could name their exact geographical origins, I certainly do not 'belong' to suburban Surrey where I grew up. But even when I arranged my mother's sail, with my seventh decade coming into view, I didn't have a clear answer to where I came from.

My relationship with my mother became characterised by distance once we lived at opposite ends of the British Isles, 612 miles apart. She used to make the journey north by train for an annual visit, and loved to explore glens and coasts with her paintbox. But the journey became too much, and her visits stopped. We had intermittent phone conversations, exchanging any news, our recent weather, our gardens and books. But always it was up to me to call.

I went to Cornwall once or twice a year to visit and the pressure-cooker proximity often made us prickly with each other. I was drawn, always with her blessing, outdoors and away from the overheated house onto the cliff paths to walk alone amongst violets in all seasons, above the dramatic chasm of cliffs falling to white sand and turquoise sea, breakers smashing against granite. It was as if I had to keep the bounds beaten of the known places, the names recited by our family: Lamorna, Penberth, Porthgwarra, Porthcurno, Pendeen. My relationship with her was conflated with my love for where she lived.

I often felt a longing for those places at other times; a feeling keen as the ache of a *person's* absence. This plucky peninsula flung out into the Atlantic had worked its way into my bones over fifty years, freighted with memories of growing up, family holidays, motorbiking trips, climbing and walking with friends, a former partner. These days, though, it was particularly associated with my mother.

Eager to get outdoors soon after each arrival, my first walk always took me west along the promenade to Newlyn. As the enclosing headland of Mount's Bay swings south, a steep hill is stacked with whitewashed and granite cottages. Below them lies a sheltered harbour dating back to the fifteenth century. This dynamic place of rope-worn quay, engine chug, the banter of men, had always drawn us to watch comings and goings. My mother might still mention in a phone call some new recognition for the former Ice Works or a rare catch of skipjack tuna. Up to forty different species of fresh fish are auctioned each morning at the adjacent fish market, including hake, turbot, mackerel and cuttlefish as well as the unsung megrim sole and spider crab.

I would continue beyond Newlyn with open sea now to my left for a mile or so, passing the old Penlee lifeboat station. It was after launching from here in December 1981 that the whole crew of the *Solomon Browne* were lost while attempting to rescue those onboard a stricken coaster during a Force 12 hurricane. When a father and son volunteered for duty, the lifeboat coxswain turned the younger man away: 'No more than one from a family on a night like this.' The son was told, 'You'll go next time.' Because it was Christmas, two children and a pregnant woman had been on board the coaster in addition to the crew.

All lost.

Always I paused here.

The compact, hill-backed village I would reach next – Mousehole, pronounced 'Mowzle' – was depleted that night of husbands and brothers, fathers and sons. It was a place rich in tradition just before Christmas, with the male voice choir singing in the pub and illuminations turned on in the harbour. 'Stargazy Pie' was baked, filled with seven varieties of fish, pilchard's heads breaking the crust on 'Tom Bawcock's Eve'. In the time our family had known it, the village had become gentrified by the many visitors, second-home owners with Farrow-and-Ball-painted plaques on cottages squeezed into tight terraces between harbour and cliff. Fishing families had been edged out.

Nevertheless, when my walk brought me here, I would enjoy drinking coffee on the harbour wall and sometimes, if the tide was right, watching a group of women gather around a pilot gig. They would launch through the narrow harbour entrance between two piers with a cox and six rowers aboard, each with one oar. The sleek, long shape caught the eye, as did the unity of the crew's rhythm forward and back. The gig cut out into sparkle and grew smaller against a wide horizon.

My mother always took pleasure in seeing them too, these boats that were once a necessity for pilotage and sometimes used as lifeboats. Rowing them has become a sport but with an authenticity that hefts it to a particularly Cornish tradition. An association of pilot gigs was created in 1986, running regattas, courses and standardising the boats. Clubs have been established as far away as the Essex coast although the greatest concentration remains in Cornwall, Devon and the Isles of Scilly where the world pilot gig championships are raced each May.

I'd often feel a tidal drag of longing on those visits, these walks. I wished to be more than a spectator, to 'belong' to a place circumscribed by tides; a place where the social mix included rowers, fishermen and old sea captains who enjoyed a long salt-lineage and could read the sea's subtext. The physical exertion of rowing, the camaraderie and the close contact with the sea appealed deeply. If I lived here, I'd seek the bravery to join the rowers.

I was dimly aware of a parallel movement developing in Scotland, with a different style of coastal rowing boat. But I lived as far inland as is possible.

My mother's rug-covered sitting-room table always held a display of large hardback books arranged face-up. Botany, American history, painters and ships. When I visited, I'd sit in an armchair leafing through them. I realise now that I should instead have been paying more attention to her, telling her about my life or listening to her stories.

I'd learnt of *Bessie Ellen*, on a visit the year before her sail, from a new book amongst these titled *Braunton: Home of the Last Sailing Coasters*. A cousin of my mother's in Exeter had written to tell her about it. The two women had never been in regular contact, so a special excitement following the cousin's visit to a museum at Appledore in North Devon must have prompted the letter. It included a hand-written list of ships' names that had been owned at one time in the extended family, including *Three Brothers*, *Sir Francis Drake* and rather pleasingly, a *Linda*.

Curious, my mother had sent off for the book, which I leafed through on that visit. It recorded vessels of the late nineteenth and early twentieth century with a home port of Braunton, where my Granny had grown up. These were small wooden sailing ships which distributed vital cargoes, mostly around the coasts of the Irish Sea, Bristol Channel and West Country, and were remarkable for continuing to use sails so late. Such vessels had been seen as merely utilitarian and then, with the introduction of the combustion engine, became obsolete and forgotten. Their histories had only recently been considered worthy of recording.

I flicked through the book, enjoying the photographs and paintings, the potted history of each ship which included exchanges of ownership, the fitting of motors, and finally their demise through wreck or abandonment. The ownership of a surprising number was attributed to Drakes – perhaps Granny's father, uncles, grandfather – as well as attributed to surnames like Chichester, Newcombe and Huxtable, families my mother understood us to be related to in some way.

'But how exactly?'

She grimaced at the thought of working it out: 'I couldn't tell you.'

She, and the three of us in my generation, knew we came from a seafaring family with many Francis Drakes amongst our forebears and a supposed connection back to the sixteenth century piratical one through our maternal grandmother – but none of us had ever explored how much of this was true.

Initially I was surprised by my mother's interest as she'd distanced herself from her own mother in her early adulthood. She hadn't known her Drake grandparents, had not nurtured relationships with other relatives on her mother's side as far as I knew, and was unfamiliar with Braunton, where they had all come from. But somehow the appeal of these ships suggested for her a legacy that she did value.

According to the book, the first owner of *Bessie Ellen* was a Chichester. This observation prompted my mother to pull from a shelf an 1830 illustrated collection of Tennyson's poetry, the flyleaf imprinted with her great-grandmother's monogram: Emma Chichester. At the same time she excavated a rudimentary family tree she had sketched as a teenager.

Although *Bessie Ellen* was a much larger vessel than she had sailed on before, my mother said she had felt 'at home'. Perhaps it was also in her blood and bones, she said – this great-granddaughter of master mariner Francis Drake and his wife Emma Louise Chichester.

I exchanged e-mails with the skipper-owner.

'Linda, she was brilliant!' Nikki wrote.

On first reading in the Braunton Coasters book that a youngish woman had 'rescued' *Bessie Ellen* and made her fit for sailing holidays, I'd imagined someone rather well off and aloof. But it was soon clear Nikki was warm and genuine, simply delighting in her ship bringing enjoyment and adventure to others.

It turned out they had not been able to tie up at the Newlyn pier after all. All the clients had to get into a RIB to cross the harbour and then climb the rope ladder slung over the side of the ship. My mother not only managed it, but loved the experience. I wrote to Nikki of the family connection and she told me what she knew of the Chichesters – a lowlier branch of them than those at Arlington Court – and she said: 'I would love to meet you and hear more about all the stories, and if you do get the urge … come for a sail – wherever we are.'

A few days after my mother's trip, Nikki forwarded a photo of the 'amazing older lady' taken by another client on board. I ordered a print and sent it to my mother. In the photo, she's caught sitting sideways on the wheel box, bare hands broad and strong on the wheel, concentrating but relaxed and looking ahead. I can see that she's well wrapped up, afraid of being cold. A small handbag is slung crossways over her shoulders. No great luggage. She looks confident and fearless. If I didn't know her I would have taken her for a younger woman.

She was evidently proud of herself. Despite her apparent determination to throw off the past, the Drake family connection seemed to add value for her. And she loved *Bessie Ellen*. I was delighted to have helped bring about such a meaningful experience. I wondered if I was behaving in more of an adult way with her now, rather than forever playing the tetchy teenager?

For both of us the sea, the coast, seemed to be a compulsion. For me it was linked in some obscure way with a sense of melancholy – my territory in literature and music – unnameable feelings about water, salt, and the curved horizon. This was too mysterious, vague and uncharted a connection to easily discuss, but it attached itself to my interest in timber and canvas, the materiality tangible in these seafarers' lives.

My mother had always seemed to me in some way unknowable, unreachable despite her incredible flair and competence at so many things through my childhood and beyond. Although descended from these mariners, great navigators of the Atlantic and the Bristol Channel, I recall an incident, probably from the early days of her remarriage, when I was about eight. I was still timid with Hugh, my new stepfather, and short of words, standing listening to him whilst my mother sat quietly nearby, a little abashed.

'Your mother's a silly old stick, isn't she?' he said.

He went on to tell me that the previous day, while driving home from the boarding school where she'd returned my siblings after their day's leave, she had got lost. So lost and confused that she had 'handed herself in' at a police station. He poked gentle fun at her, but there was an implication that she'd had little idea *who* she was and this didn't seem funny at all.

This loss of direction happened as she drove Surrey roads and lanes not so far from home on a route she knew well. There was nothing dotty or whimsical about my mother at that time. I found it disturbing. Perhaps all these years later, she was still seeking her bearings within her family too.

I had long loved historic sailing ships in a blind, unknowing sort of way and I think my mother had too. Because I was curious, I bought my own copy of the Braunton Coasters book.

Although we'd been a nuclear family in inland Surrey, my higher education was in Exeter where my mother had grown up and my 'Granny Michael' (née Drake) still lived at the time. I carried on living in the area for some years afterwards, calling it home, and initially getting involved in museum work. I helped refurbish wooden vessels at the Exeter Maritime Museum as a volunteer and even sailed on one or two of them. Although my grandmother, 'Granny', had grown up in Braunton and spoke of it often, I was too young to take much notice and she died when I was in my early twenties. The family connection to North Devon and the knowledge of all those master mariners seemed lost.

As I leafed through the Coasters book, I took note when the names Drake and Chichester appeared against Braunton vessels. If they also had some link to Scotland, I was even more interested. Two in particular caught my eye. *Emma Louise* had been built in Barnstaple in 1883 and was later associated with both Aberdeenshire and far-north Wick in Caithness. The first owner was my great-great-grandfather Francis Drake, and the ship named after his wife. Later, their son, Granny's father Robert, owned shares too.

Alongside details of each ship's history, the book presented the vessels in colour plates as captured by 'pierhead painters'. These are no Turners, even though they portray the vessels riding the waves. The ships are stylised, flattened, seen beam-on to display their best attributes. The composition is formulaic; the maritime background of each looking much like another. But each ship is unique in colour, length, beam and rig. Typically self-taught, workish men with access to materials, pierhead painters could make a living by appealing to the pride of local shipowners, capturing their precious beauties as if in the controlled space of a racehorse paddock rather than the wild sea. Yet the paintings were accurate, and became important keepsakes for owners.

Although smacks and schooners also sailed from Braunton in this period, most ships featured in the book are gaff-rigged ketches – two-masted with eight sails. They could be sailed by just two men (and usually a boy) and were agile, so suitable for coastal waters. The rig is comprised of four smaller triangular foresails including three jibs curving, when wind-filled, from the bow sprit. The gaff is a spar that supports the head of the mainsail, raising the stern end of the sail to create the distinctive diagonal shape. It leaves a triangular gap between peak and mainmast, into which a topsail can be fitted. A smaller gaff sail, the mizzen, is hoisted on a mast at the stern, also with its own topsail. Generally, more canvas means greater power, but different combinations of these sails would suit different conditions and the captain, knowing his ship intimately, would judge this.

Pirate, with her rascally and unusual name, was the second Drake ship with a Scottish link. The pierhead painting in the book, reproduced courtesy of a John Hartnoll, displays her with all eight sails hoisted and tautly trimmed whilst a steamer chugs in the background across a choppy sea and yellowy sky. Along *Pirate*'s black hull between bowsprit and sloping transom, is a long line in white, curling into decorative flourishes fore and aft, and of course, bearing her name. Two small figures are visible on deck, one at the wheel, and another just before him, close to the shorter 'mizzen' mast. My forebears perhaps.

From 1900 Francis Drake owned *Pirate*, with Robert and his brother Francis (junior) taking her on a few years later. She had originally been built in 1888, and first owned, in Stromness, Orkney. It puzzled me that the Drakes would look so far away for a ketch that was fundamentally the same as those built close to home. But this cross-Britain axis seemed a loose echo of my own adult geography, the far north and the south-west of Britain reflecting my life in Scotland since 1990 and, before that, in Devon from 1978, as well as my mother's locus in West Cornwall. The connection was pleasing and prompted my first response to this boat-shaped ancestry.

Invited to contribute to a community arts project in Caithness commemorating the maiden voyage of the emigrant ship Westland from Scotland to New Zealand in 1879, I printed a special page to fold into an origami boat. I copied onto one side of the page an Admiralty chart of the Pentland Firth, the northerly stretch of sea between the Caithness coast and Orkney whose tidal race is amongst the fastest in the world. Onto the other side I printed the tricky tidal waters and encircling land of the Taw-Torridge estuary and Bideford Bar, home of my Drake forebears. I called my folded ship *Pirate*. She was hung on a mooring line from the ceiling of Thurso Town Hall with a harbour-full of others from around the world.

My blog post about this paper ship put me in touch with someone working in the Orkney Archive at Kirkwall Library. Coincidentally, on the archive's own blog they had recently commented on a record they'd found of the transfer of a locally built ship named *Pirate* into the ownership of a man from Devon.

'And guess what his name was?' the archivist had written on the blog. 'Yes, Francis Drake!'

I relished this echo of my own delight.

Giving expression in words, images or materials to an object, past event or place connects me to it viscerally. By giving it attention, the 'spark' of it stays stowed inside me, valued, and sometimes demanding further exploration. This small creative act with a piece of paper and the embryonic story of my family's ships, their strange geographies – their tragedies and presumed joys – led me on to the journey documented in this book.

I am no natural seafarer. As a child I was afraid of water. After any day in which I'd glimpsed a pool or river or pond, I dreamt of crossing a high bridge over a stretch of water in the family car. The bridge at some point would collapse but I always woke before hitting the water, disturbed and tearful.

My memories of learning to swim remain full of clamour; chlorine-tinged and with children's screams echoing wetly from tiled walls and rising up into a glass roof above brick. Fierce, adult shouting was also part of the clamour. The source has remained Churchillian-shaped in my memory after nearly sixty years: Kennedy, a military commander who tested my readiness to swim, aged seven. The minimum age was supposed to be eight but my mother must have been particularly keen for me to learn. For the test, he pushed me with a long bamboo cane, away from where I clung to the side of the pool, into water in which I was out of my depth. It was literally 'sink or swim'. Somehow I passed the test. I seem to remember that 'passing' didn't mean you *swam* on finding yourself 'at sea', but that you didn't cry. I can be pretty sure that I *did* cry. I was a timid, wailing creature as the youngest, always left behind on walks and complaining that things 'weren't fair'.

The short, weekly drive to the military baths in Aldershot from our Camberley home gave my stomach time to somersault with sickly nerves. I suppose I learnt something about swimming there but I didn't thrive. When everyone else in my class was aiming for their 200 yards' badge, I only managed 75 and left it at that.

At around the same age came my first attempt at sailing. The location was a flooded gravel pit where family friends kept a dinghy. I remember gripping the gunwales with white knuckles when the vessel heeled over as wind filled the sail. I probably cried then too and spent the rest of the day playing on a boat pulled out onto good, solid land, which suited me much better. That day became memorable because I was knocked breathless when I fell heavily backwards onto the ground and for the first time felt my mortality.

It wasn't until we began going to Cornwall each summer through my teenage years, and I spent two weeks with salt-stiffened hair, on and off body-boards and hurling myself against the surf, fizzing with exhilaration, that the sea gripped me. Sometimes I'd challenge incoming waves, jumping them. Once or twice I lost my balance, and was dragged in a white and gritty maelstrom, unsure which way was air.

The ferocity of my dreams was startling when I returned from these sea-lashed wildernesses to the brick bounds of our Surrey home. Each dream differed slightly in the location and how far I'd committed myself to the water; up to my ankles or already swimming out of my depth. Thematically though, the dream was consistent. The sight of an approaching oversized wave turned me for the shore whilst at the same time sucking me back into its undertow. I was unable to make my escape. I didn't know of tsunamis then, but it seemed my subconscious did: waves which broke with exaggerated force, crashing high inland and tumbling me in the watery, unbreathable chaos.

Although when living near Exeter I often smelt brine, the open sea itself was a journey away. While at art college I took sketchbooks out onto various beaches to observe the sea from the shore. I seemed to be preoccupied with anticipating when and where each rolling wave would shatter into surf. In pencil or paint or charcoal I began trying to capture their power and in particular this moment just before their breaking. One day a tutor, Peter Pay, looking at my drawings, remarked that if I was interested in waves, I should look out for the work of Wilhelmina Barns-Graham.

'There's an exhibition of her work on in St Ives at the moment. Why don't you go?'

I needed little more encouragement; I collected my friend and fellow student, Jane, and we hitch-hiked to St Ives with a tent. Looking back, this shows the same restlessness that still drives me – the need to make every enquiry into a physical act, taking me away from home on foot or bicycle or by sticking out my thumb. On discovery of Barns-Graham's work, particularly her seascapes, I fell into her spell. She used pen, ink and oil on card, parallel lines acting as contours to capture marine muscularity. She had a way of freezing in time an energetic sea so that it became sculptural, landscape-like, but never exactly still. In one image of a wave at its point of curling and tightening, the centre of the maelstrom feels claustrophobic and inescapable. My chest constricted. When I returned from St Ives, my task seemed to have become to solidify a series of waves into Plaster of Paris as if in an attempt to make the sea safe.

My mountain fastness home for the last thirty years makes me an inlander. Despite this, from certain Perthshire hills on a day of westerlies I fancy I can scent a low-tide tang funnelling through the glens. Iodine and seaweed. When winter brings a cormorant inland and I glimpse it on the Tay River wrestling with an eel, or when, in March, oystercatchers return, they summon me salt-wards, filling me with longing to be where land and sea meet.

I am a walker, a mountaineer. I spent a few years documenting a series of adventures on foot which bound memory to earth, rock and ice. This seemed to be my territory, the underfoot reverberations of land and the past, this *Doubling Back,* as I called the resulting book. In one of those journeys, I followed my own father on an Alpine climb because when he died I was too young to have retained a memory of him. The journey gave me a sense of connection to somebody I *should* have known.

Once my mother had taken the helm of *Bessie Ellen*, I was nudged towards finding my own place in our seafaring line, following the ships' wakes. As a writer of memory, place and movement, my mission began to raise its head from the deep.

The sea would be new and alien territory, but I reassured myself there was also land and houses from which all those master mariners must have launched themselves: a physical place, stories to discover of Drakes, Newcombes and Chichesters. I would picture their cargoes and their journeys, imagine their lifestyles and inhabit the places they interacted with. Perhaps I could rescue our collective seafaring past from amnesia, excavating what we ought to have known more about – the ordinary people in our family who had working lives that by today's standards seem extraordinary.

My usual method when on the scent of a writing project has been active, place-based, self-reliant and solitary. But this one should involve my mother. Although her mind remained lively, I knew I wouldn't persuade her beyond her rooms, the Penzance promenade, shops and library. I would have to explore for us both and report back to her about quays, harbours, sea roads; men called Drake with rough-skinned hands and eyes turned to the horizon. It wouldn't be a detailed genealogy. My impulse was to fit myself and my mother into a broader geometry of lives and places.

Reflecting on this departure eight years later, I glimpse, flashing darkly beneath the surface aim, the submerged notion that I might win my mother's approval. I've struck out independently all my adult life, yet there seemed a need in me even at this stage of adulthood to be 'mothered' – to have her affection and approval confirmed.

Braunton was only 120 miles from Penzance so if I went there to explore, I would also see more of her, perhaps overcome the reserve between us and my childish urge for distance. A shared project might give our remaining years on the planet together a purpose – something for us to talk about. As she was in her mid-eighties the implication of doing this was 'before it's too late'.

I mustered my forces. The 'explorer', archivist, detective, memorialist and daughter opened the door and stepped out.

Getting My Bearings

October 2016. A train took me from Exeter to Barnstaple, where salt and freshwater mix and a grand stone bridge spans the Taw River at the final feasible point. I could see from the Ordnance Survey map that beyond this point the river rapidly widens under a high flyover and joins a broad eight-mile-long thoroughfare of sand, mud, gravel and sometime-water. It then collects the River Torridge and continues out to the infamous Bideford Bar and thus the open sea.

I caught a bus for the 5 miles from Barnstaple to Braunton, crossing flat fields that edge the north shore of the ever-widening estuary. A plateau of silver-mud spread, fringed with small, seeping creeks and sparkling with scattered seabirds: low tide. I glimpsed a winding ribbon of continuous water, sometimes close, sometimes far toward the other shore. It was a strangely exciting sight from the top deck of the bus.

And then I was enclosed by shopfronts, amidst traffic-carved crevasses, screened from sea or salt-scent. I walked away from the Squires fish and chip restaurant, up through narrowing crooked streets, whitewashed cottages, into old Devon: St Brannock's Church and the Black Horse pub at the top of the village. Close by was a small bed-and-breakfast run by a woman who had just passed her eightieth birthday and was surrounded by cards and balloons.

I began my exploration the next day by visiting the museum in the centre of the village. Within the small, cluttered interior were model ships, displays of photographs, navigational instruments and ropes. Songs and films played on a loop and interlocking lives were captured in fragments, implying a whole community heritage. Where I found the name 'Drake' in records collated from local newspapers, I made quick notes of marriages, births and deaths. I tried to match the names to my mother's sketched family tree and I learnt where the graveyards were.

A pictorial map of the North Devon coast hung on the museum wall. The sea itself, blank in the maps I use for walking, was dense with tiny stylised ships, each one named and representing a wreck between the eighteenth century and as recently as 1981. It left no doubt about the menace of these shores. The longest list was reserved for the narrowing entrance to the estuary; so extensive that it had to be treated schematically, the vessels' names pushed way out to sea with an arrow attaching them back to their wreck location. The Bideford Bar had taken, amongst many others, *Reliance* in 1869, *Dasher* in 1850 and, presumably one of its own, *Torridge* in 1853.

Another map from 1889 revealed the 'Great Field' in an intricate tapestry of stripe and colour. This is arable land between the coastal marshlands and Braunton which has been farmed, unfenced, and under a strip field system since medieval times. It is one of only two examples remaining in Britain and needs protecting not just for its agricultural use, but for its historical significance. I recalled then, the only thing I was aware of 'knowing' about Braunton as I grew up, that my mother's cousin John Drake owned some land here.

It soon felt more urgent to discover the place outside the museum. I had never been here before, had no bearings, knew no one and arrived with an unclear enquiry. I knew only that moving my body through a place is often an answer; *the* answer. I only had a couple of days.

Using a map from the museum and the new knowledge gained from their records, I soon found the white, plain-fronted Georgian house in Heanton Street on a sloping terrace of similar houses with sash windows, three up, two down. My Granny, Dorothy Louise, had been brought up here by her father, Master Mariner Robert Drake, and mother, Annie Lock Drake (née Roach). Robert's father Francis had earlier raised his own fleet of sons and daughters in the same house. It was from here the men departed to sea, and in Granny's case to London and sometime later, marriage. Although for twelve years I'd lived only 40 or 50 miles away in the Exeter area, I had never visited her birthplace either with or without her. The generational fracture seemed to have made it irrelevant until now; our maritime legacy near-mythical rather than 'true'.

I stood and smiled at the blank windows that gave nothing away, surprised by how easy it had been to locate the stone and slate of a home, converting an address on paper into a real building within which named lives had been nurtured. Spurred on by this find, I went to look for the graveyards.

I found the first owner of *Bessie Ellen*, John (known as Jack) Squire Chichester in the Congregational Churchyard close to Heanton Street. He had a flamboyant stone carved with a massive anchor and chain which bore a scant version of the story of his accidental death on *Bessie Ellen* in 1920.

My mother had only the vaguest memories of being taken to Braunton as a young child. She'd written to me before this trip asking if I could find out anything about the Verneys in Braunton. As a child she had, with her mother, visited a great aunt called Evelyn in a humble thatched cottage called the Myrtles.

'I was probably paraded around dressed up like Shirley Temple,' she'd said in a phone call, her voice sharpening. This had become a repeated complaint against her mother, especially since sight of a studio photo of her aged about eight that I'd used on her 80th birthday card – her blonde hair coiled and lacquered at her ears.

This great aunt Evelyn had been related to her father's family – nothing to do with Drakes or Chichesters – and I'd felt a slight irritation that this interested her more than the seafaring heritage and 'our' project. Nevertheless I photographed a Verney grave for her in the Congregational Churchyard.

A short walk across the village, in the graveyard known as Christchurch, a Methodist/United reformed Church, was a stone for William Drake who died in 1940. The sketched family tree showed he was one of Robert's brothers. My mother had told me that her great-uncle William and his wife Mary were considered rich and successful. They had moved away to the south coast in Torquay with their two daughters. Nevertheless, their sense of connection to this village brought them all back to be buried here.

I'd expected, because of records from the museum, to find here my more immediate relatives, Robert and his father Francis. But despite hours spent searching stone to stone to stone, I left disappointed.

I would beat some bounds instead.

I found my way down to the southern edge of the village and to Velator Quay. It had been built in the 1870s for new, and larger, cargo ships to load and unload following the straightening of the river Caen that allowed them access well inland of the estuary. The quay was empty now.

It was low tide and the narrow, silted-up creek (or 'pill' as these tidal reaches are known within the Bristol Channel) tipped over its small, relict vessels onto mud. The width of the Channel seemed crazily confined for the number and size of ships that belonged here in the late nineteenth and early twentieth century.

I decided to walk towards the Taw-Torridge estuary following the South West Coast Path raised on a flood-defence bank beside the pill. To my right, west, lush cattle-grazed land was crisscrossed by drainage channels reminiscent of reclaimed land in the Netherlands; fields known as The Marshes.

I came to a junction where the pill shoreline was interrupted by a large sluice gate. The road and flood bank veered away west here, following the original path of the Caen River. But the footpath crossed over the sluice and, staying close to the shore, followed two edges of a triangle of marshy land known as Horsey Island; land reclaimed from the sea in 1850. It was now providing a habitat for egrets and herons (and at that time, according to a bird-watcher I met, an off-course pelican).

The pill met the estuary at a harp-shaped point of land, and I looked across to where the Torridge joined the Taw. Opposite me, on the far side of the doubled estuary, distant white cottages clambered up the streets of Appledore. At the most seaward point of this village, an orange lifeboat was moored. Everything else spread around me, sea-level flat, a mosaic of mud and water.

I walked the estuary shore towards the coast following a cobbled wall defending the freshwater marshland of Horsey Island from salt water. Where the path met the road and flood-bank again, stood the so-called 'White House'.

Lonely, on the edge of no-man's-land, it tells of some former status. Historic maps, I found, suggest its real name as Crow Beach House or Ferry House.

Before walking on towards the Bar and open sea, I turned around to read a sign for walkers approaching the sea wall in the other direction, forbidding cyclists and dogs without leads. I was intrigued to see it signed 'By order of the Marsh Inspector.' I'd been struggling, as I walked, to rationalise this mesh of low land and water against the OS map. Now it seemed this liminal place between Braunton, the estuary and the coast 'proper' was overseen by someone with arcane knowledge, mystic authority over the balance of water and land and over all those who ventured here: a Marsh Inspector. I tried to imagine their appearance – would there be a uniform or special hat? Perhaps they'd materialise out of marsh-fog only when circumstances called for their special skills.

In the evening I went to the Black Horse Inn for a meal and pints of brown beer. Men flooded into the bar in waves and then the younger ones left to play a skittles match in another pub. There was a softness both in the voices of the older men remaining and in their playful words.

'Hello Bill, you rascal,' one man was greeted.

Memories returned of my years living in Devon, of the ways of speech, such as asking a location – 'Where's that to?'– or describing men passing their time 'yarning' on the quay. It seemed a long time I'd been away and I sat in the warmth of their sociability, listening, slurping at my pint. Across the road, the bells of St Brannock's church rang above the thatched lychgate, pealing in gloriously cascading layers as if a wedding was being celebrated or there was something else joyous to report. Apparently they were simply practising; the usual Monday night.

Back at my B&B, Thelma asked me to photograph her with a particular eightieth card, for the new man in her life who lived at some distance. On learning of my interests she found me a pile of relevant pamphlets. It included a typed manuscript, the life story of a former neighbour Mrs Clarke (née Howard) who had grown up at the Black Horse Inn after her father, a blacksmith, had taken on the lease in the early twentieth century.

She wrote of her brother, so beguiled by the sight of a full-rigged sailing ship at one of the local ports that he went aboard to ask, 'Do you need a boy?' They did, and he left for Peru the next day, not to return for two years.

She also wrote about Horsey banks, the defensive cob-bled wall I'd walked earlier beside the estuary: 'About this time a terrible thing happened. Owing to gale force winds and rain, Horsey banks, at Velator were washed away and the lower part of the village was flooded and, being a tidal river, whatever was done to stop it, the next tide would wash it all away again'.

This was 1911 and the gangs of 'strange men' who came to rebuild the sea wall were lodged at the Black Horse. She and her family packed lunch bags for them each night and cooked a large meal for their return, taking it into the tap room from which the billiard table was removed so they could all sit together. They could only work when the tide was out so their timetable shifted incrementally each day. The people who owned Horsey Banks were practically ruined and several engineers failed to fortify it until a young man with fresh ideas sank hundreds of iron bars and lodged sacks of sand between them, which at last 'beat the tide'.

Or so they thought.

Mrs Clarke also wrote of a weekly visitor to the Black Horse who came to ring the church bells. As a result, she met his brother, a Clarke from a seafaring family in the nearby village of Wrafton, the youngest of nine or ten, and the man she would in marry in 1912. He was summoned back from working on a North of England ship trading to Ireland, to take charge of the Clarke family's new ship, the *Edith*.

She wrote also that at this time the very first auxiliary engines began to be fitted to the sailing ketches, starting with the *Edith* and a sister ship. The engine used up all the space formerly in the cabin and filled the ship with fumes and vibration. Nevertheless, she said that all the local ship-owners followed suit. I knew from the Braunton Coasters book that much of the story of the dispersal of the fleet, the community and my family hung on this technological change and on petrochemicals.

For all the work on its defences, Horsey Island clearly remained vulnerable. I learned later that cattle had refused to drink from the 'freshwater' ponds over the past two decades, suggesting saltwater ingress. A map produced by Climate Central of land projected to be below annual flood level by 2050, shows Horsey Island is in danger. But so is the whole nose of land south of the Braunton-to-Saunton main road, apart from the high area of dunes known as the 'Burrows'. The area predicted to flood incorporates the agricultural land, the grazed Marshes, much of low-lying Braunton, Barnstaple, Bideford and the banks of the estuary and rivers a long way inland. It looks to be one of the most devastating alterations to the British coastline. Horsey Island is just the beginning of a major claiming of land by the tides.

My great uncle Francis, always known to me as 'Uncle Frank' because that's what my mother called him, went to sea at sixteen on the Braunton Schooner *Result*. After two months he joined the Merchant Navy, which became his life.

Result is perhaps the most famous ship of Braunton's coastal trading era, purchased in 1907 by a group of the village seamen and investors, having been built of steel in Carrickfergus in 1893 as a three-masted topsail schooner, graceful and fast. She served the coastal trade carrying clay, coal, manure and bricks. By 1914 she'd been fitted with an auxiliary engine and was requisitioned during World War I as a Q-ship, fighting under disguise in two actions and then resuming the coastal trade in 1918. Maritime historian Basil Greenhill described her as 'amongst the fastest and most useful schooners that ever sailed in home waters.'

Later her rig was reduced to two masts and her greatest fame came in 1950 when she was transformed into *Flash* for the film *Outcast of The Islands* based on a Joseph Conrad novel. The Scilly Isles doubled for the Caribbean and make-up for the crew's suntans. She returned afterwards to the less glamorous life of the coastal trade and was the last of the Braunton fleet to retire in 1967.

Following much travel with the merchant navy, Uncle Frank retired to a sea view in Sidmouth, South Devon. I remember him telling how he was woken by the telephone late one night and heard a slightly ragged voice:

'Is that Francis Drake?'

When he agreed that it was, his caller warned that he'd spotted the Armada approaching Plymouth Hoe.

'Thank you very much for letting me know,' Uncle Frank replied courteously, not unaware of his own fabled legacy.

His first son Francis died in childhood; a 'hole in the heart'. Could this have been a weakness arising from first cousins marrying? The younger son, John, chose architecture over the sea and never married or had children. And so, in our particular family line, seafaring as a calling came to an end.

'Cousin John' had always sailed on the family horizon, working in the conservation of historic buildings and travelling around the world seeking out architectural heritage; tours to remote parts of China or India. On those rare occasions we met, at funerals and weddings, and before that occasionally at his father's house in Sidmouth, he always spoke with awe of such places, barely drawing breath.

Despite some overlap of interests, my initial enthusiasm to talk to him was quickly followed, as a young person, by a precipitous fading of interest when all I was expected to do was listen. But now I actively wanted to listen, particularly to learn what this cousin of my mother's might know of the Drake legacy. It seemed to me he was the last person alive who might have internalised some of the seafaring stories for me to relay to my mother.

After many years without meeting, I'd written to John about *Bessie Ellen* – telling him of my mother's short trip. His address in a fancy part of West London hadn't changed in all the time I'd known him. I told him what I knew of the connection between us as Drakes and *Bessie Ellen* and what I had found out so far in Braunton.

A reply came only two days later in hieroglyphic stabs of black ink. 'This will be a fragmentary reply to your letter,' read the first sentence after the salutation. It took a while to decipher, but I knew something was amiss when halfway down the first page I arrived at: 'my father is still alive, b. 17 May 1904, so long in the tooth, my mother a short time ago.' His father's funeral had been some thirty years earlier, when I was living out of the country as a VSO English teacher on the East African island of Zanzibar.

One thing was clear though, he still had some sort of head for dates further into the past. He acknowledged the tangled web of Drakes, Chichesters and others. I was surprised to realise that he wasn't much more than ten years older than me. A generational gap shrank.

On a visit to London a little later I found him not at home but in the gastric ward of the nearest hospital, fully dressed and in bed with a shirt collar showing under a dark lambswool jumper. I half-expected him to be wearing shoes. And with obvious discomfort in his lower back, the angle he was propped up at looked unhelpful.

Despite all the years and his grey hair, he remained recognisable: the cheeky smile and clipped way of speaking, noisy breath pulling against his lips. There was something coquettish in his response to attention.

'You're getting like your mother,' he said, then speaking of his cat, the provision for it by carers twice a day. When I asked the cat's name he looked thrown, a hand running through his hair. Then it came to me from his letter.

'Is it Billy?' I asked.

'Yes!' He looked joyful to have recovered it.

I told him again of my mother's sailing trip and showed him a photo of the ship with all the sails belling with captured wind to slice the vessel through waves.

'*Bessie Ellen*,' I said.

There was some acknowledgement of a beautiful sight but no greater flicker of recognition.

Getting My Bearings

Beyond the White House on that first walk, I found low-tide confusion. A sandy bay of sorts with newish boats pulled up above the tideline. I edged out across sand to where timber boats had been stranded and abandoned to rot. Seaweed was strewn over pockmarked, sinky-looking mud veined by thin streams of water.

I stood within a timber hull. Although it curved around me in the archetypal shape of safety, still superficially scuffed with some red and blue paint, it was being dismembered. Tidal assaults had splintered and stripped away the boards of its hull, leaving just one or two remaining low down above the keel. Rusty nails and rivets stained the grain. This slow dismantling revealed the mechanics of the original building process. I found I didn't have a word for the still-sturdy central timber curving up from the keel to form the bow, or for the parallel timbers now exposed on each side, arcing up from keel to ghost-gunwale; timbers first providing the shape of the hull, then to be lined with horizontal planks.

It struck me how much time, money and effort had once been invested here in pale, new wood. What hope the building of this vessel had declared.

By this time, I'd had boat-shaped conversations with my friends Adam and Charlotte, who'd had long overseas careers working in international development but were now settled close to the shore of Loch Tay, 5 miles west of my home in Highland Perthshire. I'd enjoyed seeing their two children grow into interesting, internationally-minded adults, each with a watery pursuit: one now cooking on ocean-going yachts and one cooking for asylum seekers at Calais waiting for their chance at the life-threatening channel crossing.

Adam and Charlotte had long been interested in building coracles, canoes and sailing boats to enjoy on the Loch and we spoke of the growing phenomenon of Scottish coastal rowing. At any harbour or coastal town or village, we might glimpse a beautifully-shaped craft with a cox and four rowers heading into the blue. These boats had been standardised. At 22 feet (6.7m) in length, as opposed to the pilot gig's 32 feet (9.7m), a double-ended hull and wide beam, the St Ayles skiff is a stable and seaworthy design with origins in Fair Isle. Watching the small, trusty boats evoked something timeless, simple and beautifully contained.

'We could build our own,' Adam said.

'Build it?'

'Then row it on Loch Tay'.

It seemed unlikely, yet back in 2009, Alec Jordan of Jordan Boats became interested in reviving the coastal rowing regattas that once ran in the mining villages of the East Fife coalfields. Miners had built boats from timbers 'liberated' from the collieries. Jordan came up with the concept of a community-built rowing boat. The idea was backed by the Scottish Fisheries Museum at Anstruther which commissioned the St Ayles Skiff design from Iain Oughtred, described as 'probably the best small wooden boat designer in the world'.

Jordan Boats were now supplying a kit, making it an economic way to get on the sea for communities and individuals. It didn't require very sophisticated skills or equipment, its hull built with glued clinker boards of marine plywood. The idea of both stages – the building and then the rowing – was to bring communities together and thus reconnect people to the sea and coasts. We learnt there were already more than 150 skiffs around Scotland's shores.

From our heartland home, we have 60 miles of land on each side of us before reaching coasts at Oban to the west or St Andrews to the east. I had considered moving to appease my longing for the sea. But Adam was right; why not take advantage of the 14-mile length of water running between Killin and Kenmore? Loch Tay – the sixth largest freshwater loch in Scotland.

Angus Ross was also keen. As well as being a sailor and a woodsman – part of a collective who sustainably care for a fifty-acre oak and bluebell wood beside the river Tay – he is a designer and maker of exquisite sculptural furniture embodying a sense of movement and flow. He employs a team and secures high-profile commissions which have included bespoke furniture, drawing on the traditions of the sea for the Hull Maritime Museum. Yet he was ever-affable and modest.

'Is it art or furniture?' people ask of his creations.

The answer is, of course, 'Both.'

On that first visit to the Taw–Torridge shores, I stepped from the decaying hull abandoned on the estuary floor and looked around. The landmarks I'd heard most about were Crow Point, associated with a lighthouse, and the Bideford Bar, which muttered treachery at the estuary's far-west extreme. According to my 1:25,000 map, the Bar crossed the pale-blue estuary channel between a 'North Tail' and 'South Tail' of land. The shores were buff-coloured and marked 'sand' or 'sand and shingle'. Looking up, to translate two dimensions to the reality around me, I struggled to make proper sense of it.

I walked west towards the entrance of the estuary and the open sea. I took my time. On the exposed high-tide line were shells to turn and upright wooden spars of old breakwaters worn into pinnacled sculptures. The map's scant detail spoke of debatable land where the human hold is fragile and in a parry with powerful forces. Gradually the arms of 'land' fell away and I was thrown into tumbled disorder between light, air, sand, water. The shore was laid bare by low tide, gleaming like beaten lead under a bank of cloud through which a strangled sun filtered.

I knew that the grassy dunes soaring up to my right must be the Burrows, famed for the diversity of plant and animal life amongst its peaks, folds and valleys. Before myx-omatosis, rabbits were farmed here and dispatched on the London train, threaded together into long chains through a slit in the back leg of each animal. I had also learned in the museum that, in World War II, American forces practised for D-Day here, and these days the area is used by our own military forces for desert-driving training and other exer-cises. It's a UN biosphere. The map showed that from the Saunton Sands shoreline to the inland edge of the Burrows was 2km, west to east; a buffer protecting the marshes and flat farmland from the sea.

I was moving across low, flat places, at contour zero. Nothing materialised which I could define clearly as Crow Point. Perhaps I had missed it.

Despite the oddness of the angle and my confusion about direction, what was land and what sea, I noticed far out in the channel, beyond a marker buoy, a dark line of surfacing land, treacherous as a whale. A long line of waves. Presumably this was incoming sea meeting sandbanks; a churning mass of disturbed water. Rollers broke in crazed succession, each underlined in black, their white crests sprayed high by the offshore wind.

Was this the infamous Bar?

I stopped walking. My view was foreshortened by being at sea level, but beyond the turbulence close to me, I could just make out the spray-faint horizon. Somewhere beyond it lay Newfoundland. I felt uneasy, excited, stilled. It could have been any century; the only recognisable time was of the tide, the moment of furthest retreat. The sand beneath my feet, fragmented over aeons and drifted here, provided a temporary foothold. It would disappear underwater within the next six hours; water rushing in faster than I could run.

In the tight knots of crooked streets in the old part of the village, I'd been orientated by stones carved with names and dates, houses that had numbers and street names. This tumbling, the confusing boundaries between land and water, gravel and sand, offered none of this certainty.

I must have unknowingly turned a corner around the 'North Tail'. The horizon grew long and wide, the sand gradually stabilising into something more recognisably a beach as I walked the 2 miles to Saunton with the Burrows soaring to my right and the sea to my left. At the less lonely end I would find a car park, ice cream, surfboard hire and a row of bright-doored beach huts. A quite different world.

Later I phoned my mother, told her about the solid, nameable things in the village – gravestones, the Heanton Street house and Velator. Fixed stone and earth. There was the small, steep hill behind the B&B; I'd climbed it before breakfast to look across the lower land and comprehend the layout of estuary, farmland, village, Horsey Island easing in and out of connection to The Marshes. I told her that I hadn't been able to find 'The Myrtles', the home of the Verney aunt, and reported the pelican sighting, of course – she loved the absurd.

'You've found out so much in such a short time,' she said. 'That's fantastic.'

I had pleased her.

I didn't mention the ambiguities I felt whilst standing on that 'shore'.

It was true I'd got my bearings, identified some local landmarks. And yet the Bar, and its bad-tempered roaring that could be heard from Braunton on rough nights, seemed significant but somehow elusive. The men in our family must have crossed and recrossed it. It shaped their lives, and presented an unavoidable adventure in their business.

I tried to imagine seeing it up close, and from the water. Like so much about the sea, the idea both drew and repelled me.

Crossing the Bar

It wasn't until a later year, in springtime, that I had the chance to experience the Taw-Torridge estuary *from* the water. The land was hard to read. From the lower reaches of the River Torridge, I could look directly upstream along the Taw to the sentinel White House, my last 'fixed' landmark. Beyond it, and slightly raised under green hills, was Braunton. Somewhere under those rooftops was the Heanton Street house in which Emma Louise Chichester and Francis Drake had raised their family and where their granddaughter, my Granny, later grew up.

To the right of the Taw outflow at Yelland a long dark pier strode out where an oil terminal used to be. Opposite it, back on the White House side, I could just make out a small, tubular-steel lighthouse venturing way out on a pile of rocks into mud and no-man's-land, to fend off the unwary. This had to be the elusive Crow Point.

The emptying estuary was to carry us west towards the rip in the Atlantic coastline that separates Saunton Sands on the north side from Northam Burrows on the south; another grazed marsh-land which seeps between wet and dry, buffering Appledore from the sea. Around us stretched water, mud and slick sky in kaleidoscopic fragments. Although it was May, the day was gunmetal grey, cool and windy.

We'd launched from a slipway in Appledore on the southern shore, carrying the kayaks across sticky mud and slipping over weed-draped rocks to reach the water. Once afloat, with our spray-decks tightly skirted, I had seen up close that other 'landmark', the orange lifeboat that swings on its mooring just off the village. It had begun to orientate me as I worked my way around the hydra-shaped Taw-Torridge estuary: the locus of my haphazard search for submerged family memory.

Our flotilla of eight kayaks from Bideford Canoe Club turned west into the dancing waterways of the confluence. I hadn't been in a kayak for some time, and was glad to be travelling in a double with a highly experienced paddler, club leader Pete Thorn, who matched my strokes from behind. I'd been anxious as I anticipated the trip, but the motion soon felt familiar, a rhythmic roll of the shoulders and straightening of the arms propelling the vessel, warming me inside my borrowed dry-suit. My legs stretched ahead, knees wedged into the kayak's sides so my hips could tip and steer. Sitting almost below the surface, I was in a strange intimacy with the plait and shudder of currents beneath, sensing sometimes depth, sometimes sneaking shallows, as recognisable land began to disappear and the sky pressed down.

The further out we paddled, the more agitated the surface became. Looking eagerly ahead, I took in a succession of channel marker buoys. First red, which, had we been a ship, we would need to pass to our port side (left), then keeping a green one to starboard. Names were displayed on the buoys – Inner Pulley and Outer Pulley – marking sandbanks ships must avoid on their way in or out.

The Bristol Channel has the second largest tidal range – low and high differential – in the world. Its funnel shape, the great massing of the Atlantic directly to the west, and the piping in of westerly winds by rising land on either side, all increase the water's inward flow. It's what makes these Taw-Torridge waters and their interaction with land so grave. It floods in and then leaves, fast. Pete told me it was challenging to find suitable waters for novice-kayakers here, both because of the scale of the tides and the potential chaos beyond the Bar in any 'weather'. Trips have to be planned with care. Get it right and it's like freewheeling on a bicycle. Even a humble kayak might reach 10 knots in the right circumstances. You just need to be sure it's in the intended direction.

Our trip would take two and a half hours in total, Pete said. The difference between high and low water that day was 4.72m, the height of a small house. On a twice-a-month spring tide, when the sea floods highest and drains to its lowest, the depth of water in the channel can drop to as little as a metre: not a problem for a kayak with its tiny draft and seal-like manoeuvrability, but in a keeled vessel of any draft, precise navigation and timing have always been essential.

Low tide today was at 11.56am. We were to travel out on the very last of the ebb from Appledore, and come back in on the flood. The idea was that the tide would carry us each way, but we had left slightly later than intended.

There had been a pause when I told my mother on the phone about this proposed trip, after which I would travel down to see her in Penzance.

'You won't go out alone, will you?' she said.

It was highly unusual for her to comment on anything I did, at least since I'd been an adult. Even the most extreme of my mountaineering challenges or solo walks hadn't produced such a remark. She was much more likely to say something approving or non-committal like, 'Well, do have a super time, dear,' perhaps adding, 'and do take care.'

In my late fifties, exploration of the past was still demanding bodily engagement. I wanted to get to the Bar under my own steam, to see this coastal feature which seemed to be responsible for so much. I was reticent about this with my mother. I didn't explain the impulses of my discovery process – the need to feel spray or the lurch of water. I just expected her to understand.

She'd had to tolerate my displays of independence since I was quite young. Aged 17 I'd cycled off from suburban Surrey on a six-day solo ride with a tent on the back of my Raleigh. She didn't even know till afterwards as she was away with my stepfather in Cornwall at the time.

I was surprised she'd now think me cavalier enough to take out a kayak alone, especially in such a notorious place.

'Of course I won't, that would be very foolhardy,' I'd snapped, then deigned to explain my arrangement with the club.

Perhaps she had a slightly different standard when the sea was concerned. On the beach when we were children, she would insist on an hour between eating and returning to the water to swim. Cramp was the killer. And we were not to go out of our depth, but to swim parallel to the beach.

She was happiest with the sea in sight, yet always showed respect for it. On her vaguely-remembered childhood visits to Braunton she could never exactly have got to know this coast of widows from which her mother sprang; the interventions of the tide that pulsed with such violence in and out of the land and in the veins of her forebears. However, stories of wreck, men's absence, loss, must still have washed into her subliminal mudflats.

In *The Lighthouse Stevensons*, Bella Bathurst refers to Robert Louis Stevenson as 'sea-marked'. I'd never come across this term before but I take it to mean that the sea had chosen him, shaped him and his family. Had it chosen my mother as well? I wondered whether her particular fear about my journey to the Bar, strong enough for her to express it aloud, came from some vestigial remnant, absorbed through her own mother's warnings when she was young.

When I came off the phone I chastised myself for being so childishly irritable with her, especially when the whole point of this project had been to bring us closer.

Whilst the chart I'd studied fixed a sense of order and geometry, the complex jigsaw of water, sandbanks and shores we were moving through refused to steady. The estuary began to open out as we reached the marker buoy for Middle Ridge. Because we sat low in the water, the buoys we strained to see were hidden by choppy water ahead; the action of incoming wind against outgoing tide. I began to anticipate, as we rose up the slope of each wave, the fairground-ride drop down the other side. The surrounding splutter and splash seemed inseparable from the motion.

The perspective stretched and shortened as we paddled towards a big sky, the open sea. Saunton Sands stretched a long yellowy strip away to our right, and beyond it stood Baggy Point, a craggy and black fortress, with the paler Morte Point gradually amassing beyond.

Close, on our left, a corrugated stretch of shingle bank humpbacked from the sea, declaring low tide. It was prickled by mussel shells and patrolled by seabirds. We pulled onto it for a sandwich and a rest on mud that was worked into rippling contour-lines by tide and current. This was Zulu Bank, I was told, a feature whose name I knew as ominous to seafarers through the ages, lying concealed, or acting as natural breakwater, or breaching the surface. Depending.

After lunch some of the group turned back for Appledore. Three boats went on: ours, Simon's and Jake's, noses into increasingly lively waves, towards the Bar.

The name 'Bideford Bar' – like Land's End or Tower Ridge on Ben Nevis – rings with notoriety. Respected and feared. Without local-navigation knowledge and an understanding of tides, it can be disastrous, and its exact position alters with the under-sea writhing of sand and gravel. As recently as 2014, a pleasure boat capsized on an ebbing tide and one person died. What had seemed a watery playground must have transformed abruptly into a confusion of shifting land and hissing seas.

In preparing to cross this puzzle of water, sand and gravel, I'd pored over a nineteenth-century sea-chart, delighting in the textured detail applied to 'non-land'. A statement cautioned that the entrance shown was no longer representative due to the capricious nature of those sandbanks. However, it gave an account of the main channel at the time, showing depths numerically, and writhing a great white loop south around the mountainous dunes of Braunton Burrows before branching dramatically north-west and south into the two rivers. Sandbanks and their associated mini-channels, which vanish at high tide, were marked with names: Sprat Ridge, Crow Ridge, Middle Ridge. A ballast heap and buoys featured, and incoming vessels were advised to align the 'lower and upper lights': two lighthouses that once stood a distance apart close to the estuary entrance. Other features on land were offered for navigational assistance:

'Watertown in line with old Mill'; 'bungalow in line with Worlington houses.'

I thought of the map on the wall of Braunton Museum scarred with names of wrecks. If you count up the ships around the estuary entrance, cast up onto Zulu Bank or breached on Saunton Sands, despite the paraphernalia of lighthouses, guiding lights, buoys and pilots who could come aboard to take the helm with native authority, the toll is vast. An Admiralty pilot publication from 1910 advises: 'This bar is of so changeable a nature that the depths are not to be depended on; the mariner is accordingly cautioned against taking the chart ... as a guide, and not to enter without local knowledge.' But of course, there were those who tried to cut costs by doing so.

The interplay of river, sea, geology and moon must have dominated the lives of my grandmother Drake's family, determining the presence, absence and welfare of their menfolk. Their sail-cargo business continued out of Braunton well into the twentieth century. The quay built by the seafaring community at Velator was accessed from the estuary by the pill I'd followed through a mile of low-lying marshland. Before this waterway was engineered, they could only load, unload or easily reach the estuary to cross the Bar twice a month on spring tides at the new or full moon. The local story goes that if a sea captain missed his slot due to an over-enthusiastic night in the Mariners' Arms or a need for repairs, he would be held back for a fortnight, causing financial chaos for his family and crew. 'Master's lost his spring' was the justification a wife might take to a local shop when asking for credit on purchases: a request to be 'tided over'.

Even in the estuary itself their two-masted wooden ketches needed enough water to clear the hazards beneath, the tide flowing in the right direction to travel in or out, and helpful winds. Or it would have to be oars, or some other method involving heaving an anchor forward and hauling the boat on a line towards it, at least until engines began to be fitted to their ships. Rather than the hands on a clock face, the state of the tide would dictate plans. It synchronised local efforts. As many as a hundred ships went out under sail in one tide, attempting not to collide.

Before investing in ketches in the late nineteenth century and focussing on coastal journeys within and beyond the Bristol Channel, Granny's forebears sailed as part of a long-standing triangular trade taking salt to Newfoundland, salted cod from there to the Iberian Peninsula, and returning home with a hold full of wine and oranges. We think of this link between Devon and Newfoundland as Elizabethan but, as recently as 1881, the topsail schooner *Nellie,* majority-owned by Granny's grandfather, Francis Drake, went missing on a passage between St John, Newfoundland and Oporto loaded with salt cod and with five crew on board. The Drakes also reputedly traded in timber from Prince Edward Island, having a new ship's hull built there, then filling it with timber and towing it back across the Atlantic under sail.

For the more recent coastal voyages, a knowledge of the current play of tide and the shifting channel was the difference between life and death. Basil Greenhill recalls being told by an old sea captain: 'You learn all about the tides, and get as much as you can out of them.' The means of finding the channel was handed down from those living with it and by it, generation to generation, 'like a treasured family heirloom that it undoubtedly was,' according to Appledore writer John Whitlock in *Pilots and pilotage on the rivers Taw and Torridge*. Directions were oral, precise and esoteric: 'When you'm abrist the Middle Ridge, keep high light a hand spike's breadth open of the low one ...'. Nevertheless, it could change.

Unlike Braunton folk tucked away from water by an apron of farmland and marshes, Appledore's inhabitants have long faced the sea, and witnessed patterns of tide, current and weather. Perhaps unsurprisingly, the village produced many pilots, including Whitlock's family, from amongst its seafarers. For voyagers without local knowledge, this estuary was rare shelter on a rugged, cliff-fortressed stretch of coast, especially important in the days of sail alone when wind strength and direction would determine course. Pilots kept their knowledge of the capricious monster up to date. This included walking the low-tide shallows after rain to see the latest effect of freshwater ingress from the surrounding hills.

Particular Appledore families became known for piloting and before Trinity House regulations reduced their numbers there would have been great competition between them to be the first to reach an incoming ship signalling for assistance. They got the work to guide the ship both into port and, later, back out. The race demanded fitness and resilience. Rowing in 'gigs', with a coxswain pressing their crew onwards, they would race other families. Sometimes the rivalry led to the gigs overreaching the Bar and capsizing in its wild surf, with possible losses of several members of the same family.

Races were held between rival pilot gigs at other times, perhaps with gambling involved. Such racing for pleasure died out but has been recently revived; an annual race has been established on the Taw-Torridge estuary, men's crews starting close to Bideford Old Bridge and finishing at Barnstaple Bridge, and women racing back from there to Appledore.

The nineteenth-century shipyard at Appledore has survived through a declining chain of ownership, at times building ships of some size. Ferries and super-yachts have launched on the turn of a high tide, always with an expert pilot. Only one pilot now remains, doubling up as the harbourmaster, but commercial sea traffic is limited to the barges that shift clay and stones.

People these days travel, and goods are carried, by ring roads, bypasses and a new concrete bridge soaring across the Torridge Valley close to Bideford. But it is just within living memory that there were well-scored 'sea roads' between the five ports of the Taw-Torridge Estuary. So I was glad to hear of the waters being plied by small rowing craft, even if only for recreation; stitching the ports of the sprawling estuary back together again. In the past surely there were friendships forged, marriages made between its various shores?

On a visit to Appledore on that first trip to the area in 2016, I'd stayed overnight in a B&B. It was part of a terrace of houses, formerly homes to 'sea captains' halfway up the hillside of tightly-laced Medieval streets above the quay. My host Sandy, a young Irish woman, returned home at dusk pink-cheeked and exhilarated; she'd been out on the water in a pilot gig full of women; she was the cox. She seemed to sparkle still with salt and spray.

'It's wonderful, I love it – it's why I live here!'

'Did you build it yourselves?' I asked.

'Gosh, no,' she said. 'The wooden ones have to be built by expert boatbuilders to a standard design from the nineteenth century.'

She named their two builders, both some distance away in Dartmouth and Fowey. 'But we also have two fibreglass training boats for practice in the winter – they're not acceptable for racing, but the maintenance isn't such an issue.'

I told her of our ongoing discussions about a boat for Loch Tay.

Five of us had made a visit to Anstruther on the Fife coast for practical tips from the founding club, meeting in the birthplace of the new rowing movement at the Scottish Fisheries Museum. One of the St Ayles skiffs was on display there as well as a tiny model, 'crewed' by Barbie dolls.

It had been a cold and short December day and we were impressed when seven club members turned out. Between coffee, soup and cake they talked us through the mechanics of building such a boat, speaking of the quantities of marine plywood we would need for the hull; larch for gunwales and keel; Douglas fir for the oars. It would cost us a minimum of £7000 to include the life jackets, trailer, insurance and so on. And then there was the development of a club, how we would learn to row and finally join in racing and social events as part of a lively community around Scotland's 6000 miles of mainland coastline.

We were given a diagram of the St Ayles skiff. Seen side on and from above, there were four 'thwarts', each seating one rower with one oar. Footrests. The keel and 'keelson' (inner keel) together forming the boat's backbone. The diagram illustrated its distinction from a pilot gig – this vessel was shorter and swelled much more fully at the beam, the timbers of the hull gathering to identical points at bow and stern. It was, apparently, incredibly buoyant.

Finally, they had taken us to see their two boats on the quayside. Both were covered on parked trailers; each had a slightly different history. Their enthusiasm and their wish to support us sent us away warmed by conviviality into the frozen dusk.

'It's really about becoming a community afloat, isn't it?' Charlotte said later.

And that was how we decided to approach our fundraising effort.

Joseph Conrad refers to the pilot as 'trustworthiness personified', which is unsurprising when local expertise puts so many lives in his hands. This ultimate respect seems to have been in Alfred Lord Tennyson's mind when he wrote his poem 'Crossing the Bar' at the age of eighty-one from a room with a sea view in Salcombe. The central metaphor is a boat travelling out to sea on a fast-ebbing tide and crossing the Bar with ease, carrying the grateful narrator over the threshold to a peaceful death.

> *For tho' from out our bourne of Time and Place*
> *The flood may bear me far,*
> *I hope to see my Pilot face to face*
> *When I have cross'd the bar.*

Although I probably knew of this poem as a child, it was a video of The Spooky Men's Chorale singing a harmonised a cappella version of it in the Lady Chapel of Ely Cathedral that shivered me to attention. Standing to encircle their audience who sit on the floor, the music rises from the human cauldron into the dome above them. Emotion is palpable in the listening faces. It drew me back to the poem and its pairing of material and spiritual worlds.

> *May there be no moaning of the bar*
> *When I put out to sea.*

Crossing the Bar

When I was invited by BBC Radio to write a short story in response to a classic poem of my choice, I knew immediately it would be this, not least because my mother had recently passed on Emma Drake (née Chichester's) leather-bound volume of Tennyson, complete with her monogram.

'Why don't you take it?' she'd said when I went to replace it on the shelf.

I was surprised at the time that she wouldn't want to hold onto such a keepsake from her great-grandmother, but perhaps, it occurs to me now, there's an age at which we lose attachment to material things and know they will mean more to a younger generation.

I decided quickly to set my story around this Chichester matriarch's homeland and the Bideford Bar, and this sharpened my focus on further visits to the area as I wandered the places close to Braunton where sea and land wrangle with each other. My imagination built upon what I found there.

The main character for the story soon materialised: an elderly woman, daughter of a local pilot. She had enjoyed independent sailing here as a child with strict respect for tidal dangers and the Bar, but was now being curtailed from even minor adventure by arthritis and the cautions of her adult children.

Writing a fictional story required me to fully imagine this territory somewhere between the White House, Crow Point and the Bar, between firm sand and tidal rush, life and death. Engaging with it in this way, feeling it in my bones and imagination, seemed to nurture a stronger bond with the place, as fiction writing often does. But it also gave me a greater degree of apprehension on this short literal journey from estuary-port to Bar.

Sea Marked

My fascination with tides has crept up on me, returning me in my writing to shores and drawing me to drift seeds and the intertidal heroes, better known as barnacles, which open and close with flood and ebb. I thought I knew how tides worked in their twelve-and-a-half-hour rhythms, the meaning of 'spring' and 'neap' which tell of bi-monthly extremes and plateaus ruled by the moon. But I found I had more to learn about the rotations of sun and moon and earth, the gravitational pull and their angle to each other which creates extreme tides at each equinox when night and day are of equal length. I relished the science whilst remaining sure of their deeper metaphorical power.

As humans we regulate our contemporary lives by circadian rhythms, dark and light, and by the 12-hour, 24-hour clock. We seem to have become tide-blind. Perhaps it is now irrelevant, unless we are lugworm diggers, cockle-pickers, seafarers. Or, in an age in which we've come to think of this planet as being 'for us', controlled by us, and most people feel no dependency on the sea, perhaps we think we can overcome such forces with technology.

I've watched as the drivers of two cars set off into a rising tide across the Lindisfarne Causeway a full hour after the time advertised as unsafe. One car made it, one did not, and after wading to a stork-legged refuge hut, the middle-aged couple were rescued by the Coast Guard. I've watched a man, clearly not aware that the tide was rising, allow one of his three small children to wade ahead around a coastal headland, only for the family to be separated by waves crashing onto the cliff face. And of course it's hard to forget the terrible consequences of tidal ignorance, arrogance, or human callousness, at Morecambe Bay in February 2004.

Is lack of humility towards the sea a new phenomenon? The majority of us have little need for knowledge of the sea's ways or an awareness of the tides on a day-to-day basis. We seem to find the patterns too mysterious and yet we know from tide tables that they are predictable, barring the effects of atmospheric pressure, extreme wind. That our predecessors found them orderly is summed up by the word 'tidy', indicating things as they should be.

From the kayak, through spray-filled air, I could just make out last land at the 'North Tail'. On the corresponding 'South Tail', I saw two vertical figures. They stood, black and erect, close to the white line of water where incoming waves hit the Bar's shallows, making it sing out.

I stopped paddling to point them out to Pete. 'Are they surfers?'

'Birds,' Pete shouted over the roar.

I had the scale so wrong. When I looked again, they were exactly as he said: two cormorants, much closer than I had imagined.

There was nothing human out here, and had there been, they would soon be cut off by the incoming tide. Only two weeks earlier, two people had become encircled by the sea, Pete told me. The RNLI rescued them. Others have tried to jump the channel when it's at its narrowest, not realising its immense speed. I'd read of two nineteenth-century Braunton men in a similar predicament – James Hancock and William Murphy – duck-trapping somewhere out here, their bodies brought in by a search party.

We still followed the channel. Wind came from the north-west, agitating the surface against us. As we had left slightly later than intended, the last part of our journey to the Bar was in slack water, unassisted by the ebb and slowed by the wind's opposition. Pete had warned me it could be choppy today. Sometimes water was scooped into my dry-suit sleeves. Being close to the front of the kayak, as we hit each wave I took sea-slaps on my face. But now I had gathered a sense of purpose, I found myself wearing a wide smile, simply exhilarated by the growing wildness.

'You should have worn swimming goggles,' shouted Jake from the kayak next to us.

And then, paddling harder, we left the shelter of land. Pete alerted me to the whole stretch of the bay between Baggy Point to our north and south to Hartland Point; a bay holding the open Atlantic in its craggy arms. The Bar itself was now clearly visible: a stretching white line of surf just ahead underscored by something dark, and beyond it a much more confused and shifty sea. Far beyond the churn rose the pale shape of Lundy Island, 15 miles off. Beyond it, the horizon flickered, spelling enticement and promise.

Surely my seafaring forebears had felt the thrill of their forthcoming journey each time they arrived at this point and the water livened beneath them, the air freshened, the surface grew skittish? This is where they committed, where they truly 'put out' to sea. This crossing of bad-tempered groundswell and a chaotic stretch of sea marked a neces-sary ordeal between two distinct worlds – the shelter of the domestic and the wild. We were approaching that ancient threshold. It marked the beginning of adventure and com-merce; exile from home and land. The world of women and children was left closed in behind the Bar.

In the lull between tides, before the water started to flood into the estuary, we paddled the last of our journey out. We wouldn't go beyond the Bar, not today; not in this. I felt a great thrill, face wet, eyes stinging with salt, to see the words 'Bideford Bar' growing larger on the marker buoy we headed for. It had a dark green, buoyant base, open vanes supporting a light above to make the entrance to the channel visible at night. As we bobbed below this hefty steel drum, it strained on its anchored lines, leaping above us. It brought to mind an account I'd read at the museum of the men of past times relighting it when the flame was blown out by a gale, one of them bringing the boat as close as possible to the dancing buoy and the other choosing his moment to jump.

Achievement swelled in me: in being here amidst the chop and the bite of salt air to witness something of my own family story. A story my mother barely seemed aware of and Granny never could have experienced. We turned the kayaks, putting our backs to the wind. Simon took photos. I was suddenly too warm after the effort. Salty and grinning madly. Proud to have shaken off my own timidity, as if as a fragile child I'd let go of the side of a pool and begun to swim. But there was also relief that all the hostility was at my back and I was now facing green hills, white cottages on the shores, all the human infrastructure that I cling to. Past human lives remain scored here; at sea they leave no trace.

I tried to look at the estuary entrance now as the master of a sailing vessel might have done, coming in with the tide and wind directly behind. Driven in with stern raised, surfing with waves, rudder clearing the water. The ship would be un-steerable. A following wind would also risk an out-of-control gybe, the mainsail and boom slamming across the beam of the ship, causing chaos, flapping sails, splintering timber. Better to take the sails down and let the tide take you in, perhaps? But even then, with the tide running south to north across the estuary mouth as well as in and out of it, you might be sent onto Crow Point instead of Zulu Bank. There was a devil and there was the deep blue.

I'd read that in the early 1800s a high lighthouse was built near Crow Point – 86 feet (26.2m) tall, white with a red stripe and with a smaller 'low' light 300 yards to its north. Seafarers had to align the two on approach to be sure of finding the channel. Two keepers lived in quarters below the high light, taking watches rather as on a ship. One of the men would have his family with him, living on this lonely edge of dune and water and sometime-land. It must have been strange, not so far from Braunton but almost in the sea. From there the coming and going over the Bar could be watched as a daily spectacle.

But the channel entry wouldn't have been attempted until the half-tide between ebb and flood, with a minimum of fifteen feet (4.6m) of water. This safe water was indicated to incoming ships by the raising of a large black wickerwork ball at the Lighthouse, visible on approach, and at night by a light. That the lighthouse had a mortuary with space for twelve bodies to lie on slabs of Delabole slate tells the consequences of underestimating this local hazard.

When the high light became unstable in 1945, the keepers were withdrawn and both lights destroyed in 1957, leaving the low rubble I'd stumbled over on my earliest walk. Instead, the tubular steel Trinity House light 300m south of the original functions without any sense of romance.

When we resumed paddling, I was surprised to find that without any effort, without noticing, we had travelled well upstream of the Bar buoy. Tide and wind had taken us. Back within the estuary, skirls of surf were breaking over Zulu Bank where we'd had lunch. We played at catching waves in the shallows.

A turning tide often seems to bring a change of weather and now the sun blasted into our faces. Perhaps it can also bring a shift in fortune or a different way of thinking: a reliable pendulum of change. The White House appeared on the shore of the filling estuary to my left and, behind it, Braunton's roofs and spires clustered. The geography was finally clarifying.

This frequent act of ordinary heroism, this sailing 'close to the wind' of life itself, must once have moulded generations of men from the Taw-Torridge estuary and the families who watched, waited for, and lost them. And it occurred to me now that remnants of such states may still lodge like hidden channels in their descendants.

Although I'd had little luck finding the graves of immediate generations, I'd found the grave of Emma Louise Chichester's mother and father in the churchyard at Heanton Punchardon, a tiny village just outside Braunton where she grew up. Her future husband Francis Drake was also born here. Although the records become confused, Emma's sea-captain father John appears to be descended from the Chichesters of Hart Manor on the outskirts of Braunton, now remembered only in a street name on a housing estate built upon the site. John Squire Chichester, first owner of *Bessie Ellen,* was Emma's nephew.

I'd learnt a little more about 'our' ships. *Emma Louise* was one of the last wooden vessels built before Barnstaple shipbuilders Westacotts closed. My great-great-grandfather, Francis Drake, was the first owner from 1883, with a Samuel Berry owning a third of the sixty-four shares. Berry (who had been mayor of Barnstaple) was an owner of many ships, and ran a regular trade in guano from South America. In

1918, *Emma Louise* was one of the first ketches to be fitted with an auxiliary engine by new owners in Newburgh, Aberdeenshire. They sold her back to Appledore three years later from where she moved on again to the Rawles of Minehead in 1931.

She was at her most famous in these Minehead days. From there she plied up and down the Bristol Channel into narrowing waters and a canal entrance on the north shore at Lydney, Gloucestershire, to collect coal and return it to the Minehead quay where it was craned away to fuel the gasworks. She continued with both sail and engine much later than any other local ketch.

In a beautiful piece of memoir I stumbled across, Terry Winsborough of Minehead tells of being aboard *Emma Louise* as a schoolboy in 1948, accompanying a friend whose father was one of the two-man crew. Although this was his first time at sea, judging by the website where I found it, Winsborough went on to become a master mariner.

By the time of his first trip, ships using sail-power only were a thing of the past, but he still evokes an authentic journey for *Emma Louise*. He noted that, 'In spite of years of carrying such a filthy cargo she was kept clean and smart with white painted wheelhouse and deck fittings, varnished spars and gunwales. She also had a scrolled stem head under the bowsprit in the form of a Union flag which was kept carefully painted in red, white and blue.' He went aboard with only 'A loaf of bread, a cabbage, 3lb of onions and a half pound of butter. All the fresh food was stowed carefully away in the jolly boat resting on the single hatch, the coolest and cleanest place on board'. A 'jolly boat' was the small tender used to get ashore; it doubled as a lifeboat, in this case supplied with flotation tanks, dry food, extra oars and fresh water.

He tells of the engine being started by pre-heating the cylinder-head with a paraffin burner, and then cajoled into its 'tonka-tonka' beat. It was left running even when they were under sail due to this reluctance to go in the first place. They motored out into the channel, dropping anchor to wait for the tide that would carry them in the right direction. This was done '...in order to make the best progress and arrive at the next port when there was enough water to enter... a period of about two hours each side of high water.'

Written with all the open-eyed wonder of a young apprentice who subsequently opted for a life at sea, the account includes much telling detail, including about the self-sufficiency of the ship and crew. When the two boys came to throw lines to the Lydney quay, the men's mockery of their incompetence evidently expanded Winsborough's vocabulary considerably. The old long-wave wireless receiver was used 'solely... to listen for football results and weather reports in that order! There was no radio transmitter of any kind on board, and looking back, I don't think the crew would have wanted one. The fact that the vessel used to pass just a few miles off Portishead Radio Station had no significance to their lives. They had eyes and ears. Why would they want to talk to anyone ashore?'

A sense of tradition is also conveyed in the account of them sitting on deck after a sausage supper that evening. There is no suggestion of time being wasted when they had to wait due to the restrictions of tidal rhythms, but rather that there was a simple enjoyment of the journey and the ship; a sense of sufficiency and fellowship between them. That evening they were 'entertained by seafaring yarns as recollected by the master'.

Perhaps these passed-down tales included inherited memories of her first owner and his wife who gave the ship her name. I imagine Francis Drake would also have had 'yarns' to tell boys who came aboard for the first time. With his enterprise and experience, at ease with every subtlety of the wind, tide and current as well as all the variables of hull, keel, rudder and sail, Francis' commanding name would doubtless ensure his stories were shelved back across the centuries.

Francis and the other man crewing might also have teased boys as dusk shrouded the deck with tall tales of a haunting in the anchor locker. Then a boy would be sent below to bring them up a supposed loaf of bread stowed there. And of course a master must be obeyed, even one with a soft Devon burr in his voice and laugh-lines around his eyes.

With Terry Winsborough aboard, the ship made an early departure from Lydney the next morning, threading down the Channel amongst coasters, barges and tugs leaving the up-river Severn ports. As they went, other vessels steered close to them to exchange gossip and football results. I picture this as the original communications 'super-highway'; how news spread quickly around the ports of Britain. It was perhaps how a West Country seafarer might learn of a good-looking ketch for sale in the far islands of the north.

By the time they had waited out the tide again outside Minehead harbour and come ashore, their entire trip had been something like thirty-six hours, which today would be made by road in four hours: 84 miles each way.

Crossing the Bar

My friend Kate and I had been walking the South West Coast Path (SWCP) for one week each year since 2015. The route is 630 miles from Minehead to Poole Harbour via Lands' End, but we weren't walking it in sequence.

We'd met not long after I moved to Scotland in 1990, had both worked in development in East Africa and had interests in publishing, walking and occasional dancing. But now she was living in Plymouth and, for an irreverent person, had taken a surprise step by becoming a Unitarian minister. Our walks were for me a way of reclaiming my West Country haunts, and for her a growing foot-knowledge of a new home.

Just after we left Minehead in 2017 to walk west towards Braunton, we stepped into the tiny church of St Peters, tucked away on the quayside of the old harbour. A pub was to one side of it, and a gift shop in its loft. It was windowless inside, rather like being below deck on a ship, with a few rows of small pews and a simple altar on which stood a brass cross and a lectern holding a prayer for seafarers. Behind this hung a large, brass-framed painting, a feature Kate told me was a 'reredos'.

The painting depicts a broad, pale sea scene, a slight squall suggested by spray, and low clouds through which shafts of light project. The horizon is crossed by a long tongue of tapering land which I take to be the north side of the Bristol Channel – Gloucestershire or the southern coast of Wales. To the right of the scene, Jesus stands on the water in a long white robe. He is turned towards a ship which lies still, presumably anchored there, and stripped of sails. One man is left on board and three others are rowing towards Jesus whose hands rise in front of him as if in welcome or blessing.

The ship is *Emma Louise*.

She had become a common sight in the Bristol Channel and was the last working sailing ship, her crew well-respected as old-guard seamen. Perhaps this starring role in the church shows how well she was regarded, how long her service to the community; the last survivor of the local coasting trade. And it may also reflect something of our primal response to the seaworthy boat, its honesty and durability repaying the trust and great care put into its building and maintenance. The painting is kitsch but I was glad to find any traces of my family's ships. So little remains when old timber is involved.

Emma Louise's triennial survey finally showed the need for prohibitively expensive repairs – the surveyor's knife had apparently sunk up to its hilt in her sternpost. So in 1953 she took a final trip to an Appledore owner, once again crossing the Bideford Bar into the Taw-Torridge estuary, and was laid up against the quay. I've seen a photo of her in that year and in that position, and knowing the story gives the image a particular poignancy: a beautiful, sturdy wooden ship who had worked hard for seventy years and been adapted as far as she could be to the times.

Although there were good intentions by the new owner to fix her up and use her, she never voyaged beyond the Bar again.

How to Throw a Line

A few years before this quest began I had started to sail a little in the Inverness area with a now-ex. He'd bought a fiberglass boat, a 32-foot (9.7m) 'Colvic Atlantic', which was designed with a robustness attributed to fishing boats – having a wheelhouse of glass and timber – and was also equipped to sail, with a storm jib at the bow, mainsail and a mizzen at the aft to help keep an 'even keel'. We had ambitions for long coastal explorations and sea trips to the west coast and through the Pentland Firth, which although appealing to my adventurous spirit, also affected me with a nervous dread.

Having sailed a few times before, I thought it would be relatively straightforward to revise skills, but I soon realised that in the past I must have allowed fellow crew to take responsibility. This seemed to be particularly the case in the handling of lines between the vessel and the shore. Our initial excursions took us south-west from our home port of Inverness along open lochs strung together with stretches of Telford's ingenious Caledonian Canal. The route follows the Great Glen, or Highland Fault Line, and the rise and fall in elevation is negotiated by climbing or descending 'steps' in the canal, engineered through locks.

Each lock gate required one of us on engine and steering control in the wheelhouse (him) and the other (me) to throw and catch lines from the bow and stern of the boat to a lock-keeper whose face might appear several metres above me at the top of a vertical wall. I soon learnt that there was an art to this, a way of coiling the rope, holding it in preparation and knowing which part to throw first. But in those first few days I suffered multiple lonely failures, the line falling back to me or tangling in fixed rigging and then falling into the drink while the engine chugged on. The back of my skipper's head expressed fury through the glass of the wheelhouse. The boat drifted away from its intended tie-up and my face blazed as spectators gathered.

I did improve, dividing the coiled line between two hands and first throwing upwards the half with the free end from my right hand. Once that was in flight, I let the other coil pay out. The lock-keeper turned it around a cleat on the shore, and I then received the rope back and drew the boat in towards the wall. But I never learnt to be entirely relaxed about these manoeuvres.

Our first sea trip took us in the opposite direction, into the Beauly Firth and then to Cromarty at the northerly tip of the Black Isle, with Jane, an extra crew member who had extensive experience on boats. We arrived in difficult conditions at the harbour, which has two open entrances facing each other. The tide was running at 6 knots through the two entrances and directly against us, accelerated by a strong wind. Our maximum engine capacity only matched the opposing speed of the water. We made it through the entrance and attempted to edge crab-wise towards a pontoon but were being pushed back towards the harbour wall. It was important to get shelter because a significant storm was forecast that night.

Two overalled fishermen were talking at the end of the pontoon and hailed us.

'You'll never do it,' one shouted.

'Throw us your lines': the other.

They positioned themselves, corresponding to our bow

and stern, and indicated to Jane and myself exactly where the lines should fall. I knew that this was the time, if ever, to be reliable; to throw a line smartly, with precision and with enough heft for the coils to fly aloft and reach the seemingly distant pontoon. My heart thundered, my hands were sweaty on the rope. And at a signal I breathed deeply and slung back my arm, hurled the line high. Down it crashed, not far from the head of the waiting man who grappled it to a cleat as the other man did the same with Jane's precisely-thrown one. Between them, with their fishermen's strength and authority and the leverage of a half turn around a fixture, they hauled us, in parallel, to the pontoon. It wasn't quick, but gradually their caps, sea-reddened faces and tense brows clarified as we drew closer and finally were safe. Grins were exchanged, rope-hardened hands shaken. And finally they had names and blue eyes, a missing tooth revealed by a smile. From small quayside figures they became particular and unique so that we would recognise them the next day in the Fishertown Inn.

And this is how I began to think of my process. I was throwing out a line to these dimly-defined prior generations and their sea-determined lives, and hoping to gradually close the divide of water, land and time until I could see their faces. So far they remained fuzzy and undefined. Finding some archival information about my family in the late nineteenth and early twentieth centuries felt important, at least in order for my mother to more confidently 'place' herself in the thread of generations and stake a claim to Drake and Chichester inheritances. But for me names and dates were, at least at first, less attractive than our forebears' relationship with their place and its watery edges. Uncovering this hefted history felt more achievable.

By now I had fully acknowledged that I was also undertaking a writing task: a salvage operation in words. I trusted the process enough to know that routes taken by the writing would surprise me, as might what it could unearth.

I made various return visits to the Braunton area after those first ones, began to learn its landmarks and the changing moods of the Marsh, the characteristic circular 'linhay' buildings, drainage systems and sluices; sandy beaches, maze-like and shifting dune-lands, ooze and flood. Birds define this equivocal place: reed and sedge warblers, barn owls, whimbrel, marsh harriers. I walked up this knowledge, gradually accepting I couldn't fix the uneasy shiftings of land and sea, but could always turn my gaze inland to the visual comfort of Devonshire-plump hills. The variety of landscapes all gathered in one place make Braunton one of England's most biodiverse parishes.

The place dazzled me out of the day-to-day with light shining on sheets of wet sand, the constant sense of change, the lamenting curlews. Past lives insisted upwards as the keels and spars of old hulks rose at low tide, impressing on me their sense of forgotten glory, past journeys and journeyers. I learnt that every so often elephants' tusks reveal themselves somewhere on Saunton Sands from the Juba of Bristol, wrecked in a storm with its exotic cargo in December 1770.

This detail gave me pause for thought. I found conflicting accounts of the demise of the Juba, but in both cases the ship had been engaged in the triangular journey of the Atlantic slave trade. In one account this involved the death of twenty-nine slaves on the infamous middle passage between West Africa and the Caribbean islands. Despite the loss of the final cargo, the ship and the crew, a profit was apparently still made by the owners.

Whilst Bristol was one of the most significant centres of the Atlantic slave trade, the part of Devonshire traders has been more hidden. And it had not before occurred to me that the ports of the North Devon coast, and therefore its seafarers, may have been involved. Records show that at least one trader in Bideford was awarded a compensation payout at abolition in 1833 and recent explorations remind us that some Devonshire mansions and associated lives of privilege had been built upon this wealth.

My backward gaze over family and ship history so far was opportunistic and focussed on what was only just out of sight – three or four generations back, and ships built within the last 150 years. But I had to acknowledge that anyone with a seafaring ancestry on the western seaboard of Britain may have forebears amongst crew or beneficiaries of this trade.

The personal implication of this had not been in my thoughts some years before when I looked west from the Senegalese island of Gorée, at one time the largest slave-trading centre on the African coast. I was with a group of writers from Senegal and other African countries as well as other parts of the world. Some were crying.

By a strange coincidence, as I'd approached Braunton by train on my first visit, I received an e-mail on my phone. Peter Pay, it said; my tutor from Exeter College of Art with whom I'd had no contact for well over thirty years. He had come across my name, my books, and was getting in touch to say 'hello'. I'd forgotten that he lived in North Devon, not that far from Braunton.

We didn't meet on that first occasion, but he became interested when I described my mission. Being able to visit local record offices, he investigated on my behalf. He traced a convincing paternal line back from Granny and her brother, Francis: through our fairly lowly sea-captain Drakes of Braunton, including all the Francis's; to the more elevated Hacche-Drake's; then back further to a Henry Drake, seventeenth-century Mayor of Barnstaple. Numerous John and Henry Drakes then processed back to an Elizabethan privateer, Bernard Drake, knighted in Greenwich in 1586. This was confusing as 'Bernard' isn't the name rhyming through our more recent generations. 'Our' Drakes had a Francis in every sibling group and we'd always referenced *Sir* Francis with a wink and kept quiet about him when visiting Spain.

Bernard and Francis, contemporaries and both naval commanders of Queen Elizabeth, came from Drake Families from different sides of the large county of Devon. When she knighted Francis to reward him for the incredible riches he plundered for the Crown, he claimed kinship to Bernard's ancient family, Drake of Ash near Musbury in the south of the county. Peter's notes for me included a small photo of a monument in the local church, which represented Bernard amongst three generations of sixteenth-century Drake patriarchs and their wives. It was decorated with the Drake arms – a wyvern.

Although they appear to share grandparents, Bernard disputed Francis' right to bear these family arms and it led to a 'box on the ear' in court for Francis after he did so. Queen Elizabeth consoled him with a gift of his own arms in which Bernard's wyvern hangs dismally by its heels in the rigging of a ship victorious on the summit of the globe.

How to Throw a Line

I felt proud to have come from a long line of seafarers, but was puzzled. This ancestry seemed far grander than the last few generations, as we know them, suggested. Despite Sir Francis' clear excellence and audacity as a seafarer, after reading more of his slave-trading and other cruelties, I'd be unlikely to shout about descending from him anyway, even if it seemed true. Earlier generations may have thought differently. Records show that a Braunton smack, *Sir Francis Drake* was built at Westacott's of Barnstaple in 1867. Shares went first to 'our' Francis and his son Robert Drake, suggesting they may have commissioned her or at least that the name itself made her a great prize.

Peter and I later pursued physical traces in the Braunton area by driving and walking between houses and farms with a related history. We began with Sir Bernard. With kin amongst other seafaring 'greats' including Richard Grenville – captain of the *Mary Rose* – and Walter Raleigh, his prestige remains embodied in the enormous Castle Hill mansion close to South Molton whose long, white, neo-palladian façade we admired from its triumphal arch on a hill opposite.

We also struck out to villages neighbouring Braunton to which more humble Drakes, Hacche-Drakes, and Chichesters could be connected. It was interesting; a broader context to what I was really seeking. My job seemed to be to join the 'dots'. But I struggled to do so in my head, remaining quite bewildered by all the names and dates.

Before my mother remarried when I was eight years old, our one-parent family living in Suburban Surrey spent a fortnight of each school summer holiday in Exeter – a week in each of the grandparents' homes a mile or so apart. We made trips to Woodbury Common, Dartmoor, the seaside. I have a vivid early memory of being magnetised by a blue expanse of sea from a grassy plateau where we picnicked. I ran towards it with open arms, and had to be caught, not having appreciated that a cliff edge separated this grassy lawn from the sea itself.

Once remarried, my mother stopped accompanying us on this regular holiday. She drove us to Reading railway station instead and on the first occasion the three of us, with no reserved seats in the high season, spent the three-hour journey sitting on our cases in the guard's van, like wartime evacuees.

Her own visits to Exeter never resumed. Once she and my new stepfather, Hugh, had discovered West Penwith, our family holidays moved to a rented chalet in Penzance with some combination of the six children from their two previous marriages. On the way home my two siblings and I would sometimes be dropped with Granny in Exeter, but my mother didn't stay herself except to drink a cup of tea. On the many occasions they drove to Cornwall without any children, they didn't call in on her mother despite passing within half a mile.

When was it that I became aware all was not well between my mother and grandmother? Was it withheld from my child-self until Granny began betraying the details of her disappointments when I was in my twenties? As well as complaining of a husband who died and left her alone as a young woman, she told me how she'd used all her wartime rations to send parcels of cake and butter while my mother was away being a bright star at Oxford. She had sewn new outfits for her, such as a winter coat. It gradually became apparent to me that she felt gratitude or loyalty was not shown by my mother in return. Granny understood that her daughter's private secondary school education, made possible by a scholarship, had led to friendships with minor toffs; she took elocution lessons and outgrew her 'tribe'.

Granny had made the first departure away from the long-held Drake home in Braunton, but my mother took it further, throwing off the ropes that bound together the generations. Through this detachment she seems, in retrospect, to have kept aloof from our shared history.

It seemed to be very late before I first saw photographs of my mother and father marrying in 1953 and realised that our 'Granny Michael' was absent. This detail had been omitted from any family narrative. When asked the reason, my mother simply said, 'My mother didn't really approve of me'. Exactly what this meant wasn't clear, nor how it could be extreme enough to stop her attending her only child's wedding (or to be deliberately excluded). There was some suggestion that Granny thought the wedding premature, before my mother had properly finished her studies (my father was four years older and ahead of her at Oxford). It finally dawned on me that although there was only about a mile between the houses of our grandparents, some gulf of class, history or understanding divided them – we were never all together in the same place.

'She wasn't very sociable,' my mother had said to me. It was with reference to Granny's behaviour towards others during their war years when they crossed the road to share an Anderson shelter with neighbours. It was partially buried and offered greater protection than their cupboard under the stairs where she also spent time. She recalled that they stayed awake all night, making a circle of held hands to combat fear when the bombing started, then emerging in the morning to see a red-tinged sky over Haldon Hill as Plymouth burned.

But in turn Granny had told me that my mother herself was standoffish and unfriendly with the children, evacuated from Kent, who'd stayed with them. By the time Granny revealed her bitterness to me, I may have been the only person she chatted much with each week. She complained about neighbours with unruly gardens who built ugly and unauthorised sheds, and these complaints merged with those of her own life, its disappointments and betrayals, particularly by my mother. I found it both tiresome because it was often repeated, and disconcerting because I'd never heard my mother's side of this story. I didn't enjoy divided loyalties.

'My compensation is that I've got you three,' Granny said at least once. And it still worries me that we, and in particular I, failed to live up to these ideals.

To add historical and literary depth to my understanding of the Taw-Torridge estuary I read Henry Williamson's *The Pathway*, superimposing his post-World War I map of the Braunton area over my own. The novel features a damaged young veteran arriving in the area with revolutionary ideas about society. Passionate about the evil of war rather than its heroism, Williamson hoped the novel would change the European ways of thinking and reveal how young men were abandoned to become destitute and jobless following their service. It was written in his pacifist phase before he took up fascist sympathies, and published to great acclaim in 1928.

Willie Maddison is in love with Mary Ogilvie of The Wildernesse, a household with no male head that is bereaved of sons and siblings by war, but includes older relations of the 'Chychester' family. The house is on the Braunton Marshes, at an intersection of the Burrows, the sea and estuary, and with 'The Great Field' nearby.

Whilst reading it I was struck not just by echoes of the landmarks I was discovering, but by the sense of a long legacy in this fictional family. When the matriarch points to a sword hanging on the wall, she tells her son who is destined for the navy that it had belonged to his great-great-grand-father who fought at Trafalgar. She then encourages him to think of the future generations, his descendants, who will see it in the same place. This deliberately cultivated sense of lineage and secure homeland, even the spoken idea of producing another generation, was a foreign country to me.

Williamson conjures the landscape lyrically in what would today be called 'nature writing', using the seasons to structure the novel. The story concerns the young man's inner struggles with his ideas, the novel he is writing about the redemption of the world, and his relationship with Mary despite her family's disapproval. It reflects low-tide territory; that melancholy world where humans don't quite belong; where a gap is created offering risk and possibility. Willie Maddison affiliates himself to the place by repeated criss-crossing of its land and coastlines on foot, the novel showing how Taw-Torridge shores were linked then by small boat and ferry; connections mostly now lost.

It's also clear that residents had internalised tidal patterns. At the climax of the novel, Maddison waits on the sand-bank 'Sharshook' which he has reached on foot from Crow Point. It's the Autumn Equinox, meaning the *lowest* spring tide of the year. This is known as the 'Great Fair Tide' and it determines the next day as the local fair. He expects to catch a lift with the salmon boats which will come up-river from the Bar when the tide turns just after midnight. He has forgotten, however, that the salmon season finished the previous week and becomes stranded mid-channel on the *highest* tide of the year. The sea-chart makes clear the tiny distance he was from safety on the Appledore shore. But crossing the further channel when the boat doesn't show and the sea rushes in to its fullest height presents an impassable barrier: his nemesis. Mary has already envisaged the tide rushing up the estuary at speed and splashing over the buoy marking the safe channel. His sandbank will not only be surrounded by water, but overwhelmed. He is forced to burn the manuscript of his novel to signal for help as the tide rises. But his signal fails.

Earnest, but well received, *The Pathway* was reprinted many times within months of publication. Permeated by nature's moods, the Bar, the ebb and flow of the tides, the wind and light, the ambivalent marshland, it conveys deep attachment to place and a terrible sense of the aftermath of war. Even though Williamson changed names slightly, I loved recognising and visualising the exact geography of the places and pathways I was learning. And it provided new historical details such as the black hospital ship moored near to the White House, as well as a naturalist's attention to birds, moths, and seasonal flowers.

It allowed me to place Granny here in this period; I could imagine her sharing many such observations.

Before approaching the Taw-Torridge estuary on the South West Coast Path in 2017, Kate and I crossed a long, high and rugged stretch of Exmoor coast, and were forced to bypass the most westerly end of Morte Point due to Hurricane Ophelia's ferocity. When we finally approached

Braunton, we found the coast path diverted at the White House following a recent inundation from the sea. The estuary and pill shores of Horsey Island were no longer available. Instead, we had to follow the flood defence wall alongside the road all the way to Velator Quay.

After arriving at Thelma's B&B again, I left Kate and my bag there and, in fading light, went straight out, under the nearby thatched lychgate and into St Brannock's graveyard. I hadn't yet searched here for Drakes, but a tip from Peter Pay suggested that I should. The stones spread in each direction, rows and rows of them overhung by dark trees. I shuffled through ankle-deep crisp leaves, peered at names and dates, conscious that my stooped figure might alarm someone taking a short cut in the twilight. With little hope, I turned on my head-torch when darkness fell and told myself that if I found nothing within an hour, I would give up.

The time came and, tired, hungry and disappointed, I turned back towards the gate. And then, walking a line of Gothic-arched stones, a flash of torchlight illuminated the word 'DRAKE' and dropped me to my knees. Tracing the leaded inscription amongst grey lichen and moss creeping in from the sculpted edges, I read 'Robert Drake'. And then the words: 'In loving memory of my dear husband … who fell asleep in Jesus 22nd February 1907 aged 36 years'. My great-grandfather. Below him on the same stone was his wife's name, my great-grandmother, 'Annie Lock Drake who died June 10th 1925'.

I returned in the morning when I could see more clearly. Even then low light and moss made it difficult. I found several more Drake stones huddling close to the first ones as if for warmth. I concentrated on the closest relatives. Often several deaths were recorded on the same stone:

three of Robert's sisters, two of whom had only short lives. Overseeing them all was my great-great-grandmother, who died in 1900: Emma Louise, née Chichester, whose leather-bound and monogrammed volume of Tennyson poems rested on my bookshelf 500 miles away in Scotland and whose name was given by her husband to a ship.

The gravestones darkened towards the ground as if gradually morphing with it, and it was only by chance that I glimpsed a further lead-outlined name towards the base of this stone. Despite brushing the leaves away, it took some deciphering even in daylight. It commemorated a younger brother of Robert, the 'Francis' of this generation, in some further words. The only ones I could be sure of were, 'accidentally drowned off Combe Martin July 5, 1903, aged 25 years'. A shock unbalanced me when I read this. Two or three days before we had passed Combe Martin on the coast path and had a harbourside cream tea. We had reached the small town across soaring cliffs which defined a long stretch with no harbours, and included the highest cliff of the whole SWCP, Great Hangman Hill. The shores here, as seen from the sea, would have been lonely and walled by cliffs, surf slamming onto a portcullis of rock.

I was about to turn away, when I realised further words lay even closer to the ground, on the bevel of the stone's base, almost redacted by moss. The first in small capitals, referred to this Francis: 'THY WILL BE DONE' – a seemingly fatalistic acceptance. And then on the dampest, darkest part of the stone, barely decipherable, was the patriarch – my great-great-grandfather Francis Drake – and a date: '1925, aged 85'. 'AT REST.'

I shouldn't have needed such concrete evidence, but now these people and their lives seemed to draw near, confirming our ancestry as 'true' and physically earthed in a way it hadn't been before. Here were the forebears my mother had never known, who I told her of later. It all seemed a surprise to her. She had shown little curiosity in this family who were all dead before she was born. She'd had no starting point.

After my tour with Peter Pay on the Braunton side of the estuary, I visited the Maritime Museum in Appledore on the Torridge branch. I quickly discovered not only a model of the Drake ship *Emma Louise* but met the man who had built it, the Chair of the museum, Michael Guegan. He had made the model with close attention to detail including the wooden blocks through which the 'sheets' for controlling sails ran, and a 'jolly boat' or 'tender', lashed to the deck. Six brown sails were hoisted – two inner jibs, staysail, mainsail and mizzen. It was a miniature ship that I could believe in.

'This was my great-great-grandfather's ship,' I told Michael excitedly. 'Can you tell me more? About the Drakes?'

He was a small, wiry man of an age hard to place, with a broad Devon accent. He had retired as a foreman of the Appledore shipyard after forty years there and then made the museum his life. His historical knowledge of the ships that worked from within the Bideford Bar was so extensive, it seemed he embodied the active memory of the place.

'Well,' he said, 'what is it you want to know?'

I floundered. What *did* I want to know? What were they like, these seafaring men – tough, absent, hard-skinned, or longing for home and the hugs of their wives and children?

He showed me *Emma Louise*'s 'fiddlehead', a decoration that sits below a ship's bowsprit, curled into the shape of the musical instrument. It was painted with a union flag, and had apparently been originally collected by Basil Greenhill, founder of the Greenwich Maritime Museum. Michael told me of further remaining artefacts: a crest from her stern lodged somewhere. Her keel, steel-lined later in her life for the heavy drop of coal into her hold, still lies visible somewhere at low tide.

'Up Snuffy,' he said it was, with a hand gesture upstream towards Bideford.

I didn't know an 'Up Snuffy' but pictured a mud-sucked creek.

I came back to my question about the Drakes.

He laughed, returning to his response: 'Depends what you want to know'.

I realised how foolish I sounded, wanting to know something but having no idea what it was. As ludicrous perhaps as the vague notion of Sir Francis Drake being an ancestor of ours. Wrong-footed and feeling I was probably wasting his time, I turned away.

Soon after my discovery of the graves, I was invited to contribute to BBC Radio 4's *Open Country* programme about the Taw-Torridge estuary. First the producer, presenter and I went to speak about the local maritime history with Michael Guegan in Appledore. Still feeling slightly foolish, I wasn't sure I was any more informed with questions for him.

We stood on a slipway close to the lifeboat station with the sea opening out flatly beyond us. The presenter, Helen Mark, asked me first about my interests here. I spoke of my ancestry and how, as a writer, the liminal nature of the place interested me with so much permeable shoreline and the opportunity for land and water to shapeshift and beguile.

'You certainly got a different way of words than I have,' Michael said, laughing. His shortness, and relaxed dress in jeans and a waxed jacket struck me; a man comfortable in the knowledge of his own expertise. 'As far as I'm concerned the tide comes in and goes out again!'

He pointed out that the tidal range here is second in the world only to the Bay of Fundy in Canada and spoke of how a ship these days could snake its way along the channel using echosounders, but it was treacherous in the days of sail; though wide and seemingly fulsome at high tide, the estuary is, mostly, extremely shallow. With sail only, especially as a 'stranger', the channel would be difficult to locate and the ship would be blown one way and then the other.

Despite this, he said, ports in the estuary had been important – the second most significant in the country for tobacco imports in the 1700s. And then there had been a big connection with Canada.

'I've got a good memory for all this nonsense,' he said.

I was glad of it even though I still didn't seem to know what to ask.

Afterwards we went to meet a local gig-rowing club.

The rowers, in smart black and yellow jackets with 'Appledore' written across their backs, assembled around the pilot gig *Margaret James* on her trailer in the car park, long and white with black gunwales. A mixture of men and women, the oldest was eighty-three. The youngest rower, Naomi, told Helen how such gigs would have been used for everything, from delivering flowers to carrying coffins, as well as taking pilots out to incoming ships.

The crew wheeled the gig down a mud-slicked slipway and she was nudged into the shallows of this vast sky- and water-scape. Braunton was visible distantly through smirr on the far side. A mile to row. They pulled the trailer away from under the gig, once floating, and after lying her parallel to the shore, the rudder was fitted while each rower climbed in and quickly took up position, holding oars vertical. They were accustomed to this procedure, well-organised and familiar with each other, efficient with their movements. There had been plenty of banter and ribbing during the trailer-push here, but now they were silent, listening for commands.

Helen took up a 'passenger' seat close to the cox, ready to record with her fluffy microphone.

'Blades down when you've got water,' the cox said.

As depth allowed, oars were fitted onto 'thole pins' on the gunwales.

Following a further command, the rowers leant forward, oars pointing to the bow and parallel with each other, and then quickly they were off. Synchronised and moving at speed. Diminishing in size, the gig headed out into a murky afternoon towards the estuary mouth and the Bar, carrying with it my unexplainable longing to be part of such a collaboration with the sea and its traditions.

After their return we drove the 18 miles back around the estuary to Braunton and I proudly showed BBC colleagues those ranks of family gravestones at St Brannock's. I recited their names for listeners, described the stones and their moss-crawled lettering. The wind whipped up dry leaves around our legs.

To me, finding names marked on stone had seemed a miracle: *Look! They really existed. It's not a myth.* Their lives were confirmed in death by the solidity of the graveyard stone and earth. But, when asked, I found little more to add. They weren't extraordinary. I couldn't immediately think of any gripping narrative. I didn't yet know what I would do with this information.

It probably didn't make very good radio.

The producer, independently of my suggestions for the local area, had arranged to visit Broadlands Farm. The Hartnolls were one of only three remaining families cultivating the Great Field, an area of land a further step off the estuary than the grazed marshes, but similarly low and flat. Rural Devon is often characterised by its criss-crossing hedges but on this strip-farmed land, hedges were never created and many strips maintain their medieval dimensions. In theory the Great Field starts beyond the reach of the highest tide, but a 'Great Hedge' (a built bank) nevertheless protects the land from inundation at bi-monthly spring tides. At least for now.

In the farmyard bulbous orange pumpkins had been packed up in cases ready for dispatch. Potato crates were piled up nearby. We walked out onto the field with John Hartnoll, still looking good in his eighties, jovial in a baseball cap, tweed jacket and wellies and his son David, acknowledging the wildness of the day in plastic trousers over wellies and wearing a cowboy hat.

A pleasant familiarity and openness flowed through our conversation. Both men were generous in their explanations of the sharing of land, what is grown where and who owns what. How the old system in which families might own strips of only an acre or so, or even a quarter of an acre, is maintained.

Wind was driving across the open fields as John told us how each strip is separated by a grass ridge a foot wide and high called a 'launchard' which he said was 'sacred' and must never be ploughed. He said they occasionally confuse who owns which strip and accidentally plough or plant their neighbour's land for them.

David spoke about farming and sailing as dual realities for the families here in times gone by, with some members doing both. I was particularly delighted to discover that while David takes most responsibility for the farming, John was the 'Marsh Inspector'.

'Once you got this job, you got it for life', he said, telling us that it was an elected position between the current farmers and he'd welcome some younger blood. The other Inspector, still active, still farming, would soon be ninety years old. Together they were responsible for managing the routing and control of water, securing an equilibrium between land, pill, marsh and estuary; knowledge gathered through years, perhaps generations, of experience. And he explained why the coast path had recently been diverted away from the cobbled sea wall around Horsey Island.

'There's a flood door on there: kept the tide out, got into disrepair. Got worse and worse. Breached right through the bank. It's in dire straits. They're trying to do something about it now but it's a big job.'

Their surname, Hartnoll, had chimed in some shadowy memory of mine. When John referred to a cousin Frances who lived in Exeter, cogs began to mesh.

'My mother has a cousin called Frances in Exeter too,' I said.

It was this cousin who had written to my mother after visiting the Appledore Museum, sending a list of names of ships and suggesting the 'Coasters' book. She had set both of us off, first on the book purchase, then my mother's trip on *Bessie Ellen* and now my explorations. I recalled meeting her a few times, probably most recently at Granny's funeral, and remembered her as a kind, intelligent woman who had been a history teacher and seemed interested in me and my career. But exactly how we were related I had never been certain.

John and I disentangled the complex links between the families of that generation – the Drakes, Newcombes and Hartnolls; marriages made between first cousins. It was clear that in some knotty way I was 'related' to John and David. They bridged parts of my family and the generations. They were not just alive, but still here, jovial and soily-fingered, working the ancestral land.

My – until now, slight – sense of the family was materialising in flesh and blood and soil and sea; a hand I could shake and soil that bore up huge orange pumpkins. For the first time I understood how visiting North Americans feel when they come seeking and find evidence of their roots. This family has been connected for so many generations to this precise place – to Braunton, even particular fields with their own names, a long-standing connection and family legacy which I have never known.

Another idea occurred to me when we finished recording. 'Have you ever heard of a John Drake owning any of this land?' I asked, indicating the Great Field, the Marshes beyond.

They both shook their heads.

'Not unless one of the other farmers rents from him.' David took out his phone to ask the most likely neighbour, but the answer was negative.

We left via the muddy farmyard, meeting David's son who was working here for a year, having just finished a degree in aeronautical engineering. Three generations were at work on the same land. We promised to stay in touch and John said that at some future opportunity he would show me the water-balancing workings on the Marshes.

That evening, David called me. He was laughing. 'Turns out it's us that rents the field from John Drake. It's been for so long that we'd forgotten!'

Further evidence of our families interlocking materialised when I later looked up shipping records relating to the coasting ketch, *Pirate*. At one time John Perryman Hartnoll had co-owned her with the Drakes. Considering the close community once here, such co-owning of ships in the early twentieth century wasn't surprising. Sixty-four shares could be split between fathers and sons, or cousins, or relations through marriage. Commercial partnerships probably cemented matrimonial ones, or vice versa. It looked to me from what I learned from the shipping records that the families Hartnoll, Drake, Newcombe, Huxtable, and Berry used both methods to lash their families and their sea-lives together, so making their businesses secure. It probably also guaranteed plentiful crew. But they have woven a family 'tree' so thicketed with cousins marrying cousins through the centuries, that it would require a 3D model to represent even the four generations before me – which is as far back as I can maintain any mental hold on it.

Granny – Dorothy Louise Drake – whose sea-captain father Robert had died and lost his influence on her choices by then, seems to have broken the mould. Her passion for music took her to London where she lived with the Huxtables. This Braunton family had intermarried with Drakes at least as far back as 1774. By the time she married, the social and economic picture of life in Braunton was already changing; the steady chug of ships' engines supplementing canvas and creating new opportunities, bringing with it new lifestyles.

How to Throw a Line

A few days later I was further south-west in Penzance. Despite her lively chat I noted that my mother's home seemed to have frozen in time around her. Paint brushes and high-quality Italian watercolour paper, piles of books to read, second-hand ones she intended to sell on – they hadn't moved since my last visit. The bubble-wrap, padded envelopes and cardboard to package books remained crammed into any available cupboard or crack. It was as if she was awaiting recovery from something unseen before resuming her usual activities.

The house held its breath with all the evidence of a rich life intact. But, like a ship gradually listing when beached on a sandbank, the incremental decline seemed invisible to her. For the first time it struck me that these artefacts were the material reality we would be dealing with at her death.

'Good Lord!' she said when I reported to her the coincidental meeting with the Hartnolls.

'Do you know of them?' I asked.

She chewed over the name then shook her head. When I explained the relationship to Frances Newcombe she said: 'I think I'd need to see a diagram.'

Of course she was right; it does require a diagram. I need to refresh my own interpretation of this dense thicket every time I approach it. But I probably took it as a deflection. It felt like a shunning of the past, the guarded cave of memory and feeling that had been a feature of my whole family life until now. Her carapace in general was perhaps the mark of a particular era. But this stoic deadlock added to my confused feelings for her – admiration and pride against irritation and impatience. Whilst wanting her love and approval, I in turn withheld myself from her, and so created further distance.

She added details, though, that day of 'her war'. When hostilities were foreseen, she was evacuated to Weston-

Super-Mare to stay with an aunt, leaving her parents in vulnerable Southampton. Some months into her extended stay there she experienced a 'three-day calamity'. Day one, in which a telephone call told the death of her father; Day two, when everyone else had to leave Southampton due to the expected invasion; and Day three, the beginning of the war. She was finally reunited with her mother after months apart when the pair were due to move into a house on the edge of Exeter at Countess Wear. My mother said she was still walking in a daze, despite the months since the 'calamity'. While they waited for their house to be ready, members of the Newcombe family helped out: one couple, well-off through work in Australia, taking them into their large Exeter house close to the University; another providing a bicycle and thus giving my mother freedom to explore the Devon lanes and chase butterflies. My mother's recall remained sharp. She had probably told me all this before, but now I paid more attention.

Growing up as I did in a contained nuclear family, with lines to our previous generations and their homelands cast away, my new-found connection to the Hartnolls delighted me. In our immediate family we had only occasionally rehearsed the older stories, and not necessarily accurately. We seemed adrift. My roots as an adult have always felt more connected to networks of friendship. But it seemed now that I'd successfully thrown a rope back through generations; it had been caught and I was beginning to be pulled closer.

It was important, though, to have my mother's engagement. Without her involved in this project, I reminded myself, it had little purpose. But she often seemed more intent on forgetting than remembering.

The Cargo We Carry

Braunton remained in my mind a contrary location from which to run coastal cargo ships, with its remove from the open sea and even the estuary. But for the village to have grown a large and long-lasting fleet and to breed generations of seamen in such circumstances seems extraordinary.

Originally the cargo sailing ships were importing for local needs and local trading: coal and limestone from South Wales across the Bristol Channel. Bricks from Bridgwater. The ships began to grow in size in the late nineteenth century, from smacks of around thirty tons to ketches from thirty-five to sixty tons. A wave of entrepreneurship broke out and the Drakes and Chichesters were amongst the leading families involved in this revolution. Local seafarers referred to themselves then as 'Master Mariners' and often owned more than one vessel, as well as being merchants. This was certainly true of the Drake family, who seemed to buy and sell shares in ships regularly.

In the book that launched me and my mother into this investigation, the historian Peter Thomson suggests 1910 as the 'heyday' of the Braunton Fleet, when twenty-eight vessels were owned in the village and three ships could be seen dealing with cargoes at Velator simultaneously. Ships trading only within the Bristol Channel were known as 'down-homers', often running routes of several legs, for example Braunton to Neath to Penarth to Lynmouth and back to Braunton, each leg with a different cargo to deliver or lift and a different state of wind or tide to challenge the sailing.

Larger ships, including the schooner *Result* which first took 'Uncle Frank' to sea, worked anywhere within the home-trade limits of Ushant, the French westerly extreme of the English Channel, to Elbe in north-west Germany. A Further group of medium-sized ketches traded principally in the Bristol Channel, Irish Sea, and the western end of the English Channel. I picture the gruelling day for crews spent shovelling, hauling, filling the hold, and then casting off from the quay. Having crossed the Bar, with sails filling, they must have felt muscles ease as eyes turned away from the demands of land and home to the seafarers' other habitual terrain. And the horizon.

The cargo-books of *Bessie Ellen*, found by Nikki Alford, her current skipper-owner, reveal the typical goods carried and multi-port journeys made by those medium-sized ketches. For example, on November 30th 1910 Master John Chichester loaded 95 tons of oats in Kinsale, Eire, delivering them to a Mr Tonkin of Penzance on December 2nd.

'Judging by the tonnage,' Nikki writes in her blog, 'I would imagine that the cargo was loaded into sacks rather than as a bulk cargo. Oats are a relatively light cereal cargo and in damp weather (rain, snow) or heavy seas, the cargo must be protected from moisture, since wetting or damp may ruin the consignment ... It seems the ship made a slow passage down to Penzance, the distance being only 200 nautical miles. Looking at the timing of the passage, perhaps she was up against prevailing SW'lies that are the norm at this time of year.'

The next entry shows *Bessie Ellen* loading 113 tons of copper ore in Penzance for the shipper Bennello to be delivered to a William Forbes in Swansea. But she remained in Penzance for twenty-eight days, 'perhaps loading the ore, or the Master, John Chichester returning home to Braunton to spend Christmas with his family before sailing from Penzance on 30th December, arriving in Swansea for discharging on 1st January 1911.' As well as the dominant cargo of coal, typical freights included clay, cement, stone, maize, salt, and manure.

Amongst the artefacts in Braunton Museum, I came across a pile of early twentieth-century postcards sent to a Miss Eadie Corney in Plymouth from her brothers: coastal traders working in parallel with Drakes and Chichesters. Sent from Glasgow, Ireland, South Shields, Wales and Newlyn, they demonstrate the coastal dance of trading vessels. The written words are rather like text messages of today, updating Eadie on their location, the state of their loading and sailing plans, the wind direction. The sentence structure often suggests haste.

One sent from Newport on February 8th 1907 says: 'Dear sister, glad to hear from you had a letter alright. I will write to mother Sunday. I don't know when we shall load but we have a charm. From your loving brother A.C.'

A charm? The sea seems to turn us pagan, inclining us to feel our frailty and believe that a Friday, belonging to the devil, would not be a good day to sail; that whistling could accidentally raise a gale; that a piece of twine or cloth knotted three times, bought from a woman on a quayside, might provide a sea captain with three progressively fiercer winds. The third untying could be disastrous. I wonder what this 'charm' was, and where it was acquired. The wording suggests it had some bearing on their departure.

Another postcard, dated April 11th 1913, is from Penzance. A photograph from the quay shows in the foreground a bow sprit and furled foresail. On the far side of a stretch of water rises the distinctive tower of St Mary's church, a high landmark on the town's seafront not far from my mother's house.

'Dear Eadie,' it reads, 'a line to let you know we are loaded to London sailing today it's a fair wind now hope to get up pretty quick we are having a little better weather now, one thing summer time coming along, hope to be passing Plymouth in the morning, hoping this will find you well. A.C.'

These cards of few words sent during each voyage brought the dialogue between sea-journeys and family life into focus. Even women who accompanied their husbands to sea such as on the Chichester ketch, *Bessie Ellen*, would more often stay ashore. They had the family to steer as well as sometimes the business itself whilst men were away at sea for extended periods. Or were missing completely. Women, in turn, may have developed new skills and greater independence. But North Devon's treacherous coast had inevitable consequences to the destinies of marriages and families in these communities: a cargo of grief, a coast of widows.

Lines from *Julius Caesar* tell us, 'There is a tide in the affairs of men, / which, taken at the flood, leads on to fortune.' The flood tide acts as a powerful metaphor for pressing forward when conditions are ascendant. The context for Shakespeare was battle, but I was interested to come across this quotation transcribed into Granny's 'friendship album'. It was signed 'F Drake' in a beautiful copperplate hand and dated January 1917; her grandfather, retired master-mariner and owner of many ships, whose livelihood was shaped by the pulse of tides.

The Cargo We Carry

In my early twenties, when I was a student combining courses at Exeter University and the College of Art, I'd cycle or motorcycle along Topsham Road to have lunch with Granny once a week. Over these lunches she retold her own growing-up stories. I'd heard them so many times, I evaded the repetition by nodding and grunting whilst leafing through her *Daily Mail*, searching for news. I didn't ask questions.

She spoke of cycling from Braunton the 6 miles to Barnstaple Grammar School, even in the snow; mentioned friends with surnames like Incledon and Chugg. On Sundays in summer a huge crowd of family and friends would take a charabanc to Croyde Bay for a picnic. As a young woman she was famed, she said, for her 'marvellous hair and beautiful teeth' (the latter extracted, nevertheless, in favour of falsies in her early twenties). The photo I unearthed of her at about sixteen years of age shows a pretty, collected-looking girl with a softly curving pale face, dark eyes and brows, hair hanging gorgeously to her waist and tied across the crown with a wide white ribbon that matches an embroidered dress. There is, if you look closely, a surprising sense of determination in her lower jaw, perhaps a clue to how she got away from village life to study for a music certificate in London.

The friendship album was gifted to Dorothy in September 1912 by her Drake cousins Ivy and Eileen, William's daughters. It seems to have come into its own from the summer of 1914 with the latest entries made in 1919. This was a critical period both in the world and for Granny. The entries, from well-wishers amongst family, friends and teachers at Barnstaple Grammar School, reflect her as a young woman just coming of age, as if she's a ship about to be launched. There are jokes, aphorisms, advice, rhymes and literary quotes ranging through Stevenson, Tennyson, Shelley, Goethe, Wordsworth, and Dorothy M Parker. Dickens advises: 'Have a heart that never hardens, a temper that never tires, and a touch that never hurts.'

There are also some fine drawings, sketches, paintings in ink and watercolour. Amongst them, drawn in pencil with a full rig of eight sails, I recognised a ketch. The pennant flag topping the ship's main mast flies taut in the wind and clearly reads, *Pirate*. Knowing the provenance of this ship built in Orkney in 1888, the thrill of recognition reassured me of a more 'felt' connection to the past than I had found words for at the family gravestones. It was a connection made across a century or more of sea and miles. Finding this drawing felt akin to meeting by chance a beloved old friend.

It was salt-tinged, though. I'd found out that Dorothy's Uncle Francis – the one whose grave told me he was 'Lost at Sea' in 1903 off Combe Martin – was lost from *Pirate*. He had owned two-thirds of *Pirate's* shares when he fell overboard whilst hoisting the mizzen and was never seen again. There is no clue to the identity of the sketcher but clearly someone was still willing to celebrate and take pride in this vessel.

I'd found the friendship album in 'The Box', a receptacle deep and dark as the holds of the family ships. The cargo of photos, letters, bills, and other paperwork had been contained there since Granny's death in 1984. It had come with me in a house move from Devon to Scotland in 1990 and survived two or three subsequent moves until settling in my current home in Highland Perthshire in 1998. Recovered from the loft when it was insulated, it had since remained shelved for another decade or so.

Unpacking The Box, once the physical geography of Granny's life had been animated by those first visits to Braunton, represented an apology to her for not attending to her recitals of unfamiliar names and places. I suppose my life had been expanding then, just as hers was narrowing. My attention to its contents now had to stand in for proper listening. I hoped it might reveal more to me about the origins and lives of these close-knit families in Braunton.

The majority of people in the photos were unidentified. When my mother was still making annual trips to my home in Scotland, she'd spent a wet day raking through it to see who she recognised, marking the backs of photographs in pencil when she did. But largely she couldn't say who anyone was or where they were.

I recognised Granny and her brother Francis as children because I'd seen the images often enough before. Their faces are distinctive. In one particular photo, their mother, Annie Lock Drake (née Roach), comes into focus. The threesome are pictured on a slope in front of winter-bare trees. A low stone wall rises behind them. Perhaps they are in the garden of their home in Heanton Street. Frank is about three years old; white smock, fair hair, pointed chin, peering at the camera. Dorothy wears a white knee-length frock, has thick, loose, dark hair. Incongruously, she wears high, shiny leather boots. In her arms a large, clearly precious doll reclines.

Behind them both, the mother is dressed in a black ruffed blouse with a lace bodice pulled in tightly to the waist of a long, plain, black skirt. The only contrast is a small collar of white lace. Her eye sockets are deep and dark, mouth slightly downturned and brows sunk. Arms by her sides, her whole presence speaks of grief.

I imagine this to be taken in 1907 or a little later, soon after the death of her husband Robert Drake, whose gravestone I'd found with its obscure whisper: 'fell asleep in Jesus'. According to a newspaper report he had died 'after a long illness'.

I shared the photo with my mother when I visited her after my second Taw-Torridge trip. She hadn't seen it before. I asked how much she knew of her mother's loss at such an early age.

'I don't think it was spoken about,' she said. 'Not that I recall anyway. I didn't know either of these grandparents.' Both had died before my mother was born.

She sat back, clasped by the cream sofa in which she seemed to sail most of her days now. 'And anyway, when I was growing up it was the war and everyone was losing people.'

But perhaps Annie's sunken brow in the photo had struck a chord, as she began to speak instead about her own decision-making with three children under five when my father died from cancer at the age of thirty-three.

'We'd already made a plan,' she explained. 'Hypothetically. When we first married.'

The discussion had been prompted by a friend and contemporary of theirs who was widowed at a young age. I had heard it before. There was a sense that my mother had been rehearsing her stories – just as her own mother did – for so long they'd solidified into a script. But perhaps I was now a little more receptive.

In the last six months of my father's life we had to return as a family to Britain from the Netherlands, where he'd been working for Royal Dutch Shell, for him to be treated for cancer in a London hospital. I was one year old, my sister the eldest at four, and we stayed with his parents in their sizeable Exeter house. My mother travelled between there and our father in London.

'I went endlessly up and down the country,' she said. 'Feeling bad about being absent from each one in turn.'

But after he died in January 1961 it was the south-east of England rather than the south-west that called to my mother. In the discussion while he still lived, they'd agreed she should go to where friends and colleagues lived, to be sure of the embrace of a living community.

So just when a shift in geography might have healed a rift with her own Drake mother and she might have resumed her association with the coast and sea, she packed us into our green Austin Van. I still remember squabbling with my siblings over the roof-top ventilation hatch from the hard bench built into the back of this family 'car'. My mother drove us inland to suburban Surrey to make a new life far away from family – to their incredulity, I later learnt. But what we gained was parallel families to our own, known through the Shell network, with whom we shared bonfire-night parties, picnics and other social occasions. My mother took up classes in archaeology and painting; she planted the garden with vegetables and redecorated the house.

When I was a child, generational divisions were starker. My mother was always absent from my play, seeing to things indoors or gardening. Meanwhile in the wilder parts of the garden the three of us built our respective 'camps' out of packing cases. My mother came to call these our 'slums'. From there I burrowed in the bracken and ditches, climbed trees, and stood on the log pile to sing. She was adventurous with holidays, driving us to Wales without even booking accommodation ahead, and taking us up Snowdon in a blizzard when I was only seven, an unintentional summit because my brother cried each time she tried to turn back.

My godfather was an old friend of my father's from Oxford. After his divorce, when I was about seven, Hugh visited us often and soon love was in the air on long country walks, then marriage to my mother. Later an extended family of lively step-siblings materialised around me, becoming a – soon loved – part of my life.

My stepfather also worked for Shell, but in London as an aviation journalist rather than as my father had, in the Netherlands. His element was air and my mother – ever alert, ever curious – embraced his passion and the many light aircraft trips. When I joined them, usually without choice, I cowered in the back seat, trying not to look out of the window which revealed the fathoms of air beneath me. I incanted internally something like a prayer to keep us safe.

They seemed to fall in love as if they should always have been together, but there were also stresses and strains. Six children between them, a boarding school for some, another parent, a smallish house. Some strange periods followed in which my mother suffered ill-health. There was a long hospital stay and convalescence away from home during which my stepsister and I, the same age and still at primary school, stayed with family friends on school nights. Midweek, we'd walk hand in hand from one temporary home to another, carrying small overnight bags.

Then came my mother's episodes of poor sleep and sleepwalking and she became unable to get out of bed in the mornings, at least not before we had left for school. When, one morning, I needed her to drive me somewhere, it was like raising someone from profound depths. Even once behind the wheel, she was unable to speak. I didn't recognise this person.

There was another unexplained hospital stay. Ahead of a visit, I spent several evenings hand-stitching two mice for her from scraps of fabric with which she had recently tailored a suit for herself: dog-tooth-tweed in orange and turquoise. I over-stitched the seams with loops of knitting wool and embroidered on eyes and whiskers, then carried the creatures to the hospital on a visit with my stepfather. Although I was allowed behind the high red brick face of the building, it seemed children were not permitted on the wards. I was left in the waiting area whilst he carried the mice to my mother's bedside.

When he returned, he was still holding them. He told me that she couldn't bear to look at them; 'they made her too sad'. I don't recall what I then did with these laboured-over gifts but I do remember the walk we took afterwards on a wintry Surrey heath. A blasted heath, obscured by thick air and fog and a sense of terrible absence. What age had I been then – nine or ten?

Long afterwards I learned she'd been put to sleep there for three days; an attempt to 're-boot' her in some way. But I doubt it worked as the sleepless nights and late, absent mornings remained a pattern.

It was through Hugh's work and a trip to write a story about the Land's End Flying Club – at that time an eccentric enterprise – that he and my mother were first introduced to West Penwith in the early 1970s. Given a particular wind direction, a take-off from this airfield pitches you across a precipitous drop of cliffs and then over a chasm of sky and sea. They came home transformed and the next decade was punctuated by return trips. They frequented the Abbey

Hotel and its associated cottages in Penzance over the years, cultivating new friendships, delighted by the eccentrics they met with offbeat passions. They relished sea swims, admired Celtic crosses, steep flower-frothed valleys, and granite heat. She painted; he flew.

Much later I found a file of A4 pages, detailing these days in her cursive handwriting. She wrote about the way they would fly only 50 feet (15.2m) above the sea along the cliffs, startling cormorants and being waved at by fishermen. On looking down she noted turquoise water alongside the cliff, divided from violet sea-depths by a sand bar.

Back at home they navigated a tangle of teenagers, divided loyalties, the various loci of children, parents, schools. A house extension was built. In a time in which intergenerational intimacy was unusual, tensions and cruelties broke the surface but remained unaddressed. And then the six of us in my generation left home and scattered.

Hugh took early retirement in the mid-1980s and they were able to move to their beloved West Penwith. When he became ill with cancer a few years later they had a weekend stay at the 'Bristol Centre' which promoted responsibility for self-care in cancer sufferers and their spouses. The experience prompted an attempt at reparation. For my mother this was an admission to each of her adult children that she had been emotionally unable to support or comfort us, all under five years of age, when she told us of the death of our father.

Such is the cargo we carry.

Braunton's West Hill, otherwise known as Beacon Hill, offers a strategic look-out to the coast, just as it did during the times of the Spanish Armada. Women watched from here for the return of their men's ships, and perhaps in the merchant days ached as much for the money in their husbands' pockets to feed the family as for their return to the home and marital bed. Yet the documented history of this great period of seafaring – the photographs of ships in books and museums, the tales written down, the museum artefacts – seems peopled only by men. The wild places of estuaries and open sea, the shovelling and hauling, the raising of sails, is the male domain; there was a binary in this past community, and within families.

Men surely became strange with distance and with frequent communing of the soul with the sea. More often than most they may have confronted their own mortality and perhaps this nurtured a silent affinity to each other as powerful as that to their own families; to the wives who waited for them and knew they might die young.

Salt ran in their veins for so many generations that perhaps today they might be discerned as outsiders; itinerants of some sort, hard to define and never quite fixable geographically, last seen off some point or other in South Wales, or heard of in scribbled postcards, waiting for the right tide or wind in Stranraer or Padstow. Even when home, they might be visible but somehow unfathomable.

Sometimes they might have cursed their work, the harsh weather on their hands and faces, the missed companionship of skittles at the Inn, the birthdays of their children or the Sunday picnics at Croyde Bay. And yet I imagine they were bound to life at sea. The crossings of the Bar, the Atlantic opening from the arms of Devon and Wales, the promise of that complete and infinite horizon which took their own fathers and grandfathers to Newfoundland for the cod. Perhaps each time they left, they learnt afresh that they couldn't live solely amidst silver and porcelain. Their timeless association with sea, the comforting creak of timber and strain of hemp on a good ship could not be out-done by any woman or child or horsehair-stuffed sofa. They were 'off' again. And perhaps they were further distanced from wives by a love for their ship which Joseph Conrad wrote of as 'nearly as great as that of man for woman.' I wonder if, for the seafarers in my own family, this allegiance was sometimes stronger than to their wives with whom less time was passed.

I've often been accused of being itinerant by those who observe my comings and goings. I've heard the refrain, 'she's off again', as I've developed a lifestyle full of travel and work away from home – journeys, adventures, 'crossings', extending into my adulthood a self-sufficiency I learnt early. Somewhere deep inside I recognise a longing for the 'offing' but with it comes unease: drownings, wrecks, loss, and the half-life exile of economic endeavour with the sea.

In practice, I was nervous, cowardly even, when it came to the sea.

The last time I had 'sailed' (no canvas was raised) was on the return from that Cromarty trip after the difficult har-bour entry with the ex and Jane. With only limited shelter there the boat was already thrashing against its lines, and we had to leave before winds increased to storm level. A fall-ing tide added further pressure; we needed sufficient depth through the Firth and at the canal entrance near Inverness where we would reach shelter.

We'd headed east from the harbour. Sheltered at first by land, once we'd turned Sutor's Stacks on the north-east corner of the Black Isle we faced into the south-wester-lies, pitching over breaking waves which scored white corrugations across the narrowing Firth. We were apparently the only vessel out in it. Jane and my ex appeared confident despite the spray and drenched air and unpredictable motion. I lacked faith. I knew there were concealed sandbanks and, through the spray, their markers were hard to see. What if the keel cracked down on to the sea bed? There was also to be a channel between two points to negotiate and strong currents on the approach to Inverness.

I soon became silent, frozen and insular; not willing to go below and make tea. Jane encouraged me, telling me (not for the first time) how much she trusted our skipper's boat-handling; encouraging me with chart and set square to help navigate – something, anything, to occupy me. But I was that gripped child once again, longing for the security of land. This was not my element.

With delivery under the Kessock Bridge and into the more sheltered waters of the Beauly Firth, my composure seeped back. Motoring gently in between the arms of the canal quays at Clachnaharry felt like rescue from a mythic ordeal, just as it was when I was a child and Hugh had completed his noisy, vibrating landing at the airfield and was taxiing us back towards the clubhouse. I could stop 'praying' then. I was still alive.

The lock-keeper caught our lines, secured us back to something solid and said, laughing: 'Not many out there today.'

At home in January 2018 Charlotte, Adam and I called a meeting to gauge enthusiasm for the idea of building and rowing a St Ayles Skiff for Loch Tay. Despite the town having a population of only about 2000, the meeting was well-attended, bringing together people who had never met. Some were keen to build a boat; some had glimpsed those plucky boats at sea and wanted to row. Two potentially 'serious' sports rowers came too, perhaps misled by associations with my surname.

By March we were a constituted club and a committee was formed. The group included faces new and old; I'd worked alongside Adam some years earlier when he was a policy officer working internationally for WWF (World Wide Fund for Nature) in the local office where I was Education Officer. It was what had brought us both to live here. He was a good-humoured colleague with a quick wit, but also seemed highly effective. By August, with him running our skiff fundraising campaign, we were ready to purchase the kit and plans.

Early that summer ten or so of us made two evening visits to the club at Broughty Ferry near Dundee for a coastal rowing 'taster'. The *Arthur Nicoll* was one of their two boats, painted white with a sheer light-blue 'strake' (the top longitudinal plank running stem to stern). This skiff's local namesake had fought with the International Brigade against Franco in the Spanish Civil War. The other boat was *Brochty*: the familiar name for the village. We would learn before long the delights of a gathering of skiffs: the camaraderie, the catching up with new friends from across the country, the cake-cornucopia, but also the colourful glitter of a flotilla of distinctly liveried vessels, each named for some association to their community.

We were given a warm welcome and a thorough introduction to the boat and safety protocol. I noticed many competent women taking the lead. A SCRA (Scottish Coastal Rowing Association) survey had found that women made up over 50% of club membership across Scotland and that three-quarters of rowers had no significant boating experience *before* rowing in a St Ayles skiff.

It was a dazzling, blue evening with hazy views across the estuary to the houses above Tayport's shore; Tentsmuir Point reaching out into the North Sea with its low, flat cap of forest. I felt nervous as we helped push the trailers down a slipway and saw how the salt-water danced the boats into new manoeuvrability.

I had never rowed any kind of vessel before. We were shown how to sit ready for the first stroke, leaning far forward with arms straight so that blades swung towards the bow behind us. Then we were to pull the blades simultaneously through the water, leaning back as far as we dared to ensure a long stroke. The hands were then dropped, releasing blades from the water. The boat slid forward. We leant forward again. And repeated.

Being at the entrance to the Tay estuary on an incoming tide, we were raced upstream towards Dundee and our stamina was taxed on the return; not something we would have to think about on home waters. Seeing the way ahead, the cox steered, encouraged, instructed us. I concentrated on the unfamiliar catch of the long oar in slightly choppy water and the need to follow the rhythm of the 'stroke' oar, nearest to the cox, all the while avoiding 'catching a crab' and being thrown backwards off my seat (though that was said to be a rite of passage). Having side-stepped competitive sports for most of my adult life, I relished my breathlessness from this collaborative one and felt my grin spreading.

Following a hearty, shared tea, we left for the journey inland with a renewed drive to get our boat built.

Despite a desire to find affinity with my male forebears, they remained aloof from me. I had learnt little of Granny's father, Robert Drake. He called himself a master mariner and owned or part-owned various ships. He bought all the shares of the smack *Jane and Sarah* only a year before his death, as well as having a third share in *Emma Louise* and becoming managing owner from 1901, aged twenty-nine.

Sitting at my kitchen table one morning in that early summer of 2018, I looked more carefully at a tarnished tea-spoon as I passed it to my newish partner Robin, who was visiting from his home on the English south coast. I was fond of quipping that all my teaspoons had 'run away to sea' as I raked noisily through the tangle of tine and handle in the cutlery drawer.

'Look!' I said. 'The monogram.'

For the first time I'd properly seen the curled letters 'RD' etched onto the flattened tip of the handle.

'Oh yes,' Robin said. 'My initials!'

Which was true. But.

I'd had this comically assorted and evolving cutlery collection for over thirty-five years – the result of never having bought any cutlery new rather than second-hand, and never having been married and therefore given the tra-ditional matching set.

I took loose silver items directly from my Granny's cut-lery drawer after her death in 1984 when I had just bought my first house with my then-partner. I didn't distinguish the silver as 'best'. Over the years these well-used, and not over-respected, silver-plated implements have rattled along in an egalitarian way with the stainless steel on my many moves. They have been lost on camping trips, and undoubt-edly many fell down the backs of furniture as we moved from Devon to Scotland in 1990. Some hung on, though, in a series of kitchens and until the break-up and division of the spoils in 2001. Apparently, my Granny's cutlery collection had remained with me.

I stood up from the table to rummage further in the drawer, and turned up four more monogrammed teaspoons. They came up beautifully with a polish, pleasing and functional with a certain sturdy avoidance of decoration apart from the curl of the two letters. The hallmarks revealed a precise provenance: made in Sheffield by James Deakin and Sons in 1897/1898. It was in 1898 that my great-grandfather Robert married Annie Lock Roach, and so I can assume the teaspoons marked this life event. In order to arrive in my kitchen, they must first have accompanied Granny into her own married quarters in Southampton and then into her widow's home in Exeter.

These relics in my own cutlery drawer 500 miles and over a century from where they'd spooned sugar or salt or jam in the household at Heanton Street, Braunton, had been under my nose, waiting for me to value them. Some rupture in family memory caused by deaths, estrangement, denials, and dispersed geography began to feel mended by this shared domesticity. I rested the polished teaspoons on my kitchen table so that the oval bowls nested and the handles fanned out in a tail like some silvery fish.

Although the daily tides of meals and drinks still tumble together all those unmatched items, it's the silver Robert Drake teaspoons that wash up regularly onto the strandline. Far from excluding them to some ornamental position, I honour them by using them *more*. They are redolent of a family 'brand'.

On a further trawl through The Box, I found another photo of the stone wall against which the miserable widow Annie stood with her two children. This time it's ivy-covered, and three men are stiffly lined up against it. I'd seen photos in the 'Coasters' book of men on their ships, at sea, or on the quay in caps and rolled-up sleeves, but 'our' men hadn't featured there.

The family resemblance between the three is striking, especially in the two younger men in flat caps. I recalled that Uncle Frank's appearance had been very similar. They share thin faces, an accentuated curve in the brow, a long narrow nose, for each a moustache. Solemn, frozen expressions. I deduce that the grey-haired man wearing a boater on the left is Francis Drake Senior. His face is a little bulked out by whiskers. The man on the right is his son William, who seemed to do so well from his own ships. He has a white collar, dark tie, a jacket over his waistcoat opened to display a gold watch chain.

But of the three it's the moustached man in the centre I focus on. I'd found amongst my grandmother's possessions the same face in a gold locket, its case studded with a single 'diamond'. At first I thought it a different photograph because the shirt he wears has a collar. However, a magnifying glass revealed that the wings of the collar had been drawn on for the locket. He'd been respectable-ised.

It's perhaps the only photo of Granny's father, Robert Drake. He doesn't look like a man who'd have silver cutlery engraved with his initials, RD. He looks glum, country-bumpkin-humble, and clearly not accustomed to having his photograph taken. A man of the sea, captured briefly and uncomfortably on land.

It's as if three caged gannets have been rounded up and held briefly to rock and soil between narrow Devon lanes and walls. They look so ill at ease. It's hard to imagine them animate, moving fluidly on the deck of a ketch rolling in a swell or teasing the boy they send up the swaying mainmast to reach a fictitious piece of equipment. There would be laughter at the boy's expense but it wouldn't be cruel; a kindly pat on the back as the lad descends, knees trembling a little, but feeling more sea-smart than when he began the climb.

I can't help wondering about the occasion that brought these three uneasy looking men onto land at the same time. Could they have been attending a family funeral? If so, the absence of the third brother, young Francis, is stark. Had the occasion of his loss in 1903 pulled them together from their scattered routes within and beyond the Bristol Channel?

According to the Braunton Coasters book, by the outbreak of World War II, most traditional wooden sailing ketches in Britain were obsolete and abandoned. However, those from the ports within the Bideford Bar were something of an exception. Traditional sailing vessels with auxiliary engines were sometimes still making money, and the majority of these were owned in Braunton. Effectively, these were now motor vessels with a sail simply for steadying purposes.

As war began, the railways were soon fully employed in the movement of munitions, and such ketches came back into demand for coastal trade, criss-crossing the Bristol Channel with cargoes including pit-props from the Exmoor valleys for Welsh coal mines. Ten of the Braunton fleet of ketches and schooners were requisitioned early in the war for balloon barrage service. Most had to be condemned afterwards because of the damage done.

After the war, the remaining Braunton ketches lost their usefulness and had very little resale value; those still viable were sailed two-handed by elderly men with heads angled to the past. They ran on for as long as the ships passed their surveys without too much expense and could still make a profit. But associated infrastructure and skills ashore – sailmakers and shipwrights – declined, road haulage improved and coal began to be moved by land rather than sea. Velator Quay in Braunton fell into disuse.

Emma Louise struggled on, glorified in the seafarers' church for her coal run between Lydney and Minehead, as recalled by the lad who came aboard with his cabbage. But then the Lydney Coal terminal closed in 1960 and she was also out of a job.

This substantial and unique fleet had boomed for half a century (1890-1940), a period coinciding with the too-early deaths of Granny's father in 1907 and in a disastrous echo, my mother's father in 1939. The trauma of two wars meant Dorothy had to seek a way out of their crisis into the years beyond, pioneering new lives away from their home port. The modern ways of 'un-belonging' which I grew up with had begun.

Envelopes, photo albums, packages and letters became scattered across my workroom floor as I delved further into The Box that summer, trying to gather them into groups and match their meanings against a mental framework of the history. But what remained within The Box never seemed to diminish. The bottom was, almost mythically, unattainable.

This journey of discovery had already shown me that identifying a gravestone, a photo, a public record, a silver teaspoon, helps a person emerge from a historic void. But my understanding still felt insubstantial. This family, whose history is lashed to the sea, have left no monuments, no lighthouses as Robert Louis Stevenson's did. Their work carving across fickle, unmarkable seas, has been lost in the swell, their timber ships rotted into the mud of estuaries and largely forgotten. I wondered by what means I could better access the *experience* of my forebears.

I'd written in my notebook on the day I first walked beside the Taw-Torridge estuary of an intense feeling that, 'I must take to the water, get my hands on rope and timber, tackle tides and charts and my own fears.'

I'd been too much indoors during this excavation of papers; land-locked in my home in Perthshire. I felt a little like a trapped seal, flailing against containment, clumsily eager to reach its coastal element.

I owed my mother a visit and it occurred to me that it might be satisfying for us both, for our project, if I made the journey under sail, following some ancestral west-coast wake. There was only one ship of the Braunton fleet that remained sailing. Could I make this trip on the *Bessie Ellen*?

I remained uncertain, though, that I could overcome the sense of dread that this churned up.

An Inland Soul at Sea

September 2018. *Bessie Ellen* is tied up against a pontoon on Oban's North Pier: black hull, sloping transom. My shiver at the sight of her combines apprehension and excitement. Arriving later than everyone else, I climb over the rail onto a planked deck, stepping along aisles with high 'apexes' made by rope and spun steel; stays and shrouds stretching from the deck to the tops of two masts. Numerous lengths of thick, sandy-coloured rope dangle in coils on wooden pins.

I duck down the companionway ladder, arrive blind into a dark saloon lined by benches, fixed tables and curtained bunks. Eighteen unknown faces gradually take shape at its gloomy edges as I find a seat. The safety briefing is about to start as interior detail materialises: bookshelves, a rug on the floor, wall lanterns, and a ceiling decorated with luminous stars. This hold, once full of oats or copper ore, now carries humans on holiday.

I listen to how we should respond to a fire or someone falling overboard. Meanwhile the ship barely shudders, not yet betraying its element. I've chosen this particular trip at the close of the ship's summer itinerary because the journey has an authentic purpose. This 'passage' will deliver the ship from Scotland back to her home in Cornwall, powered if possible by wind in the eight sails. The final port is Newlyn in the far west of Cornwall, from where I'll be within walking distance of my mother's house. I will earn the arrival just as past seafarers did.

Skipper Nikki Alford, weathered, blonde, strong and highly experienced, makes clear the seriousness of our journey at the same time as encouraging joy and playfulness. I feel some pride that she recalls my mother's trip aboard and the correspondence we've had since about the family connection to this ship's first owner. She must meet so many people each season and manage their expectations, reactions, questions.

I remind her of the history – how in 1862 'our' Francis Drake married Emma Louise Chichester. It was her nephew John Squire Chichester who seems to have fallen for *Bessie Ellen* when he saw her hull under construction in Plymouth in 1906. He changed her destiny when he bought her by commissioning a ketch, rather than a schooner rig, and thus making her less suitable for the Newfoundland salt cod trade. Instead, launched by his two daughters Bessie and Ellen, she became one of the early twentieth-century sailing coasters running out of Braunton.

You don't have to look far into this ship's own story to realise the potential gravity of working a vessel with a gross tonnage of 87: John Squire Chichester was crushed between his ship and a passing barge whilst docking at Sharpness in 1920. Afterwards, his widow, Bessie (née Clarke of the shipping company family, Clarke, Incledon and Clarke) continued to organise *Bessie Ellen*'s cargo-shipping business and did so until her death in 1946, clearly demonstrating a head for business and an independent spirit.

Although their son Jack had been sailing with John since childhood, his father had noted his skills in drawing and writing and wished him to study as an architect (echoing the background of our 'Uncle Frank' and his son John). But Jack insisted on following the family tradition and took on the captaincy, although he appears not to have been very good at it. It then passed to John's brother, and subsequently onto others, but always with Bessie herself organising the cargoes and the business element. Her refusal to sell up perhaps speaks of the bond between a family and a ship; as emotional as it was commercial.

During World War II *Bessie Ellen* was part of the diminishing North Devon fleet, dodging mines whilst carrying cargo to Ireland and apparently remaining useful until 1947. At the end of the war, when such vessels were often abandoned, there was a demand for them in the Baltic States and she found a new home in Denmark. With a reduced rig and new engine, she ran scrap iron cargoes into the 1970s until she was laid up once again, for sale. After a false start with a restorer whose project failed, Nikki bought her in May 2000 and returned her to sailing glory.

The etymology of the word 'passage' connects it to the traverse of a mountain pass; the action of stepping; a portion of text or music. These associations bring the concept closer to my land-based and literary terrain. When I think of the many passes through mountains I've walked, I recall comfort sensed in the valleys at each end where there are homes, artificial light and warmer temperatures, even cafés or pubs. Any wind will be stilled, just as it is in harbours. But between the two, in the high wilderness, lurks the unknown and the liminal. Mist might descend, storms rage, fairies intervene. There's potential for losing the way: there may be a pathlessness of the mind alongside the unknowability of your fellow travellers.

I begin to anticipate parallels on such a sea passage. Inhabiting maritime metaphors, I am 'at sea' and 'out of my depth', small and ill-equipped with experience, afraid of feeling cold, desperate not to be a mere passenger, and, as ever, not wanting to be wrong or make mistakes. As nineteen of us claim our bunks, our only private spaces for the week, I realise there is something else less 'me' about this journey and about seafaring in general. I could never do anything remotely like this alone. It is necessarily social. We will be together for one week, not touching land until our promised arrival in the Isles of Scilly, that far western archipelago of Great Britain with its urge towards warmer coasts of the south.

Up on deck the small crew prepare the shorelines ready to cast off, the engine is on and we are introducing ourselves to each other. Before even knowing that engine and lines have been worked against each other to 'spring' us off the pontoon, Felix and Owain are telling us to take off the rope gaskets that hold the furled mainsail to its horizontal 'boom'. The wire cables or 'stays' which support the masts must be moved back. We begin our dance sequence with equipment; with each other. Everything unfamiliar. There are no winches, so *Bessie Ellen*'s sails are hoisted manually. It takes teams of six of us on each side of the ship to raise the mainsail, one team on a halyard which lifts the end nearest the mast – the 'throat' – and one on the 'peak', which lifts the sail's other end higher, to point skyward at the stern end, thus forming the traditional 'gaff' shape.

The rope runs easily to start with, needing only two of us to pull downwards, but becomes more arduous the higher the sail rises. Others join, each two-handed on the rough, thick rope. In our breathless oblivion in the midst of this, we are surprised by Nikki's voice nearby re-energising us: 'Go on! Stretch! Pull!' as if we are barely trying. We dig for sea shanties to regulate the pulse of our joint hauling, but find them lost to us. Instead, someone calls 'One, two, (heave); one, two, (heave)'. The person with hands highest dangles from it with all their weight and finally 'sweats' it by heaving any slack backwards and then easing it towards the wooden pin while someone else 'tails' it in, preventing the gained slack from escaping. Finally, the tailer is told by a crew-member: 'Make fast,' and we all let go and catch our breath. I begin to question that historic assertion about two men and a boy being able to sail one of these ships.

I ask first mate Felix how he gained all his knowledge. He is so young and so competent.

'I was born with it in my blood,' he says in his marvellous French accent. 'And in my testicles.'

With this flurry of activity and heave of our lungs and limbs, we barely notice that we are out in the sound of Kerrera in sheltered, flat water. And then the engine is off and I glance up to filling sails. I feel hugged by familiar land on each side of the narrow sound. We are underway, heading south. The casting off from land is done.

The four foresails are hauled up and then we're heeling over, seawater washing the deck, and I'm trying to differentiate between the functions of similar-looking ropes – halyards, sheets, downhauls – coiled in rows on wooden cleats on the foredeck. I need to know which is which so that I can be quickly useful when an instruction comes: Hoist! Trim! Drop! My body must remember how to do these things even in frantic moments. There are words to learn and objects and procedures to attach to them: the binnacle, a handy billy, a rolling hitch, and we are told of a marvellous, potential command: 'scandalise the mainsail', a means to reduce its size quickly in high winds. Presumably the verb was used in its original meaning from the twelfth-century Greek; 'to make to stumble'.

Any change in direction, or alteration in wind speed, requires multiple rapidly-executed actions. The ship is complex, it seems. Within hours of departure, my background family history gusts overboard. Instead of historic curiosity, I focus on a rapidly altering present in which I heave on lines to hoist canvas and my legs ride the swell wrought by a southerly wind meeting tidal flow through the Sound of Jura. I concentrate on keeping lunch on my plate (and in my stomach).

There is a lot of cake. I eat it.

'I'm sailing to visit my mother,' I tell my companions.

Watches are set. Our nineteen aboard form into groups, and are each given four hours on and eight off through night and day. A new rhythm will now overlay tides and meals; dark and light; the sea's rise and fall. A sudden seriousness.

Despite being well over a century old, *Bessie Ellen*'s small chart-room is equipped with state-of-the-art navigational gear including the electronic chart that, with a GPS plotter, shows clearly our position, speed and course on a screen. It identifies other vessels around us by name. In a column on the right is a mysterious list of other figures.

We learn that on each hour of our watch, two of us must huddle here to complete the log, entering degrees for 'true' course against what the helms-person reads from the compass. We will record figures for wind speed and direction, sea state, visibility and the log reading for our position. I'm afraid of this procedure, averse to both figures and to responsibility.

I find myself distracted instead by the beauty of the traditional paper chart, the blank yellow land, and pale blue of coastal waters fading to white expanses where the sea deepens. There is a complexity of numbered contours for depth around the coastline and isolated rocks and reefs. Enigmas abound: 'The Smalls'; 'area to be avoided'; 'the Bishops and Clerks'. Arrows and lines of shipping lanes, notes to laden tankers. The boundary between the United Kingdom and Republic of Ireland is a dotted line stepping down St Georges Channel into the Celtic Sea.

This is where we are going.

Becky, the cook's assistant, tells me she has never worked on a boat before and she is 'whimsical' about *Bessie Ellen*. When I press her on what she means by that word, she says that she feels too much for the ship, is almost in love with her. I think about ships attributed with 'souls'; animate, with distinct characters.

I'm delegated to the 'port watch' from 8.00 till 12.00 both morning and night, and our attached crew member is Owain, twenty-three years old and self-effacing, who we soon name Neptune for his quiet but omniscient beardiness. Reassuringly, Nikki will be with us too. She has written on her blog about the rigours of working a ship twenty-four hours a day and how one can become very tired. For the deck-watch, she says, 'Time passes looking after the continuous chaffing of gear, working aloft to protect spars and rigging, regular rounds and checks, along with updating forecasts and routes. Coffee is important, and the pots are always full of steaming brew.' She tells how scant opportunity for communication with the outside world (other than overheard traffic on the ship's radio) steps us into another time. Perspectives change, the past comes closer, and friendships develop in the midst of challenge. This is what is promised.

An Inland Soul at Sea

A schematic map of the deck is given to each of us; bow to stern, port to starboard, each item of the rigging is marked. Forty-seven things are named. Some of them are familiar to me from other sailing vessels. I know a halyard is used to raise a sail, a sheet will control its angle to the wind, a downhaul will drop it. But with eight sails there are many such points to learn and then there are topping-lifts, backstays, forestays, vangs. There are wooden 'blocks': systems of pulleys through which lines run and force is amplified. And I find literal meanings for things such as the 'bitter end', the final part of the anchor rope near to where it's fixed to the ship's deck, named for the bollard or 'bitt' to which the anchor rope is tied. And I discover other animate features of the ship whose names I enjoy: dolphin striker, cathead, whisker stay, gaff jaws.

The ship begins to breathe, yet there seem so many nods to death in the naming of parts. The 'deadeye' block has a macabre appearance, resembling the eye and nose cavities of a skull through which lines are guided and controlled in the rigging. There are 'shrouds' that hold up the mast, the 'deadwoods' integral to a ship's construction, and the 'widow maker', a block of the type used to multiply efforts in tensioning lines which was invented by Archimedes in 250 BC. This controls the position of the large triangular staysail, fourth in from the bow.

Back at my inland home not long before my departure, the Ian Oughtred skiff construction plans had arrived – a single roll of paper covered in beautifully line-drawn cross-sections, hand-written measurements and another throng of unfamiliar words.

'We're going to have to learn a whole new vocabulary,' Charlotte said.

'Apron', 'stretchers', 'breasthooks', 'skims', 'spalls'. And then the words for the necessary techniques: 'scarf joints', 'bearding lines', 'fairing'...

Led by Angus and Adam, work began, first to build the frame and moulds that an upside-down hull would be shaped over. Angus offered the use of his furniture workshop to prepare this and a few of us turned up to each evening session. I joined when I wasn't away somewhere. I enjoyed the long first-floor gallery scented with sweet shavings from the local native trees they work with. In amongst the forest of machinery, plans were pinned to walls for ongoing projects and timbers rested in curvaceous, swooping lines made by steam bending – everything paused mid-creation by Angus' team at 5pm.

Angus assigned tasks, so we were working on different things simultaneously. Although unimaginable then, each would be a tiny contribution to a boat. We were trusted to use some of the bandsaws and other power tools. Motors roared, sawdust flurried; our faces were grained with concentration.

When I confessed that I had wandered slightly from a pencilled guideline, Angus said:

'We'll know who to blame when we find a kink in the hull!'

In a double-garage belonging to Margaret, a member of the skiff club who was in her eighties, we erected the frame and its moulds which would shape the hull during building. The lateral 'frames' – which I think of as the boat's ribs – were fitted. Angus had laminated strips of larch, a wood famed for durability and waterproof qualities, into the two stems, each curved for the shape of bow and stern. As well as being functional, this optimised the visual qualities of the striped, golden grain. Between the stems the long, straight spine of the boat was created with the keelson (or inner keel). With this basic structure established – length and breadth, we could now see mapped out in three dimensions the full 22-foot (6.7m) length, 4'6" (1.2m) width, of our boat-to-be.

Heading south aboard *Bessie Ellen,* the wind increases in strength and turns to come from behind us as dusk settles on the first day. The land goes by, dark and squall-washed now. After dinner, my watch-mates and I dress in warm and waterproof gear and go up on deck. We will sail into the dark, beyond the end of the Mull of Kintyre, I suppose to dangle between Cumbria and the north tip of Ireland.

The early part of our watch is wet and squally. We are sailing with the mainsail swung wide out to the side on its heavy boom to capture the wind coming from directly behind us and now risen to Force 6. It's tricky, Nikki warns us. The wind speeds us on, but running with it so directly behind puts us in danger of causing an accidental gybe. This is when a slight deviation in direction, or the ship's angling caused by rolling between waves, allows wind to fill the 'wrong' side of the sail, thus pushing the boom and the mighty weight of a hundred or so square metres of driven canvas suddenly and violently from port to starboard or the reverse. In a ship of this size it can be devastating, even bringing down the mast. I am not keen to take the helm in such conditions.

Nikki sends us with Owain to fit a 'boom-restrainer', a rope lashed to keep the sail wide and avoid a crash gybe. It involves some precarious scrambling on Owain's part, and for us 'swabs' some heaving and tightening of ropes, whilst our boots slip on a wet, sloping deck. My hood falls over my eyes and hair whips my cheeks in the hurly-burly of wind and shower and dark.

Not long afterwards the restrainer falls off.

'Fit it again, then,' Nikki shouts from the helm over the bellowing and cracking of wind and canvas.

Gradually the weather improves, and we settle in. Skies clear south of Scotland (though land borders have now become immaterial). Mars rises ahead and hangs red in the rigging, acting as a guide to the helm; the Milky Way runs its road over the top of the mizzen mast. There are occasional ship lights, shore lights, and cordial exchanges overheard on the radio between the Belfast coastguard and ship masters across the sea miles.

Towards midnight I make tea and coffee for the next watch and then go to wake them; fortunately sleeping only lightly, and at the ready. I feel quite exhilarated as I return to my bunk, the ship making 6 knots down the North Channel under sail. I'm sorry to miss the connecting land and sea, this slept-geography, just after the flashing lighthouse from Rathlin Island has marked new territory approaching to our west.

Before sleeping I look at my phone, kept mostly turned off to maintain the battery. Robin has sent a screenshot of our position from 'Marine Traffic' – he's tracking us. My mother has never embraced digital technology and will have no idea where I am.

At 8am the next day, our watch resumes responsibility and picks up the geography. Ireland is to starboard and the Isle of Man to port. Sometimes the ghost line of mainland Britain appears.

We are on a bearing of 190, then change tack to 120, and when the wind dies, hoist a topsail for the first time. Then we have to gybe again, hauling everything in tight first in order to make a controlled transition. We are rolling, and with each roll to port, the mainsail rattles and the boom threatens to swing across. Stays are fastened again to prevent this but the noise and motion, the slide and crash of lunch plates from the saloon roof onto the deck, makes me uneasy. I feel apprehensive about the coming dark and our next watch as the engine is turned on for a while somewhere off Liverpool.

Time shifts into new shapes. We seem to have travelled so far in less than thirty-six hours.

There are three quiet hours on our night watch; a fleet of stars and Mars hanging again in the rigging, a bit of swell, time to chat. We are approaching Cardigan Bay when we realise we will have to change tack again and I go below to wake the next watch early: we need more bodies on deck. Owain and Felix organise us with tasks, hauling in the mainsail sheet tight in readiness, Nikki bellowing from the helm.

Then we're pulling each foresail in turn around the bow, trimming them to the shape of the wind which now drives from the other side. There are two hazards here, the first being the flying jib, the furthest forwards on the bow sprit. Two people must handle the corresponding rope that controls it, known as a 'sheet'. Taking its chance to fill, the sail can grow so boisterous that Nikki has seen it pull a single person, hanging desperately to the sheet, overboard. The other hazard is the heavy 'widow maker': the block controlling the sheets of the staysail, the largest, furthest-back of the foresails. The block dances manically in the wind, thrashing amidst a group of cowering crew until the sail can be hauled in and calmed. Heavy and unruly, it's clear how this lump of ash gets its name: it is at head height.

Soon after, the skipper's order comes that the topsail must come down. There is too much wind now. This is tricky. The ship rolls and the wind blows harder in response. And so the night goes on.

Overwrought in my bunk later, my sleep is interrupted by the rolling and righting, the gurgling of the sea by my ear, running footsteps overhead, the engine coming on, murmurings about paracetamol from another bunk.

The rhythm quickly becomes our new normal: night and day, the change of watch marked below deck with whispers, rustling waterproofs and the tear of Velcro. Someone is always sleeping, or trying to. We've become strangers to some of our fellow crew. Our only complete meeting is at lunchtime on the deck, when we pass on the events of our watch; which sails were hoisted or taken down, any crises.

The tracking device shows us as a single pink triangle ploughing a determined line south. With Ireland to starboard and Wales to port, we wave goodbye to Waterford on one side and St David's Head on the other. A mythic gateway of gnarly headlands guarded by rock-infested shallows tightens around us and then flings open, spilling us into the Celtic Sea, with no land now between us and the Scilly Isles.

The Bristol Channel gapes wide here to our left, the land parting and fading until we are out of sight of it with only the knowledge that the shores of Lundy Island and North Devon, where I might have waved across the years to my family, are to port somewhere. We've passed the last of Ireland, and are ploughing on into an abyss. There is nothing on which to fix the eye; no shore. This was what I had dreaded – being out of sight of land. And hadn't Nikki said that this was where we might meet rough weather?

Apprehension gnaws.

Accordingly, the swell we work through becomes higher and deeper. Falling and climbing, each summit is crested by scrabbles of white water, throwing sparkling confetti into the air, hissing. Helming becomes an art of anticipation as the wind behind surfs us into the hollows and we soar up the other side, mainsail slung out and filling on its broad reach, to meet a moment of suspension and uncertainty at the top of the wave. Which way will the hull be pushed or fall, the course modified by roll or wind? There is a precarious balance to be struck between the right bearing and the wind still filling the sails on the correct side.

Nikki keeps an eye on whoever is at the helm: 'Do you *want* to go to Scilly?'

'Yes,' replies the helmswoman. We all do.

'Steer for it, then. You're heading for Bristol. It's 165 degrees, not 160.'

This is typical of Nikki's bluntness but also the trust she seems willing to place in us. Her patience combines with an active desire to share the expansiveness of sailing a traditional ship.

The sun comes out and reflects up from under us, blue horizons stretch, skies clear and below us, should we dare to think of it, are the cavernous fathoms. I take the helm for a while, concentrating hard on correction and compensation, listening for the sound of a wave approaching from behind that might be angling to shift our course. Nervous at first, I begin to enjoy the feeling that when I 'play' this great ship against the wind, when I get it right, all of her 115-foot length and 3,550-square-foot of sail leans into me so that there's a visceral sense of my body and hers, strong together, working with wind and swell and tide to create speed.

I find that I can't rationalise the course by obeying the compass and the red-and-white pennant flag which indicates wind direction from the top of the main mast. It's logical but doesn't seem to work for me. Instead, I feel for it instinctively. From my solid stance at the stern, I sense our vessel gather strength and momentum. I'm filled with concentrated purpose now; not fear.

'It's about becoming one with the ship,' Nikki says, and I feel that truth in my body, like finding harmony when pushing forward and controlling a horse from its back, or like discovering as you dance to a new rhythm, that its beat and step are somewhere dormant within you, waiting to be listened to. My mother spoke of not having lost 'the knack' when she took this helm. I was dubious then, but perhaps she was right. Intuition is at work.

Being at the helm hoists you into a slightly elevated position, perched side-saddle on the wheel box. It's as if you're on a low balcony, looking through the rigging, taut canvas, the crosshatch of rope, towards something fixed, or at least relatively fixed, to guide your course. If no land is in sight it might be a slow-moving galleon-shaped cloud. At night it might be a star or planet. There is a slight sense of detachment from the rest of the crew who, when conditions are good, tend to spread out forward of the mizzen mast and chart room. Alone at the stern, there is concentration on the task as well as an opening space, an enhanced communion with the 'now' of things. Timber under hands and feet; the sky and it's whipping or steady winds; the hiss of the sea in its dialogue with our movement.

An Inland Soul at Sea

Leaning into the helm with its feedback from below divulges deep time. It sends me into a kind of alert trance; human purpose meshing with the elemental. I understand now how this position of power might become compelling.

Nikki tells us that when she's helming at night, with the deck lights on, the action unfolds on the foredeck as a dance, figures moving between the taut lines of the sheets and masts, the deck becoming a shiny, elemental stage. I've noticed that when she's helming, the one most in tune with her ship, she's often quiet. It's as if this position, demanding and commanding, responsible, takes a person into direct communion with the primal nature of the wooden vessel and its medium.

With her all-seeing 'mariner's stare' and experience with *Bessie Ellen* for so many years, Nikki has also absorbed the ship's history, recalling the Danish family for whom *Bessie Ellen* carried cargo in the 1980s but also the skipper's daughter who, at the time a baby, was kept below deck in a drawer. Nikki is heroic in my eyes, and probably to others on board. I'm moved by the depth of her knowledge and interest in all matters to do with sea and sail and also by her passion for sharing it. She's playful, adventurous, as well as blunt. 'You twat' is perhaps reserved for crew members rather than guests, but it will soon be followed by affection and encouragement.

In a quiet moment someone asks, 'How did you come to acquire *Bessie Ellen*?' Most of us think we know this story but it's longer and more convoluted than I had realised. Her first knowledge of this ship was at the age of nineteen when she worked as a secretary in a Devon yacht broker. She took a photo of the *Bessie Ellen* hulk then in Denmark and tucked it away in her jeans back pocket, never forgetting her through years of informal apprenticeship during which she sailed twice around the world working on traditional rigged boats and tall ships, once getting into trouble with Chinese officials. She had a close association with the brig *Maria Asumpta*, which went down off Padstow in 1995 with the loss of three lives; it was an accident caused by a technical error that I remember my mother bewailing. Nikki's former boyfriend had also been aboard but was rescued.

In 2002, Nikki gathered a team and went to the Ring Andersen Yard in Denmark to refit *Bessie Ellen*. Then, with a skipper's clear vision, she brought her home to the south-west of England to prepare for commercial work again, this time with a human cargo, ninety-four years after she'd run off the slip in Plymouth.

It occurs to me that there is female 'knowing' involved. She believes that this ship holds and cares for us. She reminded us that the first owner, John Chichester, nephew of my great-great-grandmother Emma, died in the aft cabin where she now sleeps. It's a quiet tragedy we sail with, but Nikki says she's convinced that his spirit watches over us too.

How many must *Bessie Ellen* have mothered since 1904.

The growing familiarity between us means we now quickly find coordination when we have to heave on and sweat a rope. We know how much heft to expect to give. We may have no sea shanties to hand but we've became more playful with each other, the heave sounded by some other harmonising groan or whine: 'One, two, (whimper); 'One, two, (whimper)'.

With blue soaring above, scattered white clouds, a sense of direction and steadiness, and with nothing between us and the Scilly Isles, something new descends, bringing people to sit on deck and stare at the horizon. The rigging creaks and voices murmur. We pass a trawler tipping back and forth between waves, haloed by a great flock of sparkling gannets with sharpened black forewings, each bird pitching, tilting, folding itself into an origami dance.

Now out of sight of land, we have all entered a new space, dreamlike and reflective, as we sit on our bearing heading south-west into the Atlantic. Time has collapsed, marked conventionally only by the hourly logbook filling by those on watch and by the music of the ship: drumming in the staysail and the squeak of the gaff. The ship's dry timbers are warm on bare skin; grain meeting grain. As late afternoon turns to early evening, the sun illuminates the windward side of the sails, highlighting parallel rows of stitching. Shadows of the criss-crossing lines and reefing ties, the rungs of the rigging ladder swell and flatten with the canvas. The visual rhythm of this patterning and its constant change is mesmerising. All is gently swaying as we roll, with the music of wind buffeting, the sea-shift, the creak of timber.

The ship is a pip between Heaven and sea, between two distant shores; the hull cupping our small human community which will only survive by communicating and co-operating in the face of our great irrelevance here. We depend on each other. And if anywhere can show us that the world is fierce and wild and has its own momentous longevity, I realise it is here. At sea we know we are tiny. The sea doesn't care about people flushed from their homes by fires sweeping across Australia, or about the spread of a virulent virus around the world, or war fomenting in the Middle East. It will continue.

It strikes me that so many at sea in the past have shared this raw experience: the generosity and flexibility of timber around them when land falls away and canvas catches wind. And it feels like a transcendence, reaching back to a common experience; being part of a community which accepts its own fragility. We are one instrument made of timber, hemp, canvas, the elements of sea and wind, and a group of humans who are no longer strangers to each other. Each component of the instrument has its rhythms of manoeuvring and guiding and is bound by physical laws, working towards the same end.

It comes with a feeling I've sometimes had in high mountain environments. I feel my place, but don't exactly feel small or vulnerable; simply in the right proportion to my environment. I am not cowed, but elevated by it. It is perhaps the furthest one can be from the humiliating sweat and scrum of an airport departure hall on a busy evening, each person ritually denuded, stripped of shoes and possessions. Does the human at sea have the chance to become his or her best self?

Perhaps this 'empty' place is the equivalent of the highest point of the mountain pass. It is the most alien to human life and nearest to the sky and all it holds. It brings a surprising joy, knowing that all will be downhill from here and the destination will draw closer. In the mountains it's at this point one might lay a fragment of sparkling quartz to honour a mountain god or a holy spring, or add a simple stone to others on a cairn. Is there an equivalent at sea, to give thanks for a safe passage, the major work nearly done?

The call of the open sea is strong. If we turn right now, west and north-west, around the southern tip of Ireland, we could head directly for Newfoundland, recreating a journey taken repeatedly by the Drakes before they threw their resources into coastal trading. If one had enough stores, might that enticement, the curiosity, lead one to turn the wheel, to just keep on going?

To my left, the other way, lies Lundy Island, near mythical now in my mind and not visible to the eye. It tantalised me for a whole week's coastal walking between Porlock and Bude, shape-shifting, gaining and losing heft and distance with the weather conditions, teeming with stories of pirates, wrecks and general lawlessness of humans and nature.

In the seventeenth century Moroccan corsairs settled on the island, using it as a base for raids on the local coast, where they reputedly captured people for the Arab slave markets in North Africa. More local pirates found it a useful place from which to prey on passing merchant ships, forced close by the fast tides of the Bristol Channel and its treacherous shingle banks. In the late eighteenth and early nineteenth centuries Thomas Benson, member of Parliament for Barnstaple and Sheriff of Devon, diverted shiploads of convicts intended for Virginia to Lundy, to use as his personal slaves. A shorter journey than they were expecting. The island became known as 'the Kingdom of Heaven' when purchased in 1834 by William Hudson Heaven as a summer retreat. After World War I the owner Martin Coles Harman proclaimed himself King and issued 'puffin' currency.

Will I ever reach it, or will it remain elusive like the islands between Somerset and Pembrokeshire, a whisker further up the Bristol Channel? The 'Green Meadows of Enchantment' are not usually visible to humans unless seen by accident or by air, and occasionally by sailors who join the revels of the fairies but find, when they look back from their ships, that the islands have once again vanished.

The land has shrunk back, no longer my touchstone as it was when my eye sought the security of grey headlands, mountains, islands. The points of reference are close in now and mostly within the timbers of this ship. It is this 'us' that's central to the experience, the mini-world we've formed; a speck of sand within the stretching oceans and swirling continents of the astronaut's perspective.

Wouldn't my forebears also have inhabited this ageless space, enjoyed the quiet and camaraderie after the urgency of changes of direction, or the frantic preparation for landfall? They would know how a boat at sea for more than twenty-four hours becomes a capsule, a mini society living by new rules and a new sense of hours.

Despite a period of subdued voices as we focus, we are soon crowding at the rail to whoop hundreds of dolphins past as they course under our bow. They soar, surf, roll, transforming under greenish translucence from arrows of speed and current to lozenges of mouse-dark and pale skin as they surface. The stream goes on and on, apparently performing for us, mothers with young finally at the rear of the long cavalcade. Nikki tells us they always see a pod like this between Lundy and St David's Head.

Then: 'Whale!' Nikki's cry goes up as a long, dark platform of back slips above the waterline next to us, spray from its blowhole punctuating the course of its mysterious mission away from us. Flurries of swallows flee winter, low over the waves, and there are gannets, gannets, gannets, often in pairs, flying in perfectly-synchronised attitudes and angles.

There is now a sense of it being just us, in harmony, getting on and getting there. Purposeful and yet with little to do.

An Inland Soul at Sea

That night our watch is calm as we follow the north coast of Cornwall, leaning over the rail to watch phosphorescence sparkling off the hull, and hearing the hiss of dissipating waves. It's obvious in this half-light that the swirls of white lace cuffing the hull as it rises and falls would suggest magical beasts to anyone out of sight of land, cast off and sleep-deprived in this timeless space of swell and sky, timber and canvas, as a cargo of sleepers rolls below. I think of the Scottish beliefs about 'lucky' ships' timbers; that some – including the oak that makes up significant parts of *Bessie Ellen's* original construction – are female and faster at night. When dolphins carve through the phosphorescence, faster than the waves and our own eight knots, they are spangled arrows of motion. There are shooting stars with long colourful tails and a crescent moon rising above the land. When we come off watch, we huddle, whispering, in the dark fore-cabin, each with a dram of Oban 14-year-old.

It seems soon, and yet so much later, that I come up onto deck and find the engine chugging, sails furled, as we slip gratefully between the Islands of Scilly only seventy-two hours and 520 miles after leaving Oban. It is dawn and a ravenous hunger is preparing us to share a cooked breakfast for the first time in three days. Nikki has never before done the journey so quickly. The voyage makes us feel the distance, remember that Britain is made of islands and the sea historically has been scored with such vital routes.

We begin to assess our rope-burnt fingers, bruised shins, before trying out newfound sea legs on solid ground. We are tourists, taking showers on the pier at St Mary's and then a boat to Tresco to visit the garden followed by a long pub lunch. We are happy together; the land rising and falling as a sea under us.

There will be beer that night and lemon syllabub. All of us sleeping simultaneously. And snoring.

I've been taking pride in telling my fellow shipmates that I'm sailing to visit my mother. She first came to Scilly in the 1980s to paint with her friend Joan. They were entranced by the miniature scale, the brilliance of colour, the semi-tropical plants. As I've travelled towards her, I've saved up snippets to tell her – so much to report when I arrive at her house, as well as catching up with sleep. Not for the first time I feel shame at the way I sometimes behave with her, withholding my experiences, hopes or fears; being irritable. I tell myself that as a nearly-sixty-year-old it's time I behaved like an adult rather than as a diminished child. And after all, this is our joint story.

On our approach to the mainland, I phone her.

'Hello dear,' she says. 'Where are you?'

She seems surprised I'm phoning whilst still on board. I suggest she walks the few minutes to the Penzance promenade to see us sail across Mount's Bay before we enter Newlyn Harbour. I'm expecting enthusiasm from her, and realise how much I want her to share in our arrival. It will remind her of her own enjoyment of sailing out beyond the prom on *Bessie Ellen*.

So I'm disappointed to hear a little reluctance in her reply.

'I'll see what I can manage,' she says.

The strong, dry deck of my hope shudders under me.

The final time we change tack, bearing down on St Michael's Mount topped by the castle and scrambled over by tourists, we don't need to be told what to do. On the foredeck, each of us in my team are stationed beside a sheet controlling the fill of one of the triangular foresails. Those on the port side are ready to release. While on the starboard side, we will quickly pull each sail around the ship's bow, take in the slack, then 'trim' them in careful release until they arc into a sequence of powerful crescents. We know to duck when last of all the large staysail will come across the beam of the ship. Its brute block, the 'widow maker' guided across by hand.

We each have our part to play, are braced and ready for the command. Bouncing through spray, the ship listing with graceful power, above us an azure sky. An audience is gathered ahead on the rock, cameras ready. We are thrilled by the machine we make with ourselves, sails, creaking timbers, wind and water. We are shiny with smiles.

Nikki is showing off her ship, taking her in close, at speed, before we go about. We are quick. Slick. She trusts us. It seems we have 'learned the ropes'. And by now, after six days on board, we are each deeply and irredeemably in love with *Bessie Ellen*.

On the Penzance promenade, my mother, twice-widowed herself, stands with a pair of binoculars and watches.

Holdfast Women

Back at home in Perthshire that autumn, work continued on the St Ayles skiff. With Angus and Adam's steady work on laminating, planing and shaping, together with the less-skilled tasks for the rest of us at weekly gatherings in the garage, an upside-down boat developed. Marine plywood planks were, one at a time, glued and clamped into over-lapping positions, gradually forming a 'clinker-built' hull. The garage-workshop grew cluttered with dried-up pots of epoxy glue, brushes, rags and tools.

'Industrial-scale' stocks of sandpaper and masks which would protect our lungs waited, in advance of the next slow, dusty stages. The long, pale creature sat diagonally across the space where Margaret's car would usually be.

'Just a few months,' we told her.

She remained endlessly supportive of the project; a tiny woman, these days supported on a walking stick, she had a lifetime of adventure behind her. At eighty-three years of age, she'd abseiled down the face of the town's old cinema as a fundraiser for its restoration.

The arrival of winter brought cold temperatures, too low for glue to set in an unheated garage. We were forced to take a break and Margaret's car remained outside in the elements. But by the end of March 2019 we finally had an upside-down hull and, with a ritualistic group heave, we turned 'her' over for the first time. A landmark moment, a halfway point or more, when the building instructions directed us to celebrate.

Another opportunity for rowing came. On a bright April day, when pockets of snow were still lodged in the hills above Loch Tay, the Lossiemouth Coastal Rowing Club visited us with their pretty cobalt-blue and yellow skiff *Loxa,* launched two years earlier. They towed her 110 miles each way to be with us. Many of us took a turn to row with them that day on our home waters.

The exhilaration, and our new waterborne friendships, brought us bright-eyed and flushed to the formalities of our second AGM.

Whilst in the South West again, eighteen months after the passage aboard *Bessie Ellen,* I visited my mother's cousin, the one who had first launched our curiosity with a poetic list of ships' names. She was shrimp-like in her armchair, becoming deaf and blind, but still attentive. When her son referred to her age of ninety-one she seemed amused, as if he must be teasing.

Her voice had only a slight Devon twang. Like me she had studied at Exeter University, less than a mile away from where we sat. Afterwards she taught history at Totnes Girls' High School.

'You were at Maynards?' she said, conflating me with my mother who had won a scholarship to the Exeter private school. It was as if she slipped fluidly between generations, mothers, daughters. We were effortlessly both unique and the same. Russian dolls.

We spoke of her father, a Hartnoll, who was a Trinity House pilot. He was attuned to tide times and the incremental movements of sandbanks on the Teign estuary – another place with a dangerous bar. I believe her father died at sea but she didn't mention this.

Being in Exeter, and with family, provoked memories of Granny's death there in 1985. A fall had admitted her to hospital after she'd lain on the floor overnight. A neighbour – the one who always invited her in for Christmas so she wouldn't be alone – found her. She must have been unwell before that because I was approaching her gate with a plant of some sort in my hands when this neighbour hailed me.

'You can take your plant to her in the hospital,' she said.

Did I detect in her voice a hint that I was at fault? That I'd been less than dutiful and caring, too tied up with my raggle-taggle life 10 miles away, making a family of my friends? I was paying attention much too late. I realise now that a different sort of family would have made sure she was absorbed into the festivities of the younger generation; would have kept an eye on her as she became prone to falls, alone in her house.

I visited her in the hospital more than once. She looked pleased to see me, but at some point called me 'Jill'. This was my mother's childhood name, which she had cast off, identifying herself in early adulthood by her middle name, Jennifer, as if beginning a new life.

On my final visit to Granny, she was not conscious and I didn't stay long. It seemed pointless to sit beside someone who didn't know you were there. I had no knowledge about death or dying and learned nothing about her condition from hospital staff, perhaps because I didn't feel entitled to ask; not sufficiently 'grown up'. I didn't know she was close to death. I didn't know that even in such a state a person may be aware of a presence at the bedside. It seems that acts of care were hidden to me.

I remembered that she had come to look after us in our childhood home when my mother went to Canada to visit friends. I must have been about five years' old and suffered a nightmare during her stay. I can only remember the terror I felt, not the substance of the dream. Perhaps it was the recurring one of the bridge high above a river. She came into my room to comfort me, and as I was afraid of returning to sleep, she remained sitting at the head of my bed so that each time my eyelids fluttered open, there was her reassuring presence next to me in the dark. It seemed almost worth a nightmare for this loving attention. She had done better for me in my early days than I did for her in her later ones.

My mother must have understood more readily than I did the seriousness of Granny's condition. She drove from Surrey to Devon to visit her before unconsciousness took hold. It was the first time they'd seen each other in twelve years and it was the last. She didn't attend the funeral. I don't remember the reason. A duodenal ulcer was recorded on Granny's death certificate.

The will revealed the wreck of their relationship. My mother had been bypassed as a beneficiary and the estate came directly to my generation with the three of us as executors. We took on the work of organising a funeral, house-clearing, contacting friends and family in her address book. Grown-up tasks.

Living so far from my mother, my visits to her had now become linked to my Braunton forays and were an opportunity to share with her what I'd learned. I was a loyal cat, bringing to the doorstep the morsels of our family legacy like dead mice, and then skulking back to the wilds.

On one occasion late in 2019 I left her house almost as soon as I'd arrived. I probably didn't even explain why I'd arranged to go to Newlyn Harbour and how it seemed to be relevant both to a fascination with tides and to our family geography. But my mother knew all about my 'itchy feet', and had always encouraged me, once her own coastal walking stopped, to get out and enjoy the place where she lived. She did not complain.

I'd come across a short book, *The Newlyn Tidal Observatory*, co-authored by a man called Richard Cockram who I had arranged to meet to see evidence on the ground. Together, we looked across the harbour entrance to the South Pier where a tatty red shed stood next to a small lighthouse.

Essentially the shed covers a well that was designed into the pier when it was extended in the late nineteenth century. For over 150 years a self-recording gauge inside it has taken hourly measurements. Such equipment, with mechanical floats and stilling wells, was once the primary means of determining sea level. A brass bolt implanted on the floor of the shed became and remains, the benchmark which gives us land-height measurements all over mainland Great Britain. This is 'height zero', which informs construction of roads, railways and the calibration of contours on maps (though rising sea levels are likely to mean change).

I've seen the distinctive 'pi'-shaped Ordnance Survey benchmarks carved into walls and onto obelisks in various places across Britain. There's one close to my home, high on the pass near the slopes of Schiehallion. Coincidentally, it was on this almost-symmetrical mountain, isolated from other peaks, that contours were 'invented' as a by-product of a gravitational experiment 250 years ago by Astronomer Royal, Nevil Maskelyne. Mathematician Charles Hutton joined him to map the mountain, connecting elevation readings into rings, and so revolutionising mapping.

These initiatives link the mountain that rises into its distinctive point on my home horizon at the centre of Scotland to the small fishing village on a far south-west taper of Atlantic-lashed land. Each time I check contour height when I'm hillwalking or stand at a trig point on a summit, I throw a mental line to Newlyn's south pier, to my mother and her adopted country.

After the meeting with Richard, I walked back along the 'prom' to spend time with her. I found vegetables in the fridge-cooler marked with a 'best-before' date of months earlier. Fancier cupboard condiments – pomegranate molasses, balsamic vinegar and vacuum-packed chestnuts – lay unused. Perhaps with fewer opportunities or reasons to leave the house, she was less aware of the seasons passing and so, the years.

I hesitated to do anything with such items, partly for fear of undermining her independence but also because the condiments were redolent of one-time passions. As a young wife in the '50s she'd been an early adopter of the Mediterranean dishes championed by Elizabeth David, and she'd gone through a 'Madhur Jaffrey phase' in the '80s, cooking Indian food from scratch with whole spices and insane amounts of oil (until cholesterol became an issue).

These days she was resisting the efforts of her children to look after her. On that visit she refused point-blank to put the door keys we'd cut for her into a safe outside the door in case of an accident inside.

Yet she seemed bright, if lacking curiosity in any of my news, favouring the repetition of stories of her own.

A while before this visit my mother had written to me, with reference to my passage on *Bessie Ellen*: 'I think you and I have a bit of the Drake/Chichester in us.' The simple statement had sparked up a sense of pride – as if it confirmed me a place in the lineage. It also threw between the two of us a line of commonality, rarely voiced: a warming in the mother–daughter relationship. I remained a needy child craving her mother's love.

Then I read: 'I'm so pleased you are writing up your trip on the *Bessie Ellen*.'

Had she misunderstood my wider purpose? I wanted to connect us to those sea-dedicated families; the men so much away from home, and to gain familiarity with the place they sailed from. My project didn't just concern one sailing trip.

Her mention of the surname Chichester sent me to my bookshelves where I picked up again her Victorian book of Tennyson's poetry. I was sorry I couldn't picture the Emma Chichester of its monogram. I knew from public records that she'd been born in 1840, two years before the wedlock of her parents. She had presumably been given the book as a young, unmarried woman.

There seemed no further way of knowing her but I could, at least, share with her the heft of this book in my hands. I creaked open the green, cloth-covered boards embossed with a gold inlay of flowers, butterflies and scallops. The pages of tiny print looked well-read – some loosening now from their binding; delicate pages which may have inspired Emma's journeys of imagination over a century before me.

I noticed two things for the first time. The first was a folded piece of yellowing paper caught between the pages of *Elaine*. It held a pressed plant cutting, its multiple, tiny, bell-shaped leaves grey now as they dangled inflexibly from a fragile stem. A botanist friend identified it as *Adiantum* or maidenhair fern, found on sheltered sea cliffs, but rare.

I supposed this could have been put there either by Emma herself, or later by her great granddaughter, my mother. A keen amateur botanist, my mother was fond of telling us about the time she had gone aboard the *Endeavour* during the ship's visit to Penzance – 'the finest tall ship replica ever'. She was determined to be there because of a lecture on Joseph Banks and the plants he introduced to Britain from the wider world including eucalyptus and acacia. She described how the audience sat on chests in the crew's 'mess' around tables that swung from ropes. Hammocks were slung above their heads and slides projected onto a sail. Perhaps her love of plants and poetry was passed down from this great-grandmother.

The book then fell open at a particular illustration of a bedraggled, bearded castaway scanning the horizon from a rocky coastline, captioned: 'Down the shore he ranged, or all day long / sat often in the seaward-gazing gorge. / A ship-wreck'd sailor, waiting for a sail.' This striking, Crusoe-esque image was illustrating Tennyson's narrative poem 'Enoch Arden' which tells of a merchant sailor who absents himself at sea, leaving his wife and three children in order to better support them. Missing for at least eleven years, he's assumed to have died and so his wife agrees to marry another. After the island castaway is finally rescued by a passing ship, he arrives home to see his wife through a window embraced in a happy family scene. He leaves without revealing himself and dies of a broken heart.

It's a classic tale with mythic depths that surely would have resonated with Emma Louise Chichester's own experience of domestic life while the men were exiled to salt and wind. So many uncles, sons, brothers, fathers, nephews, absent and unseen, lost in one way or another to the sea; the women apparently as steadfast as the bollards securing ships to the shore.

Although their lives are more explicit, traceable through records of ships, crew and ports, the seafaring men of my family remained just out of my reach. It was the strength and independence of the women like Emma Louise which, though absent from any written history of the sea, became more animate as I allowed my imagination in amongst known facts.

I pictured her with her plant-collecting and Tennyson, as a matriarch supporting her husband Francis and with a family branching widely both before and after her. Coming from a group of seven siblings born across seventeen years, Emma bore seven children herself over fifteen years. Her marriage to Francis bound together two significant Braunton seafaring families; the merchant coffers were presumably growing but always at risk, too, in the event of the absolute loss of a ship.

Francis became well-established as a man of perseverance and energy; his was a life marked by the heft of the ships and their timbers. He and his three sons were tapping into the boom in coastal trading with cargoes of oats or coal or cement, commissioning the building of ships or buying existing ones, even acquiring one from the far north.

Emma Louise's life was marked by the reliable rhythms of the men's departure and, hopefully, their return on the tides. But the potential brevity of life must have preoccupied her, as diseases threatened and the sea both gave and took. Two daughters died before her. Her last-born son, Francis, only just outlived her before the sea took him from *Pirate*. My great-grandfather Robert died not long after this, making her son William – with the gold watch chain – the only male to live a full-length life, becoming prosperous from the same business. Her granddaughter Dorothy Louise, my Granny, was born just six months before she herself died.

Would Emma Louise ever have had the freedom to wander the Burrows alone, to press rare plants or still herself long enough to dip into a book of poetry? Solitude would be a rare thing. Families were laced together by blood and trade – the Berrys and Hartnolls, the Newcombes and Chichesters as well as all the Drakes, meaning she was hardly ever out of the Church with all the funerals, christenings and weddings. That was her role, to bind families tight as her tatting, and I imagine that her keen awareness of human fragility might have made her as loving as she was stoical, just as Granny had been. I glimpse her at ease, coming in from a garden with a handful of fragrant carrots, bouncing a cousin's baby on her lap, or ruffling the ears of a pet terrier.

When she died aged sixty in 1900, twenty-five years before her husband, she left him £162 9s & 3d, worth over £23,000 today. A woman of some independence. I wondered whether she had invested in the ships herself and was able to confirm this at the record office in Barnstaple. I carefully turned each page of the massive leather-bound shipping register of a century before, deciphering the copperplate writing. It revealed the cusp of the twentieth century to be a busy time in terms of transfers of ship shares in the family, and particularly for women. Emma Louise herself took over all sixty-four shares of the Bridgwater-built *Maggie Annie* from her son, William Drake.

The register also revealed more about *Pirate*'s ownership. Initially, as the ketch was sailed from Scotland to be re-registered locally to Braunton, all sixty-four shares belonged to Francis Drake Senior, her husband, but he soon transferred forty-three shares to their son Francis and twenty-one to a Holly Berry, 'spinster' of Barnstaple. When Francis Jr died intestate, his brother Robert became *Pirate's* managing owner. But a third of the shares were still owned by Holly Berry right until the ship was broken up in 1928.

On Robert's death in 1907 his forty-three shares in *Pirate* were transferred to his wife (Granny's mother) Annie Lock Drake, and it wasn't until 1914 that she sold them on. This meant that for seven years, two women were the joint owners of *Pirate*: Annie Lock Drake and Holly Berry, presumably considering themselves businesswomen, and employing a master to sail the ship.

Having begun my exploration by focusing on particular ships and the men with lives referenced in records, history books and museums, I was now coaxing the submerged lives of the women of the family into greater clarity. They were more geographically fixed on solid ground, and apparently more photographed, but otherwise had lives far less documented.

To discover they were shipowners pleased me.

Back inland in Perthshire, another winter came on and low temperatures halted the boat-building work. Nevertheless, our new rowing club was now scenting the fulfilment of a much-imagined skiff. We were also getting to know the nature of the coastal rowing movement we would join; established clubs and rowers were outstandingly generous toward our humble casting-off and also taking great interest in the first boat to have a freshwater home-port.

But just as we would have resumed building work in spring 2020, Covid-19 and the first lockdown struck. A brief reprieve in the autumn allowed us to apply the first coats of paint after endless sessions of sanding, but soon we had to hit the pause button again.

With my mission in the south-west also frustrated by a travel ban, my explorations were forced indoors. Instead of roaming shores or planning sailing trips, I began to pay The Box more attention. The piles of papers, collapsing packets and fatigued elastic bands soon spread a new sea around my workroom floor as I mined the wreckage of a line of less-celebrated mothers: the women left on land, belonging behind the tangled wrack-line. In coastal culture, these were the lives more often marked by longevity.

Some had been corralled into a studio and made to keep still for a camera. Printed on yellowish, thick board with the elaborate insignia of a Barnstaple studio on the reverse side, a portrait of a long-chinned, ringleted matriarch, Agnes Roach, surfaced. This was Granny's other grandmother, wearing a high-collared, dark dress covered in beaded brocade. Her eyes are small and pale, close together, accentuating the broad chin. She is perhaps in her fifties here.

With so much time alone and a diary swept clean, I spent days excavating further – funeral cards, letters, photos. Agnes frequently rose up from the depths, remaining recognisable at different ages by the scraped-back hair, the central parting. Her two daughters appeared with her, first in girlhood and then as mothers themselves, each with a white-flounced infant on their laps. The baby held by Annie Lock Drake – which must have been Granny – had a familiar look. Eight months before he died, in June 1960, my father had taken a photo of me as a one-year-old in the Alps. Granny and I share the same round-faced, broad-browed, wide-eyed look.

A newspaper report told me that Granny attended Agnes' funeral along with members of the Chichester, Hartnoll and Drake families. The cause of death was heart failure. I was shocked to realise that Agnes's daughter Annie died only two years later. Both had lived for many years as widows.

Raising my head from the spread of photographs and arriving back in 2020 and Highland Perthshire, I looked forward to a time when I could travel again, and visit my mother with these photographs, having more certainty about who and what was represented. I would spread them out for her and we would name the people who helped make us.

'Good Lord,' she would say. And perhaps she'd vaguely recall a story or two.

I'd begun to scent my own ancestry, my mother's, in these women's lives; an *expectation* of loss that perhaps forearms us towards self-sufficiency. Like my mother, Annie (her mother's mother) had no choice but to continue living with a widow's courage. In later studio photographs she wears a white blouse and sits with a folder on her lap. She's looking quite the businesswoman; stern and serious, with the same cinched-in waist. By now she is majority-owner of the ketch, *Pirate*. The 1911 census also reveals her occupation as 'boot-dealer'. Perhaps this explained Granny's shiny, high boots as a girl in the photo of the grieving threesome in the garden. When Annie died, at only fifty-two, she left a sum of money that would represent over £170,000 today.

My mother had questioned on a number of occasions, both by letter and in person, by what means her parents could have met. Perhaps she was referring to their divided geography, but I wondered if there was something else lurking beneath the question. Did she consider them poorly matched in some way, in education or accomplishment?

Granny's life spanned the first three quarters of the last century, including the widespread introduction of the combustion engine, space travel and major changes in the expectations of women's lives. It bridged a huge change in social culture between a stable, intermarrying group of families remaining in one place and their scattering following two world wars.

That little girl pictured in long leather boots after her father's death won a scholarship to Barnstaple Grammar School and evidently grew into a fine young woman who had musical talent. Out of the apparently bottomless Box came a photograph of her at fifteen in a white dress with a thick rope of plaited, black hair to her thighs. She sits on various beaches amongst crowds of young people picnicking, about to 'bathe', as she called swimming. She is relaxed and smiling in front of the camera. Suntanned cousins are arranged in age order on a beach as if rowers in a gig. Her skinny-legged brother Francis (Uncle Frank) is cross-legged at the front.

The North Devon Journal I consulted named Granny as a mourner at many funerals, as well as a bridesmaid for her Drake cousin Ivy in July 1921. The reporter went into raptures about the bridal dress of ivory charmeuse, the overdress of georgette embroidered with silver and pearls, a wreath of orange blossom. The bridesmaids' dresses were of 'apricot crepe de chine draped with turquoise blue georgette and a striking effect produced by their veils of gold lace and wreaths of fruit.'

I found photographs to match this description: Granny, serious-faced at twenty-one, standing with the other bridesmaids behind the plump-faced, prosperous-looking, bridal couple. I wonder if by then she might have felt 'on the shelf', and overshadowed by this showy affair of her cousin's.

Growing into her adult self during World War I, she lost friends and potential husbands. I have a vague recollection of her speaking of a sweetheart from Braunton. A young man's thin face with large ears and a long Roman nose punctuates the piles of photographs, one of them signed: 'Hope you will not burn this. Love Billy.'

Not yet married herself, she left Braunton for London and the Royal Academy of Music, staying in Northwood with the Huxtable family, part of the Braunton diaspora with whom the Drakes had intermarried, owned ships and sailed over generations. She passed her music 'certificate' in 1922. All this I recovered through the congratulatory letters and telegrams preserved in The Box.

Granny was twenty-five when her mother died. She'd told me many times that when her mother was dying, she spoke of her children, Dorothy and Frank, as her 'two angels', always by her bedside. Granny was 'worn to the bone' by the nursing. She had lost her grandfather Francis Drake two years before, her father seventeen years before that, and grandmother Agnes six months before that. At the prime of her life, she must have felt surrounded by death, living amongst legions of women wearing black.

She'd kept four letters from her future husband – my grandfather – Ernest, in two separate envelopes. Three of them date from September and October 1921, two from Basingstoke and one from Bristol where he was studying at university. He progresses from commiserating with her on something unlucky (I imagine the result of her music exam the first time she took it), to commenting on a piece of music they have shared, to reporting on playing tennis and moving lodgings to somewhere without a piano. 'That will mean periodic fits of the blues,' he writes.

Shortly afterwards comes a birthday letter, referring to recent time spent together, trains caught in different directions and the fact that he couldn't sleep when he arrived home because he had been 'bubbling over!' A couple of weeks later he answers a letter from her in which he says he's glad of something she has told him. He reassures her that nothing she can say will ever make any difference to his feelings about 'the only girl'. He goes on to say that he feels very sorry for 'Billy', but having ascertained that Dorothy and Billy were not engaged, he had dismissed 'it'. It seems Billy had not: 'that's rather a queer idea of his that I ought to have written to him'. He asks her not to worry about it or to blame herself. If it would help for them to be properly engaged, she has only to say the word.

By the time he writes in March 1924 from Southampton, he addresses her as 'Dear old Dot', a letter which tells of theatre he has seen and the accompanying music. He excuses her for some irritability she's confessed to, and promises that he won't tease her when they are married, offering to love all the bad temper out of her. 'Anyway, we love each other too much to fall out. You're a wonderful darling girl, and I'm the happiest chap in the world. How can you think I shall get fed up with you when I want you so badly I don't know what to do?'

They married in London, rather than Braunton, in 1926. I think with the loss of so many immediate family members, the Huxtables had become a surrogate – as well as more distantly biological – family who took a lively interest in her. I became sure it was they who introduced her to Ernest in Northwood, though his family origins were just along the coast from Braunton at Ilfracombe. Both pianists, I imagine the youngsters being invited to play duets before dinner.

Her marriage then removed her permanently from Braunton as his work as an industrial chemist with Pirrelli's took them to live in Southampton. And so her separation from home-port was cemented.

This part of the story I would be able to report to my mother: how her parents were drawn together by music and the extended family.

Photos from the summer of 1939 show the couple radiant and suntanned on cliff paths, Dorothy smiling with her glossy hair coiled in two plaits at her ears. Ernest, the grandfather I never knew, is handsome in a white open-necked shirt and sleeveless jumper, long pale shorts and walking shoes. I see my brother in his face, and when he smiles and his lower lip curls outwards, my nephew. My mother walks hand-in-hand with her father, or riding piggyback, pretty and smiling in a short white dress and a ribbon around her head. The happy threesome are on the beach, riding donkeys, all smiles and affection, blazing with health.

At a time so defined by loss – and with her brother Frank away at sea – I imagine this new security and love must have been vital to Granny. How desperately unlucky must she have felt to lose this husband, a fit man with whom she had just returned from a walking holiday, to a heart attack two days before Britain joined World War II in September 1939. The family pattern of male partners dying young had continued to assert itself even after they stopped taking to the sea.

I recall the angry tone in Granny's voice sometimes when she spoke of his death, as if it condemned her to be a young widow with a single child who went on to desert her too. She spoke of him 'dropping dead', from which I had pictured it happening on the holiday itself. But I realised now from the letters and death certificate that they had just returned home to Southampton. A press clipping I found reported that, 'when in bed after returning from his professional duties, he suddenly gave a groan, turned over on his side and, before medical aid could be obtained, had passed away.' His great interest in music and his accomplishment as a pianist were noted. The floral tributes at the funeral are listed in another press clipping, and include: 'To my darling with love from Dot.' When I read, 'To my dear daddy, with love from Jill,' I wept.

I wondered if, as they walked on that holiday, Granny and Ernest had been savouring final freedoms, knowing that a storm was closing in. She had sometimes suggested to me that she would have had a better life if she'd married someone else – perhaps 'Billy', the young man with large ears and a long face.

At eight years old, my mother had been evacuated from home before her 'dear daddy' died. I found letters she'd written to her mother during this period, asking about the cat, Bunny, reporting how many strokes she had managed to swim with encouragement from her aunt and the latest activities in the school she was attending. She never did return to their family home in Southampton.

Along with some paperwork about death-related financial matters, The Box offered up bundles of sympathy letters from friends and family far and wide in Britain, and one from St John's Newfoundland, Devonshire seafarers' diasporic home. Many letters refer to Granny's previous worries, troubles and bereavements. Doris and Jack Huxtable remind her, 'your dear mother lost your father when she was much younger than you'. The letters reflect the chaos of the forthcoming war, referring to the 'situation' or 'crisis', and write of decisions they must make to stay put somewhere or travel elsewhere or evacuate children, given 'the new reality'. Her brother, Frank, is often mentioned as a tower of strength to her, going to her side immediately on hearing of the death.

'Comfort yourselves,' one friend writes. 'It's better for him to go like that than to be killed in war.'

Ernest had served in World War I in Field Artillery, and was twice mentioned in dispatches. Following the armistice, he worked in France for about a year with the Imperial War Graves Commission. This new war looming and Ernest's concern about it is cited several times as a possible factor in the suddenness of his death: 'Did he upset himself with this war I wonder?' Many invoke comfort in faith, time and the needs of 'Little Jill'. By now her school was closed by war, and my mother's teacher in Southampton writes that 'little children can never realise these sad happenings and it is not right that they should'.

Mother and daughter might have returned to their intricately-wrought net of families in Braunton. But perhaps by 1939 it was already too dispersed to hold them. Instead, they moved to Exeter, 40 miles from Braunton and linked to the sea only by the river Exe, broadening and salting to their south. This was the same house I had known, where Granny hung up a string of seaweed as a weather-forecaster in addition to a barometer she tapped daily, made trays of clotted cream, and kept a piano at which she gave lessons.

As she aged, my mother complained with some bitterness about how she was treated at this time – her mother's absence for several months after her father's death, when presumably she was sorting affairs and dealing with the inquest.

Today we might question the attitude taken to my mother's childhood grief, but it strikes me now as a familial trope, a pulse through generations. A mother's emotional withdrawal from her bereaved children seems also to have been my inheritance. Perhaps we would now be able to discuss this and she would recognise these patterns, understand her own mother better. Let go of some bitterness.

The Box continued to turn up things I hadn't seen before. Some were poignant, such as the cards from my child-mother to Granny, presumably cherished. They often featured her drawings, which grew rapidly in competence. Even at twelve or thirteen she could execute in pen and ink a scene of racehorses in motion that were anatomically balanced. And frequent appearances were made by a black cat on cards addressed to 'Mistress' from 'Bunny'. This impersonation seems to have recurred on all celebratory occasions.

I also found Christmas cards sent to Granny from Rijswijk in the Netherlands where my sister, brother, mother and father went to live in 1958, and where I was born a year later. The front of each card bears a drawing or print of a local scene by my mother, but the message inside is written in my father's hand. He signed for all five of us. It is not a cold greeting, but not personalised either. Distance was well established.

Sea Marked

I would have said that Granny had never been abroad until a photo album showed her, in the Netherlands, cuddling a two-month-old me. My brother and sister also gather in adoration. My father had apparently 'bumped into her' in the street close to their Rijswijk flat, quite by chance when she was on holiday visiting her brother Frank who was also based in the Netherlands at the time.

I'm not convinced by this 'chance'. For a woman whose life narrative emphasised her loyalty and duty to her own widowed mother as she declined into ill health, I imagine the 'modern' separation from her only child must have been Granny's ghastly wound.

I looked up from The Box, arriving back amidst a sea of wreckage on my workroom floor and recognising a visceral shift. Those straining lines of rope with which I'd tried to draw my vessel of enquiry closer to a quay, sharpening men's faces, trying to see the colour of their eyes, were loosening now. I released them back into their unknowable oceans. Instead, hand over hand, through supposition and imagination, through evidence in The Box, I was drawing the women closer. Whilst I remained uncertain of the eye colour of the men, I felt a blind confidence that Emma Louise's eyes were brown, sunlit with flecks of green; the hazel of Granny's and my own.

Outside in the garden a choir of blackbirds and sparrows sang, sovereign in a trafficless summer. There still seemed so many silences, gaps, ellipses, in our family story, so little continuity. Sometimes I wondered at my mother making a discrete island of us, surrounding us with submerged truths and offering only the flimsiest link to what The Box cried out: place, connection, pride, love. She had been quite purposeful in her opting out of a line of forebears.

I looked now at my temperament, *ours*, with a new clarity. Our mother-daughter relationship was central; the spine – or keel – from which we could restructure a ship of family memory. Shared joy at being aboard *Bessie Ellen* had begun it – the creak of sail and haul of hemp lines. Now there seemed an urgency to weave us both back into the wider story of the place, the time of sail, the women's losses and beyond; to take up our legacy and mend the fractures.

I determined to report back to her, lay out more generously the shared past in photos, drawings, letters and discuss how it had shaped us and even our relationship. I might brave some of my unanswered questions. Doing so could readjust the dynamics between us and perhaps step me into proper adulthood. I would no longer whine like a left-behind child or retreat to delve alone in ditches.

I buzzed with purpose. But it wasn't something I could do on the phone and, with Covid-related travel restrictions still in place, I didn't know when I might next be able to see her.

A Blaze in the Dark

My mother died, suddenly, apparently in good health and spirits, in early November 2020. The news tipped me into an icy plunge. Living alone, and at a time of enforced solitude, I sat stunned by my fireside that evening. I went to bed late then woke from a heavy, dream-filled sleep; knowing that something had changed, taking a moment to realise what it was.

Over the next few days my brother, sister and I made plans, let people know. When I called the newsagent to cancel her paper delivery, the rich voice of the Cornishwoman calling me 'darling' collapsed me into sobs. I spoke with one of my mother's dear literary friends in Penzance who was sitting beside a white lily with a candle burning for her. 'So many people loved her,' she said, and we agreed how marvellous it was that she had been able to be herself and independent to the very end with her home, books and intellectual capacity intact. News was coming in of the US elections – Trump declaring a false victory, Biden elected. She would have been riveted to this. Always engaging with the world and especially US politics.

It was November, the season of death. The first long, strong, loving hug came (illegally) from a dear friend on my doorstep; Robin was always available at the end of the phone. The days submerged me in numb depth with occasional gulps of air and snatched light.

Inevitably I thought back to my most recent visit to my mother; a quick train ride down for the day from Plymouth. Remarkably, I had managed this only two weeks before, taking advantage of a brief relaxation in Covid restrictions. She'd been mostly housebound since the beginning of March, foregoing her involvement in two local book groups, but in at least one case keeping up with the reading and writing implied, and sending in advance a handwritten piece to be shared at the group's virtual meeting.

She had told me on that visit, and I believed her, that she was perfectly content in her enclosed world. As an only child she'd cultivated a rich inner life. She was reading and watching TV a great deal, going out for short walks. She said that her kind neighbour looked out for her and sometimes brought her bin back into the yard.

We shared a lunch of focaccia and various salads I brought with me and she ate with appetite. I had promised myself that I would give her some company and show her warmth on this visit, not be my withholding, defensive self. On recently reading Diana Athill's *Somewhere Towards the End*, I had paid attention to her words about the pointlessness of excavating old people's perceived wrongs when they can no longer be acted upon. I instructed myself that it was time to celebrate my mother rather than blame her, and to help her through the present times.

We chatted about this and that. I told her I had a book coming out in the spring and she asked me something about Robin, who she had not yet met. Though always reserved with her about matters of the heart, I told her a little. How despite the physical distance between our homes, we'd found commonality in our backgrounds: we had both been at the College of Art in Farnham in the 1970s, had a friend in common in the Western Isles, both loved mountains, literature, and had enjoyed semi-itinerant, travelling adult lives. Each other's friends seemed similar in attitudes and lifestyles. What I didn't tell her was that our emotional bond was swiftly clinched on meeting through sharing stories of our squally childhoods.

Later, she and I walked the short downhill slope to the promenade and the whole of Mount's Bay opened up. We looked east towards the Lizard and then turned to walk west towards Newlyn as we usually did. She had something to say, as always, about the sea conditions, still thinking as a painter and commenting on the unexpected hue of the sea in different states of light. She got a little out of breath but walked with determination.

It seemed impossible that she had died so soon after this visit, and yet I must have known her death was coming sometime soon. Otherwise, why would I have started to keep her letters – written in the famous sloping hand not so unlike my own except in Biro rather than fountain pen. I had noticed that she had long since stopped dating them by year, as if it was no longer of any consequence.

On that final visit I didn't fill her in on the discoveries I'd made through The Box, my breakthrough into the women's territory of love and loss; our shared legacy. I hadn't been able to carry all the accumulated proof in photos and documents, and the visit was too short, I'd told myself. Soon, when circumstances were easier, I would.

This omission was a complex additional layer to my grief.

Our initial work at her house was governed by practicality rather than sentiment. My sister was the first brave enough, free enough to travel. Covid restrictions stopped us being there at the same time and so I followed soon after, taking the long cross-Britain journey to the far south-west with Robin.

A Blaze in the Dark

On arrival at her house, fearful about the shock of a bodily absence on the pale sofa, I stepped into the sitting room and picked up the photo of her at the helm of *Bessie Ellen*, taken four and a half years earlier when she was eighty-four. I welled with pride and loss, put it back for the time being where she had displayed it on her bookshelf. I also noted the partly-complete *Guardian* crossword still resting beside her perch. I wanted these things that conjured the joys and habits of a living person to stay in position forever.

Robin and I stayed in a tiny tin-miner's cottage. It was six miles away, perched above the lash of the Atlantic in a village on the north coast near Pendeen. From here, in the last light at the end of some of these days of work in her house, I walked out onto the cliffs. As the sky blackened, Pendeen Watch, my mother's favourite lighthouse, pulsed four white flashes per minute into the silence. A frill of illuminated surf echoed this signature from below, bright and reassuring. I stood with damp turf under my feet, eyes on the horizon. A depth of dark feeling coupled uncomfortably with fondness for this place which was so much hers and would continue without her and perhaps without me now that I would lose my familial foothold.

She had loved to come here and paint, or just watch.

We undertook essentials over ten days – the clearing of fridge, freezer and stockpiled cupboards of tinned food, discretely-hoarded packaging materials dating from her time as a second-hand book dealer. Everywhere were signs of her increasing inertia. There were specified items in the will to identify, valuations of contents to arrange, estate agents to invite in, and a need to leave the house clean and tidy for viewing. And there must be a funeral.

We worked hard. Nevertheless, I was frequently halted by surprising or poignant finds. The Chinese dishes decorated with fishes that I remembered from my childhood, three lead shots from a ship called Juno wrecked off the Scilly Isles in 1797, her scribbled notes of trips with me in Scotland, and a whole collection of my airmail letters to her from Zanzibar.

Her passionate association with the sea sang from the many paintings she'd produced of West Penwith over thirty years, where you can never be more than six miles from a coast. When she'd moved to this new landscape her favoured painting materials changed from oil paint to gouache – a medium which could conjure the vital shock of lichen and hyacinth as well as being more practical in terms of its quick drying when painting outdoors. The paintings always included sea, always seen from the land.

I stacked these in a curtained bedroom, gathering them from around the house in the knowledge that many more were dispersed across Britain following gift or sale. And then there were all the others that remained unframed in sketchpads.

Amongst the books and papers abandoned on the table beside the sofa, her handwriting filled an A4 page entitled 'Inheritance'. It had probably been set as a theme by one of her literary groups. In a few brief paragraphs, her words connected this place, where she had come to live in later life, with her childhood garden. From the latter she had climbed over the back hedge and walked up to the top of the hill in order to see a distant chink of sea at the Exe estuary.

Pride glimmered in what she wrote and the piece included history new to me, such as a couple in the family who sailed to North America thinking to settle there, stayed six months but, not liking it much, sailed back again. She acknowledged the perceived normality of growing up in a family preceded by all those Francis Drakes, the shipowners and master mariners of Braunton. She had understood their proximity to disaster. In the final lines, she noted the sea now at the bottom of Cornwall Terrace, two minutes or so walk away from her Penzance home of thirty years. 'I can look down at an ocean slamming against the land in a fury of foam, or squint at a sheet of dazzle on which lolls the light-bitten silhouette of a yacht.'

And finally she wrote: 'The ocean. My inheritance.'

The chance to fill out my mother's life in her own words had now passed. Stories were frozen as first told. Or they would remain untold. However, the person she had been before she had us children now began to gather a richer patina as relatives and old friends contacted us with tributes and memories.

Those who knew her in the earliest parts of her adulthood commented on her beauty and sense of fun, her clever dressmaking and fashion sense. A contemporary of mine, my first friend and next-door-neighbour at pre-school age, remembered her cartwheeling across the garden. 'The sexiest lady I ever saw,' she said, and praised her great fortitude and adventure as a single mother and widow at the age of twenty-seven. Later she sent me a photograph taken in our Surrey garden, in which my mother is looking up from a book with a youthful smile. I recalled the parties she cooked for, orange juice laced with vodka, her dancing to The Beatles and the Tremeloes; an early adopter of miniskirts and hold-up stockings.

Sea Marked

Friends and neighbours local to Penzance came forward too, commenting on her smile, her great cheerfulness. Many were library associates. After the death of my stepfather in 1993, she'd become more involved with the town's independent Morrab Library. Within easy walking distance of her home, the fine white building from 1818 was housed in subtropical public gardens surrounding a pretty Victorian bandstand. With its rooms floor-to-ceiling with books, unique Napoleonic memorabilia, a photographic archive of the area, and a special collection of books by and about women in Cornwall, it could have been formal and austere. But it was always full of activity and laughter, people pursuing research passions, making poetry or prints, people who not only loved literature but also West Penwith.

It was here she organised events and became Honorary Librarian, acquiring a circle of like-minded acquaintances and friends with the independence of mind this area seemed to nurture alongside its botanical diversity of palm trees, carpets of thrift and luxuriant dank mosses.

There were so many decisions to be taken in such a short time after her death, including about the funeral. I thought too late of asking for 'Crossing the Bar' to be played for the committal of her body at the crematorium. We had Elgar's 'Nimrod' instead, suggested by my brother. Anyway, the poignancy of Tennyson's words, that melody by the Spooky Men's Chorale and my own investment in it might have floored me. But I'm pretty sure that the poem, the song, would represent her attitude to her own crossing – another adventure, a brave anticipation.

I read out a poem I had written about her in 1995 whilst on my first writing workshop. The advice from the tutor, Liz Lochhead, had been to trust material observations to convey emotion for the person. I'd included the way her mug of tea always clunked against her spectacles at each sip; the pockets full of sand she returned home with; her climbing the stairs to tell Hugh, in his sickbed, the colour of the sea today. My brother read an early poem she'd written, 'Spring Supper' in which she slices mushrooms and peppers indoors, whilst at a distance the garden pulses with the sounds of children who rehearse 'the terror / of warm shadows / and watch the hollies darken / to the black of myth'. My sister read 'Water Music' by Elizabeth Jennings. She had found it left beside information about funerals, as if in request. The poem is full of flow, estuary, gulls, sea music, and closes: 'I would like my death / to come as rivers turn, as sea commands. / Let my last journey be to sounds of water.'

Summoning the tides. Crossing the Bar.

We processed from the chapel to 'Penny Lane' by The Beatles. Just us three, our three partners and my brother's three children – two generations. Others who loved her watched a broadcast in their homes. Whilst she had never volunteered any opinion on how she should be seen off even when we encouraged her, I think she would have approved of the small event we created; enjoyed it even.

Over this period of her death, the funeral, the correspondence that followed, I recognised how much of my mother had 'belonged' to others. Her oldest friends from university, the friends from Camberley, and kindred spirits more recently at her local library. It seemed that as a daughter, my view of her had been both short and narrow.

I return in a loop to the that now-familiar question: was my mother 'sea-marked'? Was Granny? A person who the sea has chosen, perhaps standing in peculiar attention to it and waiting to be called. In Robert Louis Stevenson's case it seems to have developed in him a need to 'be a nomad, more or less, until my days be done'. Although some women accompanied their husbands to sea, as Mrs Chichester did on *Bessie Ellen*, few others in the early twentieth century could claim such freedom. In women perhaps this 'marking' has more often taken a slightly different form.

Coastal women were surely not naive about their sons and husbands and fathers and uncles. Watching from land, they would understand the fatal impact of that split-second decision or this unexpected current, even when they had never experienced it themselves. Women perhaps knew they were marked out as widows-in-waiting, and developed hardiness in order to withstand responsibilities alone later. Might it also develop in them not just fortitude but a kind of spirituality, a turning to poetry or music or visual art?

My mother had risen to the widow's challenge, apparently stowing away grief for her father and then for her first husband, both of whom died in their thirties. She showed strength as a young single parent, moved house and resisted family counsel about where to go, choosing her own course.

My own interpretation is that when she found new love, someone to lean on and open to, the caulking leaked, her cargo of stored grief destabilised her. I believe she became truly happy, as her 'Inheritance' piece suggested, with her responsibilities to children more or less concluded, and with the breakers of the south-west audible from home. She could go to a different coastal point each day to walk and paint, looking out from land to sea, judging its temper, and noting the surprising hue at the horizon against the foreshore; the interior of a wave against its foam.

During these initial ten days in her house I came across a written version of a painful incident from her teenage years. In the year or so before her death she had told me this story several times and its telling fractured her usually bright and cheerful demeanour.

Now I found it as a poem entitled 'Post-war'.

'I walked with him, my older cousin / newly home from POW camp. / He said nothing.'

Jack Huxtable says nothing for four stanzas until on the fifth he suddenly speaks at the dinner table about a dream in which he was being chased by Alsatian dogs. But the focus of the poem is really her mother's reaction to this.

'When my mother cackled, thinking it hilarious, / he reverted to saying nothing'.

And the final stanza: 'I knew then / that I would never defer / to her again.'

I wonder what made Granny laugh. Was it nervous embarrassment about this disclosure of his unconscious, his internal terror, at a time when superficiality meant survival? A stutter of truth unlocking a stiff upper lip?

But my mother did not try to justify it. I recalled how her lower jaw set, her lip curled as she spat it out: 'I could have killed her'.

She believed that her own father died young due to 'broken heart syndrome' – a reaction to a surge of hormones triggered by an emotionally stressful event, in his case the gathering storm of World War II after his experience of the first. She'd told me that her mother moved things in the house when he was out at work to see if he noticed, a sort of 'Pelmanism' which was said to disclose shell-shock. Perhaps she thought her mother incapable of compassion to this cousin who was experiencing the same mental torture from wartime horror that killed her 'dear Daddy'.

Mother and daughter were never properly reconciled, it seems. Perhaps this would have to serve now as the explanation for their strained relationship. A closing of one link in the story's chain.

The loss of a parent, and perhaps especially a mother, opens a black hole whatever the quality of the relationship. A certain kind of madness descends. A black armband might have warned of my need to be treated carefully.

I gathered snatches of news subliminally, such as developments in the worlds of literature and connections to our story of sea and ships, saving them for a letter or a phone call to her. But these impulses could no longer be delivered, and I regretfully acknowledged all the times I'd withheld such sharing, even at that final visit. I began to learn the loss of a fundamental rung in the ladder of years and generations; the person who would know something I can no longer ask about.

When Granny died, I'd kept her linen-bound *Recipe Cuttings Book*. On certain pages her handwriting is still comfortingly familiar in fountain pen: recipes for chocolate-chip cookies, chocolate potato cake, cake without sugar. The war is evident in 'utility Easter eggs' using soya flour and a drop of almond essence, mock cream. Tucked amongst the pages are the recipes she clipped from newspapers for sardine cream pie, tangerine marmalade. At some stage long ago I started to use the folder myself and I like to see my handwriting alongside hers in the cake section: her orange fruit cake, made with orange squash and peanut butter; my devil's food cake with a great deal of cocoa.

The book has become a working receptacle for my own cuttings and handwritten recipes sourced from friends and relatives over the years. I find there, in my sister's distinctive handwriting, a recipe for Bakewell Pudding, and my mother's handwritten recipes for Moong dal and Saté, recalling her palette-prickling culinary adventures. I like the fact that this book has become a growing, dynamic store, embracing the influence of all four of us in the kitchen over the last century: grandmother, daughter, granddaughters, a post-rationalised intimacy in scraps of paper. The opportunity of a collaboration across the generations, person-to-person, was now lost to us, divided as we were between those living and those dead.

My mother's heart suffered a fatal arrhythmia and before that it was surely broken by the premature deaths of two husbands, one of them a young father. Did I inherit my, literally, back-to-front heart, flipped over into an abnormal position at the centre of my chest? Granny lost first her father, then mother, then husband, then a living daughter. And lining up amongst her forebears were all those young widows and their losses. Are broken hearts our legacy? Hearts physically deficient in some way or loaded with loss and sadness even before we know why.

My memory spat out something from a long time before. Both my sister and I when young had voiced some reluctance about marrying. Our female inheritance was the seafaring burden – our men would die young. We've never been a superstitious family and yet this uneasiness amounts to the same thing. Plumbing the unconscious now raises the wreck of an idea – we are all still living as a community at sea.

Transgenerational trauma is a relatively new concept in psychology, and not without sceptical treatment. It's been

particularly applied to families uprooted by grave distur-
bance: people sold into slavery, Holocaust survivors, refugees,
colonised communities. But could it be that seafaring families, braced as they must be against loss when human life is
so fragile, have passed down a particular propensity not just
for forbearance, but amongst women an armoured acceptance of repeated 'abandonment'? Men made strange by their
rhythms of departure and return, as if they are only partly
domesticated and partly owned by the sea, doomed to follow
their ancestors out there. They'd scan the horizon and tides
uneasily if on land for too long. And then die prematurely.

My choice of partners over the years has perhaps followed this echo – one a commercial diver who departed on
long work trips away; another with a boat on an island several oceans south; and now Robin living on the south coast
of England. Always an element of 'away-ness', of the coast,
patterns of separation and reunion. Had I been unknowingly practising the old ways of that coast of widows?

Perhaps such ancestry moulds a certain emotional dys-
function, fashioning it into a shield of self-sufficiency. Even
in early childhood I was aware of carrying a burden; always
anxious, a worrier, feeling the loss of someone or something
or some place that I couldn't identify. There were ghosting
absences as I played alone amongst the bracken and ditches
of our wild garden, making 'tea' from rowan berries for my
imagined guests. On reaching my eighth birthday I'd asked
my mother to get rid of my dolls and soft toys – I had some
idea that this great age should put me beyond emotional
dependence on such props.

Depression, anxiety, guilt are sometimes said to be the
indirect result of high levels of maternal stress. I'm aware
now that the three of us were inconveniently young when

our father was dying, and in the aftermath of his death my mother must have been absent for long periods, literally and emotionally. As a child I had a sense of being a nuisance, 'unwanted' in some way; a childhood state transforming in adulthood into a fragility around intimate relationships despite craving them. A pushing away and pulling to.

I am gregarious yet recognise my own introversion in a physical need to retreat in order to be myself. I've found comfort and affinity in the melancholic. In music and literature my territory is failed love, solitude, the seashore, dereliction and wreck. Even while still at school I was drawn to Hardy's tragic heroines, Shakespeare's Juliet, and still I'm mesmerized by Fado music, by 'Song to the Siren'. My early writing adventures seem to have been a way of fashioning something that sings out of loss.

Without children myself, without father or mother, my thinking now seemed too contained to one life. I could look to my role as an aunt, and someone who cares about friends' children. I can look to the words with which I chart our family past for those who generate new lives and endeavours. Does being a writer make of this role a duty; is it partly why we write, so that others can remember?

In the wake of my mother's funeral, I travelled back north on a sleeper train in late November 2020, back home to certain solitude and short days, dark nights in Scotland. I was deeply exhausted and at night lurched between sleeplessness or dreamless depths. When dreams came, they were sometimes disturbing; one night I accidentally swallowed the new-born baby of a close relative. I failed in attempts to pick up the tails of my freelance life and writing, tried to be gentle with myself, taking long walks carrying a flask of tea and a mat on which to pause somewhere. I had virtual get-togethers with friends, or huddled on their cold doorsteps with coffee.

My hands urged to make something rather than to work with words. Some years earlier I'd taken a day workshop with artist Brigid Collins who specialises in building beautiful artefacts with coloured tissue paper stretched and lacquered over simple frames. The semi-transparency creates panes of luminosity. They often reflect the structure of books and respond to literary works, notably Kathleen Jamie's poetry of place, landscape and natural order.

I began, as Brigid proposed, with nothing planned other than what the materials in front of me suggested. In this case it was lengths of slim tree branches stripped bare and polished by westerly storms on Loch Tay and dumped on eastern beaches close to Kenmore, where I went to gather them one raw December day. Pale, luminous, contorted, I had no idea yet how I would use these wands. I had also plucked a stately bullrush and this suggested itself as a mast – light and, unlike the driftwood, unrelentingly straight.

I tore coloured tissue paper into irregular strips and shapes, laid them over each other and shellacked them into glossy strength, stretching the paper between a thin wire on one side and the mast. I used coloured markers to write onto the paper lines and words of Tennyson's 'Bar' poem. It began to transform into a single, 18-inch-tall, sail. From wire, paper and shellac I also made a black pennant flag with a white cross to signal my mother's allegiance to Cornwall.

I'd had a vague notion of launching what I called the 'Mother Ship' bearing a candle on to Loch Tay on the shortest day of the year. Just before it, further Covid restrictions were introduced meaning that mixing with others was only allowed on Christmas Day itself, and Robin would no longer cross the border from England to join me. I lost energy. The vessel remained unfinished and anyway, it would never have floated.

When the day of the solstice arrived, I decided to observe it with vessels of a more immediate form, folding golden card into origami boats and writing lines from 'Crossing the Bar' onto their sides. Then I set off for Loch Tay into drizzle and low cloud as dusk began to settle early in the afternoon. Where the road peaks just a mile or so short of Kenmore, I rallied when a haze of diffused luminosity appeared ahead. Rather than radiating from the sky, the surface of the 150-metre-deep Loch, a vast unquenchable bowl, was up-lighting the shoreside foothills.

My friend Elizabeth met me in a car park at the north-eastern edge of the Loch and we assembled the paper boats, tealights, matches. Though not permissible this year, over recent times a group of us had always gathered at winter solstice and focussed on things we wished to part with, throwing a list into a roaring hearth indoors. Then we'd usually record wishes or intentions for the year ahead.

We launched six boats bearing candles as dark settled onto the water. They moved slowly away from us – a small yellow-flamed fleet against the black water. Despite the calm night, a surprising breeze or current carried them out as we sang along to 'Crossing the Bar' playing on a small speaker. Our ships crossed Loch Tay in a south-westerly direction towards a conjunction of Jupiter and Venus that had glittered through recent clear nights. That night, though, the sky was occluded.

During the preparations for this bright flotilla, I'd been struck by the lozenge-shaped indentation that opened up in each of the card boats, flat enough to hold a tealight level, a kind of 'deck'. Into one of these hollows, I'd added a small chip of quartz with its properties of triboluminescence to carry away a message of light across the water. I couldn't help conjuring the image of a person cradled within this hollow of boat. It echoed the miracle of my body once carried inside the body of my mother, in turn held so carefully within her own mother's. I saw us as a fleet of boats, each contained within the next, back across time, stacked within our mothers.

This small ritual, the handling of physical materials, lighting a flame and the sisterly support of Elizabeth at a time of year I always consider sacred, brought me exponential comfort. It was surprisingly uplifting. I had *done* something, marked life and death rather than letting its peaks and troughs pass unobserved. The conveyance of water felt not just appropriate but necessary in order to make it a passage, a crossing, blazing and optimistic. I felt almost celebratory as we stood and watched, chatting with food and drink, the flames slowly diminishing across the water.

One boat – my own that was carrying unwanted things from 2020 – flamed most brightly; the card had caught fire even as I launched it. Still, it didn't sink but burnt on the water, radiant as a Viking 'burial'.

I turned away from the Loch-side into the darkest part of the winter: a Christmas largely alone with enforced interiority. I was miles away from my remaining family members and from Robin. My mission with the family ships, with Braunton, with all those entwined cousins, ship-routes, dates, had no urgency. An opportunity was now lost – I had at least in part been throwing a line into the past for my mother.

For Mum.

There now seemed little point.

Ancestral Anchor Chains

A period of darkest days and a travel ban beat me down after Christmas 2020. My memories are dim, retrievable only through consulting my journal of the time. I can see that I had occasional company from friends as I roamed on short, numb days and sat looking west from various local hilltops with flask and muffin. I was a slightly new person now without a mother. I'd gained both a bleak awareness of my own mortality and a certainty I was no longer a child.

I also felt painfully cut off from the sea; a second mourning.

The River Tay, a five-minute walk from home, became my daily solace. Following the Moness Burn down to it, I watched at the confluence of the two, the way the waters resisted each other or intermingled in neat plaits, depending on the Tay's height and ferocity or on recent rain and run-off from the hills. Together, the two waterways left me, bucking in a white-ridged roar over rocks and disappearing around the corner towards the estuary and open sea at Dundee, 50 miles south-east.

I wrote onto a piece of timber six lines of a triolet poem which began: 'Dear River, do not pass me by, / but take me with you to the sea.' I cast it afloat here, imagining it being washed up later on a salt-soaked coast somewhere, where I would like to be.

I toyed with the 'Mother Ship' again. Without any real need now for the vessel to float or have a keel, I was liberated from function. I bound together some of my pale wands into a long low triangle of hull. It was rustic and irregular but I faced it with segments of an old map of the Taw-Torridge estuary to complement the words from 'Crossing the Bar'. Finally I fitted the bullrush mast and lacquered sail.

It reminded me of a type of simple, rickety-looking fishing boat I'd known in Zanzibar; the *ngalawa* – a traditional, double-outrigger canoe of the Swahili coast, propelled by one large triangular sail. I felt satisfied with this rough experiment and it still sails now on a table in my sitting room, a reminder of the 'letting go' of a soul to cross from one life toward the deep and wild seas of her voyage.

Initially in this exploration, my interest in ships and the Drakes had leapfrogged over my mother to earlier generations; the past of Granny's childhood and the boom in sailing coasters. But now these links between generations were fractured by my mother's death. My own childlessness felt stark; an omission. I'd failed to build a bridge through time and generations and now dangled, unattached to either past or future. I wondered how I'd been supposed to know that this building forward was important when no one ever spoke of it, or revealed the rewards of motherhood rather than its stresses and strains.

Perhaps I've been judged as a result. I came across an article on non-parenthood in which Maria Popova observes that despite millennia of human civilisation, we are 'still succumbing to the tyrannical cultural message that opting out of parenthood is a failure of ambition or magnanimity or social duty, or simply a symptom of a profound character flaw. Being childless by choice – like being alone, like living alone – is still considered by unspoken consensus the errant choice.'

As I read on, I realised a connection to the writing life. Popova quotes from female writers anthologised by Meghan Daum in *Selfish, Shallow and Self-Absorbed: Sixteen writers on the decision not to have kids*. It includes Sigrid Nunez who views parenting as a trade-off with creative and intellectual achievement. In her view many of those willingly childless were the children of unwilling parents. She references Alice Munro who wrote about the impossibility of being both a 'real mother' and doing the difficult job of writing, at least assuming that unconditional love should be offered to a child. I heard a deep, dull toll of recognition.

Remaining childless was never exactly a decision for me, but more the haphazard result of my preoccupation with freedom to move and a fear of being tied. To some extent it was also *because* I had a choice. Being of the first generation after my mother's with this liberty in some way made it feel a feminist duty to live differently. In my twenties I made a determined departure from the previous generation, growing into adulthood as an activist, a vegetarian and a pioneer for justice and ecological living. I believed I had greater things on my mind and wider aspirations than settling down and having children when, anyway, the world needed a reduced population.

Nor did I understand from my early life that one's own children could bring joy. I recall an incident in a neighbour's kitchen when I was pre-school age. The mother of a young brother and sister spoke of her caution driving the car when they were on board. One of the children said something like, 'You wouldn't be careful if you had robbers in the back, would you?' And the mother agreed, implying love and care for them. I stood listening, surprised by this open revelation. Were children not mostly an annoyance to their parents?

Sea Marked

My opportunity to be a mother had slipped between the cracks of relationships, the time never seeming right. And it didn't seem exactly necessary. I'd seen my mother struggling, never loving in a conventional motherly way, but clearly determined to do a decent job, enabling freedom and adventure in our lives whilst also carving out creative activity for herself. There was certainly no notion passed on of a duty to leave a human contribution to the future, to cultivate and nurture new life or pass something down the line. The rewards are evident to me now amongst friends and members of my family: my brother and his children, my stepsisters with theirs, and now their new grandchildren. The joy of new life, building a mini society, the plaiting of a rope with other families who share round faces, wide eyes.

And then there's the continuity of memory.

Our few family myths didn't feel real or true: humorous nods to Sir Francis Drake; the interest we took as a family in *Gypsy Moth IV* in 1967 when Sir Francis Chichester (who in name might have had some connection to us) single-handedly broke a number of records including fastest voyage around the world by a small vessel. But we'd also taken a lot of interest in the Apollo moon landings in 1969, just because it was ground-breaking. The real players in our family, including it seemed, my own father, were lost in the muddied waters of memory, casualties of a will to forget.

Perhaps there's an age at which we crave an understanding of where we have come from; want to clarify the passions and ventures of our forebears. In 2008 I'd pursued my father's footsteps high into the Alps to bring him closer than the black and white photos kept in a closed drawer had done. He had been the shadow under ice, rarely spoken of in my childhood.

Ancestral Anchor Chains

My lifestyle hadn't changed significantly between twenty and sixty years of age; marked by restlessness, travel, interesting work. At the age of forty, approaching the end of my fertile period as a woman, my first book of short stories was published instead. I walked away from a twenty-year-long relationship, went to South America and began to write a novel. As if writing were the foetus. Perhaps I made the subliminal decision to leave a legacy with words rather than through making more people.

Since then I've carved out a freelance life in writing and teaching, experiencing none of the pivots and rites of passage of my friends who have grown their own families. Not having children myself has made me feel ageless in a way, at least until now. Until this hinge of my mother's death.

My striking out unencumbered and alone felt for the first time less strength than weakness. Perhaps the whole point of family, something I have failed to learn and observe for myself, is security and longevity. Although there's no regret in my choices, traditional family patterns might have brought me an understanding of my part in a historical succession.

I recall the kindly questions of people I've met whilst working in East Africa: 'How are your children?' or 'Where are they?' I learned to invent a husband, for convenience and evasion, but I'm not a natural liar and my quick thinking didn't extend to another generation. Shock and expressions of sorrow followed when I said there were none. Perhaps, I see now, they were concerned about the rupture I was causing in the forward procession of my family. Or is it more self-interested than that? One of the characters in the novel *Stay With Me* by Nigerian writer Ayòbámi Adébàyò says, 'Sometimes I think we have children because we want to leave behind someone who can explain who we were to the world when we are gone.' Perhaps a writer feels less need of this.

Some friends have told me that their daughters have made difficult, conscious decisions not to bring children into our broken world. I wonder if this makes them 'good ancestors'? Australian philosopher Roman Krznaric describes the current behaviour of adult generations as pillaging the inheritance of future citizens. We're dumping our problems on them, pushing crisis away from our own lifetimes as if the future is a postcolonial country. Out of sight, out of mind. For him, being a good ancestor means assigning rights to future generations; a way of thinking in long-term ways often lost now to short political gains. We need to make a vault for seeds in the Arctic, build a future library, see to it that we don't 'foul the nest'. Perhaps losing access to collective memory through a family line, not having a strong sense of our pasts, encourages short-termism.

Knowledge can be passed down effectively through human generations but that may not include emotional intelligence. Thanks to my own family I value learning, walking; know to be kind to animals, to appreciate the arts. But I seem to have missed the lesson on cultivating loving parenthood. I didn't learn that I might foster a new generation and in doing so pass on particular values.

I find myself wanting more from the concept of a 'good ancestor'. What does it mean for me? Is it as prosaic as labelling the photos and documents I've unearthed – the ones I've been able to match with names – on a sketchy family tree? Perhaps I should encourage the younger generation of my family to come and view the strange archive that spread its mysteries across my work-room floor. Maybe they'll remember some of it later, might even pass it on. If any of it matters at all.

Or does this 'good ancestry' mean that as well as looking outwards, back in time, future-wards, we must also look inwards, addressing the tangle of psychological blocks, pressure points, fault lines passed down to us by our parenting? Perhaps my mother tried to do this, to unknot some of those tangles, but did so only very discreetly. I don't know how to break passed-down cycles three generations on from the seafaring life of this family that seems so inevitably shaped by loss. A family short on emotional expression and long on contained suffering.

My mother always made it clear when I was a teenager that my educational and life choices would be my own. She admitted to no preference. So it hadn't occurred to me that a parent might feel their own legacy truncated by the diversion of their offspring. Not, that is, until reading in Bella Bathurst's *The Lighthouse Stevensons* about the heartbreak of Robert Louis' father when his only child abandoned his place in the engineering dynasty. His mother apparently noted that, 'It was a cutting short of his own life, as he had looked forward to its being continued in his son's career.'

I've sometimes interpreted my mother's lack of steering as disinterest. Now I'm forced to think again. Towards the end of her life she'd spoken of feeling controlled by her own mother, dressed up like a 'doll', and perhaps pushed into the sciences at university as opposed to the arts; browbeaten when she opted for an early marriage. My brother and sister were clearly marked out for sciences, each brilliant and high achieving, whereas when my education demanded choices and I was torn between arts and natural sciences, as my mother had been, the school timetable was too inflexible to allow both. I chose the arts, and despite my mother's own strong science background, and that of my siblings and my father, my creative pursuits never amounted to a rebellion and were tacitly encouraged.

I now begin to understand her standoffishness as a way of allowing me freedom to make my own choices, bending far from her own mother's style. She enabled me to rise as an individual beyond the ancestral.

What began as a study of our seafaring past now sank my gaze in fathoms-deep shadows. With my mission suspended, I'd packed away The Box and reshelved it. Even if my discovery process in the south-west had still felt relevant, with lockdown, I certainly couldn't reach the Taw-Torridge estuary, Morte Point, the Braunton Pill. They might as well have been on a far continent.

I dreamt of my mother, sitting with a small smile and long, cat-like eyelashes. I dreamt of approaching the edge of a bridge high above a big river with someone beside me who at the last moment jumped over. Snow came and I took out my skis once or twice on forest tracks. There were short social occasions, flashes of fun, always outdoors. The light grew daily. The river ran. I noticed that if I wrote I felt more energised, happier. I spent oceans of time alone.

In February a focus presented itself for my wanderings in the wintry wilds. A commission. I was to make three short videos to prompt creative writing outdoors for children who were being educated at home or for teachers to use once schools resumed. Now I spoke to the camera on my phone rather than mumbling to myself as I roamed.

On lengthening days I witnessed the woodland cathedral; slant light raising an illuminated vault of bare trees;

the psychedelic shock of sunlight on moss. For the camera, I demonstrated how to compose a riddle by laying words written on slips of paper and shuffling them into new orders on a floor of dead leaves. I crouched next to a small burn, writing words onto pebbles and letting the flow of water rearrange them.

I also climbed to a ruined crofting village, demonstrating a way of exploring a place through the senses: the tumbled walls, the guardian rowan tree. It was a day of big skies and low sunshine crashing into the back of my eyes. Later I took to my bed with visual disturbances and a terrible, first ever migraine. My mother had sometimes suffered from these too and that affinity gave me some perverse comfort.

These tasks that took me outside (except for the hours and hours of computer-editing), returned me to my childhood 'fossicking' (as my mother had called it) in the dead leaf-litter and sludgy ditches of that Surrey garden. My serious play.

'Be yourself,' I heard her say.

This is what I recall now – the snow-shafted light outlining things, the tinkling and clatter of water, a robin shrilling from a high branch. Tightly corralled, I circled a tiny portion of land around my home.

Old sea-songs were sung again at this time, rousing minds and bodies with the beat of manual work and evoking the days of sail; collaborative songs bringing a cappella voices into harmony. One in particular brought fame and a recording contract to an Ayrshire postie; 'The Wellerman' sung by Nathan Evans reflected whaling days, but was technically not a shanty.

Shanties specifically helped synchronise manual labour for hauling on halyards or anchor chains efficiently, actions performed by all on one beat. It required a leader and the led, human co-operation and accumulated strength. Perhaps such songs appealed again at this difficult time (in addition to reminding us of our wild days of travel and the pirate in our souls) because of the need to combine our strength rather than stake out individuality.

It was whilst living on the island of Zanzibar in the late '80s that I had the most sustained contact with coasts and sea, even when it was just glimpses of a sail-filled turquoise bay as I cycled from one place to another. On a white sandy beach at the north point of the island I witnessed one of the larger local *dhows* being hauled up the sloping beach away from the tideline. This was for the regular caulking of the hull with fire and tar. A string of twenty or so young men were spaced along a line, their hauling coordinated by a single caller at its head who used a numerical language which was not the one in day-to-day use on the island. It seemed to be some throwback to the days of the Omani Sultanate; an African-enriched form of Arabic. Call and response. On a given syllable the men leant into a collective heave. The boat slid a step up the beach. Incrementally they arrived, making a beautifully articulated machine of sound and movement.

I saw this long before I had a means to easily record voices, or even take digital photographs. But I was entranced. An efficient collective act by barefoot men with *kikoi* cloths wound around their waists. The spectacle probably replicated the methods of their forefathers. A chain of human strength and co-operation, a rhythm, an incantation.

As someone who had often found it easier to be alone, who'd been stranded on a nuclear family island, I wonder whether I recalled this because of some yearning for a line of connection, an articulation of effort with others.

Five months after the death of my mother, I answered an unexpected phone call from a number in Sussex. It was Sue, a cousin who had been keeping a watchful eye on John Drake. He'd been contained in his West London flat with his cat, Billy, and with carers visiting.

Sue was phoning with bad news. John had died the previous day.

The circumstances were a bit vague, and no cause of death had yet been given. There was a bit of history to his decline – another hospital stay following a fall meant that remaining alone in the flat was no longer appropriate without full-time care. Whilst arrangements were being made, he had been moved temporarily to a care home where he died a week later, despite being only in his seventies.

Although my relationship with John was distant, sadness washed in because now my mother and John – first cousins, children of siblings Dorothy and Francis – were gone, we'd lost the anchor of that generation in our branch of the Drake family.

He had asked for a London service at his local church, then a cremation on Topsham Road in Exeter where we'd said goodbye to both his parents and to Granny, and for his ashes to be scattered on 'his' land at Braunton. I took pleasure in being able to help with the location through my coincidental meeting with the Hartnoll family, providing an address and phone number. It gave a sort of legitimacy to the exploration I had done and evoked again those flat, silver-scored marshes stretching low to the shore of an estuary raced by fierce tides.

I was moved by John's ancient tug of belonging to a place, a specific portion of land, through the hemp lines of ancestry and his evident sense of a connection. But I also recalled that, in the lifetime of my nieces and nephew, John's land and resting place will lie underwater if climate predictions are accurate.

John's church minister phoned me about the content of the funeral. I suggested 'Crossing the Bar' as a relevant reading for John, whose land was just upstream from the Bideford Bar. He also asked if I had a photograph for the service sheet. This returned me reluctantly to The Box.

In one of the photographs I found, he's with my mother when she's fifteen or sixteen, smiling in her maturing-in-to-adulthood phase. Tall, dark and with a strong brow and full lips, it must have been clear by then that she was going to be a beauty, qualities retained into her old age with her elegance and long silver hair always gathered off her face into a bun. John is still a child in the photo, some years younger than her, and has the same slightly scrunched-up smile as the one I saw in hospital, the eyes saying: 'I know you find me sweet'. His older brother Francis is in some of the earlier photos too, but didn't live many more years after they were taken.

I wasn't able to attend John's funeral in London, but my sister went on our behalf. I hoped that his name, the last Drake in our immediate family line, would not be lost.

Around this time in early 2021 several large cardboard boxes arrived, couriered from Penzance. I'd chosen to keep a small number of paintings that I associated with Cornwall or with my mother, including a few of her own representing different seasons and places I recognised around West Penwith or Scilly.

From her vast and luminous book collection I could have taken several yards of contemporary poetry or the New Naturalists series, but I chose eclectically. There was a tiny paperback guidebook to remind me of Weissensee in Austria, a lake where we had holidayed when I was seven, arriving after a memorable drive five-up in a mini. We'd found accommodation in a chalet at the end of the lakeside conurbation, enjoying from there the nightly rattle of crickets and a stream rumbling out of the Alps. We waded flowery meadows, ate unsalted butter on breakfast rolls and cooked on a camping stove on the balcony in the evening. We swam in the lake under a thunderstorm. My mother introduced us to such chance adventure.

There were also boxes containing items I'd personally gathered together after her death with no time to look at them properly. Files, loose papers, large hardback notebooks covered in her handwriting from a period in the 1970s and '80s when she had written poetry. She was placed in one competition and won another.

I didn't know the majority of these poems. Some showed her workings, reflecting careful word choices or nuances of meaning. Mostly the poems are observational, with only rare attempts to capture emotion. However, 'The Lake' reflects an incident on an earlier Austrian holiday with three young children when she first understood my father was seriously ill. It shows him in pain with only one good hand. After the children – us – 'slept, snug / in the plump, hay-scented feather beds', they go to the lake, and although he dismisses his problem, 'her mind awoke to fears / like an invasion of moths'. Another poem remains in fragments but has a title, 'The Absence Shelf' and her notes explore aural metaphors for a painful gap: 'the cans on the shelf full of silence', 'the air the bird has just quit'.

With neither father or mother now – orphaned – I thought back to his absence in my own young life and in the family stories we rehearsed. No photographs of him had hung on our walls. We had his canvas tent with wooden poles as a plaything in the garden; an antique bulbous compass. The lack of visible artefacts made him seem immaterial. It had sent me to search drawers in the bureau for evidence of him when my mother wasn't looking. I teased out, and quickly, guiltily, put back, albums of photographs. There were mountains, boats, picnics, and a smiling man who looked a little like me with a Siamese cat sitting on his shoulder. By keeping them in the dark, I suppose my mother felt able to press on into the future.

My mother's books began fraternising with my own, revealing the commonality of our interests in writing, painting, walking, the natural world. Why had I never properly acknowledged this? We'd both sought expression in visual art, the written word, treasured time alone and yet needed conviviality, or approval from others. Whether or not this shared territory had also led to the uneasiness between us, this recognition now steadied me. We had common ground; common sea. We had both carried unacknowledged grief from our childhoods into adult life.

I unpacked numerous sketchbooks going back to our family trip to France in 1966 and her first visits to Scilly before she moved to Cornwall. What struck me was not only the similarity of style with which she and I worked on paper but the choices for focus – the stacked granite blocks of the cliffs, dilapidated farmhouses, church towers, sea horizons interrupted by vertical landmarks. Amongst these I found her many attempts to capture in pen, pencil, paint, the curl of a wave; a gasp before the hollow roll explodes into surf on a beach. It resonated with my own visual fixations as an art student. Perhaps these efforts, this moment, embodied for both of us a profound unease.

Her poem 'Beliefs of Coastal People' halted me. In four stanzas of six lines each, she had associated aspects of the human life cycle and farming with states of the tide. The first is a birth at the time of 'the tide's brimming', the second concerns the sowing of clover, the third the drawing of cow's milk. But it was the fourth idea that had also long intrigued me.

In this one,

> *'... the old man on his cot*
> *watches over the ocean of his sheet*
> *the bent figures of his unforgot*
> *dead friends rowing to meet*
> *him. Slips out of his blue web*
> *of veins. Departs on the ebb.'*

I'd originally learnt of this phenomenon of coastal people dying on the falling tide in James Fraser's *The Golden Bough*, a book that has been on my shelves for many years since I 'borrowed' it from my mother in my early adulthood. Always fascinated by folklore and worldwide customs, I was struck that we both, independently, had taken note of the tidal influence manifested in the human pulse, in life and in death. And didn't this also evoke Tennyson's 'Crossing the Bar'?

Both she and her cousin John, being 'sea-marked', surely themselves had left us on the ebb.

All of us with ancestry in the British Isles are likely to have seafaring forebears and something of that sensibility in our DNA. To watch a horizon and feel some inexplicable longing or dread speaks of this collective past. As Robert Louis Stevenson said in *The English Admirals*, even a man from

Bedfordshire with no experience of ship or sail finds that as the ship begins to move, they swagger, 'with a sense of hereditary nautical experience.' In his view the sea has an undeniable connection to death in our culture, regarded 'as a kind of English (sic) cemetery, where the bones of our seafaring fathers take their rest until the last trumpet ... no other nation has lost as many ships, or sent as many brave fellows to the bottom.'

Whilst walking one of our annual stretches of the South West Coast Path back in 2018, Kate and I had paused for the night at Morwenstow in North Cornwall. We stayed at the Old Vicarage, a magnificent and echoing building with Victorian roll-top baths and a billiard room. It was former home to the famous Reverend RS Hawker (1803–1875) who believed in fairies and also documented the smuggling and wrecking that was rife along this stretch of coast. Kate and I squeezed into his clifftop eyrie a little further west the next morning. Created in a rugged niche between rocks and lined with shipwrecked timbers, it was from here he observed the sea crashing onto rocks below, and further out, its traffic. It was also where he smoked opium and wrote.

He became best known for the rescue of shipwrecked sailors, and rewarded those in the community who went to their aid or recovered bodies rather than ransacking wrecks for treasure. Most famously, the *Caledonia*, a 200-ton brig from Arbroath, was wrecked here in 1843 after carrying a cargo of coffee from Rio de Janeiro to Syria, Smyrna and Constantinople, and then loading wheat at Odessa to deliver to Gloucester. This was what brought her up the Bristol Channel, pursued by an increasing north-westerly gale. In the depths of the night she hit 'Vicarage Cliffs' and all but one soul was lost.

Hawker saw to it that bodies were carried up steep crags and buried in the graveyard where later he erected the *Caledonia* figurehead, a Celtic warrior-woman leaning into spray and defended from storm by her shield and sword. He took in and nursed the one survivor who told him the causes of the disaster: they had allowed a cook to come on board with a black bag, a bucket was lost overboard, and they had departed from Rio on a Friday.

Tradition tells seafarers not to wear clothes dyed with a lichen. After all, 'what comes from the rocks returns to the rocks'. Land animals are similarly dubious. If you see a rabbit on the way to the ship, return home. Despite this, a photo in the Braunton Coasters book shows three crew members on the St Austell with, between them, four small terriers in arms. The men's faces and clothes look blackened by coal. Perhaps Braunton men, or men regularly ashore on coastal journeys, were more comfortable with this dichotomy.

According to my mother 'Uncle Frank' had always sailed on Merchant ships with a cat on board – believed to bring good fortune, or to foretell weather (or perhaps just kill rats). He told her of an occasion when one cat or other fell overboard from a vast ocean-going vessel. Frank and the captain locked eyes and with a slight nod, a purse of the lips, agreed to turn the great ship around and execute a rescue. Did they simply love the cat or was superstition at work?

Braunton folk must long have been affected by what the next tide might bring in. The passage of ships on significant journeys just beyond the Bar broadened imaginations, brought in news, goods, and sometimes fatalities. One story is told about a cart arriving in Braunton carrying the bodies of seventeen drowned Dutch seamen. The following week the bodies of twelve unknown sailors were found on Saunton Sands. All had to be buried within the parish.

The loss in 1799 of one particular ship on rocks in Morte Bay still haunts the coast's graveyards and reverberates down the generations within the Bar. *HMS Weazle* was a naval ship preventing smuggling and protecting North Devon coastal traders from privateers. Appledore became *Weazle's* 'home port' for a number of years. Whilst it provided a sheltered harbour, the captain could only get out over the Bar when high water, a leading wind and daylight coincided, which was infrequent in winter. The crew were well known in the village, or recruited *from* there and their 'gaiety' had apparently been noted. Some crew members had time to marry local women. Even unconnected Appledore residents would have enjoyed the sight of the mighty sloop going out and returning over the Bar. Deep bonds of affection between ship and village can be assumed.

On a passage from Falmouth back to Appledore, a hurricane-force north-westerly storm battered the ship and she hit rocks after changing her intended course and firing distress signals. The total loss – estimated to be between 90 and 106 men – had a profound impact locally. A number of Appledore children grew up never having known their fathers. Some property and seventeen or so bodies were washed up over the next month; one man identified by initials on his stockings.

On the day following the wrecking, an unidentified woman was found amongst the washed-up bodies; a very uncommon 'passenger' on such a ship. The implication of bad luck may have sent mutterings twisting through the steep, cobbled streets. I don't know whether it was any more unlucky or dangerous than having a clergyman on board, or mentioning knives, eggs, cats, pigs or hares (though it's possible her drowning simply coincided with the wreck).

Amongst the details collected by Bob and Ann Brock about the *Weazle*, I read that the crew list, as far as it could be known, included a number of men who came from the east coast of Scotland and Shetland; once again illustrating the fraternity of our coastal geographies. And I learnt that a 'widow's man' was always to be found at the head of the muster lists on such ships. This was a fictitious character justifying pay that would later support a woman made widow by the voyage.

In the case of the *Weazle* the amount would have been very far from sufficient.

After looking out that photo for John's funeral, The Box once again spewed teetering piles across my work-room floor as if trying to entice me back to a wrecked project. I couldn't altogether ignore it and then the historic dialogue between coast and sea surfaced into public view. I paid attention when it was reported that the well-preserved wrecks of two nineteenth-century cargo ships had been added to the National Heritage list for England.

Both vessels were found in the shallow waters of the south-east, and were so far unidentified. One on Goodwin Sands off Sandwich, Kent had been carrying a large consignment of coal when it sank, possibly after a collision. The other, discovered during a routine survey of the Thames estuary, was on the West Barrow sandbank and heavily laden with Cornish roof slates at a time when North Wales slate was the norm. This detail may suggest the specification for a particular building, perhaps in time making it possible to identify the ship.

Despite the slightness of my connection, I was cheered to know that these workaday vessels were now to be honoured and protected. It had taken the best part of a century for such vital ships – part of one of the largest industries in the UK – to be recognised as of heritage significance. Coastal trading vessels had simply been considered too mundane, and perhaps the wrecks too numerous.

Taking out the Coasters book again, a brief survey of the Drakes' wrecked ships shows my namesake, poor old *Linda*, foundering off Hartland in January 1900 following a collision with another local ship, *Sarah and Jane*, which only lost the bowsprit. Their *Marjorie* was believed to have been sunk by a U-boat in 1917, and *Mouse* lost on a trip from Swansea in 1915 with a cargo of basic slag after the captain refused the shelter of Ilfracombe due to its high harbour charges. Overwhelmed off the infamous Morte Stone, Captain Henry Drake and one crew member drowned. The third member had missed his train for Swansea from Barnstaple and so survived. The 'crew' had therefore been only two and perhaps this was not untypical.

Families such as mine going about their work between coasts, people minutely attuned to tidal rhythms, with multiple skills and an inherited allegiance to both land and sea, wet and dry, seem overlooked in social histories. They were often going relatively short distances, carrying cargo from North Devon to Wales or traversing the coasts of Somerset or Cornwall. They worked at all times of year. Ships were frequently caught out even in waters close to home by the interactions of swell, wind, current and tide, at least until engines were fitted, which gave them a greater chance of escaping problems. Their job was to interact frequently with the shore, even if briefly. It was their enemy, although a necessary one.

Writing elsewhere, I've pictured all 11,000 convoluted miles of coastal Britain outlined by a prickly band of barnacles which open and close with the tides. Now I added to this mental picture. Just a little inland from the barnacled frontline I imagined a similarly dense line of women, standing, facing the horizon, looking out towards departing or returning ships which carried their family livelihoods, their loved ones' souls. Facing the primal on a daily basis, they were stoical and, like the barnacles, tidally attuned; a psychological feature of the coastal landscape. These women were perhaps as irritable as the sea when arguing with the shore and, like my mother, often freighted with grief.

I looked up from the book and through the window. The trees and hills of Highland Perthshire lurched me inland. I'd scented salt, been rolled by the swell, feared sudden shallows. And just like that from my land-locked home, I found myself summoned back, called to connect with people and their coastal nature to whom my mother had subliminally belonged; to seek the seams of history where sea and land meet.

It was time to cross some version of the 'Bar' that had recently kept me too contained.

The Sea Road North

I took the opportunity to sail with *Bessie Ellen* again in the summer of 2021. Ten days at sea between Ullapool in Scotland's north-west and the Orkney Islands to the north-east should dislodge a long period of stasis. Such a journey could no longer relate directly to my mother, but my search for family connection to the sea was driven by an instinct that said 'yes' to adventure. I knew she would approve.

'Don't worry about me,' she'd have said from the safe harbour of her sofa. 'Go and have a lovely time, dear.'

Ullapool was 90 nautical miles further north from Oban where I'd begun the previous, southbound, voyage on *Bessie Ellen*. But still, I'd have linked the majority of the western seaboard in these two journeys.

Griefs were left on shore as we got underway, attention turning instead toward expansive views, the daily routines of the ship, shrieks of 'dolphin' or 'whale' or 'hoist the mainsail'. The need to act as part of a team was welcome after so much solitary time. Rafts of comically upright puffins became a familiar sight, as did the guillemot pairings of 'watchdog-dad' with infant. When they became separated, the youngster could be located by its hysterical cheeping.

The smirry coastlines were also soon rousing memories as we threaded through the Summer Isles. Amongst my mother's scribbles on the back of shopping lists, sketchbook covers and envelopes, I'd found one dated Summer 2002. From my home in Aberfeldy we'd picked up my friend Claire and driven to Achiltibuie, stopping (so the notes tell me) for fish and chips in Ullapool. 'Blowy night. Rattling windows,' she wrote of our rented cottage. On the Saturday we visited the cliffs on the western headland at Reiff: 'Stunning views, blue sky, warm — walked over plateaued cliffs ... sea indigo blue. Orange sunset under clouds.' With her delight in colour, she had also painted there.

Aboard *Bessie Ellen* we turned north at Reiff, tracking a landscape of fantastical verticality that erupts from Coigach and Assynt's low-lying plateau. From the sea I reconsidered familiar landmarks: the spire of Suilven when seen end-on, Lochinver, the beach at Clachtoll, the Old Man of Stoer and the famous lighthouse nearby, then on past the vast scoop of Sandwood Bay. The land here held many memories of former walks and climbs but there was opportunity to make new ones.

Nikki had reduced client numbers from the usual twelve to just eight, and the health of all on board was confirmed with regular Covid tests. Spending time in our small, new community gave me a taste of a 'free' life after so long without travel or novelty. The ship held us within her crucible. To meet new people and take a journey together mostly insulated from wider society felt simultaneously 'safe' and brave. Our only visitors were great skuas (or 'bonxies' to give them their northern name), seabirds who arrived singly to circle the ship. They settled on and lifted from the rigging, repeating the circuit as nonchalantly as is possible for a hook-beaked dinosaur, then circled again as if delivering a message of some sort in deep, throaty cries.

With little necessary action in light winds, we slipped in and out of conversation, finding different perches around the deck on the closed lids of lockers or the saloon roof. It allowed room for thoughts to stray over the patterns kaleidoscoping across the sea's surface.

I thought about my great-great-grandfather Francis Drake sailing his new acquisition, the ketch *Pirate*, in the opposite direction, home to Devon, perhaps with some other family members in his crew. With no firm information about this past journey, the current timber-creak and copious time of our northerly passage tickled my imagination.

After leaving Orkney for the south-west, might Francis and crew have found shelter and supplies in these far-flung mainland ports of Kinlochbervie, Lochinver, even Ullapool? Perhaps Francis stood on the quay side-by-side with other seafarers or with shellfish pickers on the shore, 'yarning' of this and that. When the locals learned his name he might tell the story of his grandfather, another Francis, remembered for fighting a duel at sea.

He comments on the bonxie, seen on home waters too when on its migratory passage: 'Proper pirates,' stealing fish from birds even twice their size. Or they chuckle together at the sight of a raft of puffins and compare local names for them.

'Sea Parrot's what we say,' the locals tell him, 'or Tammy Norrie.'

And Francis gestures to their west at the sea road almost visible to him, carrying trade to Newfoundland. 'Over there too,' he says. 'They calls them Sea Parrot or Clown Bird or Hatchet Face.'

And he adds how down home in the Bristol Channel, it's said Lundy Island is named for its many puffins – still arriving each April – from 'Lunde' in Old Norse.

'Shows how much we got about in the old days, don't it?' he says, and shakes his head as he recalls, only twenty years before, his *Nellie* gone missing on a passage between St John, Newfoundland and Oporto, loaded with salt cod.

And with a relative of his on board.

They stand quietly then, distracted by watching the youngster in Francis' crew, clumsy with the rope he'd been told to coil, until Francis can stand it no longer and strides back to the ship.

'Boy! You'm like a cow handling a musket!'

Maybe they remember him in one northern port or other, even absorbing his stories into their own local lore.

Nikki introduced activity to bring us together, dangling the bosun's chair from a boom extension over the port side, and 'ordering' some of the male members of her crew over the rail to ride with their backsides just above the deep water. Some were briefly 'dunked', but in fair play she took her turn. Still, I imagined the wry nod of Emma Louise Drake across the years, to see this revolution in gender roles; old skippers' pranks for new boys now 'played' on grown men. I imagine she would laugh, not unkindly, along with us.

I took my turn too. Sitting close to the water on a single plank felt surprisingly safe in this calm version of the Atlantic and I could have remained daydreaming there, travelling companionably with a kindly sea, watching the bow slice up a clean wave just ahead. Above, the lovely triple curve of the jib sails arced in a visual rhyme.

The Pentland Firth corridor, where the Atlantic and North Sea meet, is infamous. At its eastern end between Caithness and Orkney one of the most powerful currents in the world runs at up to 16 knots. Tidal swell can form waves several metres in height. There are named features such as The Merry Men of May and The Swilkie, the latter a Nordic name suggesting 'the swallower'. It forms a whirlpool and tidal-wave allegedly created by a sea witch grinding the sea's salt with a giant quern-stone down below. In the days of sail, this strait would have been avoided where possible.

I had worried that winds, tide or weather rather than witches would force us away from the decisive turning point at Cape Wrath, and so *away* from Orkney. Instead, the air's stillness silked the sea into gently shifting rolls as we turned the point easily. The lighthouse overlooked us on its grassy platform, and a view of angular north-coast cliffs now opened up; steep, dark slopes leading up into low cloud. Nothing happened quickly but I sensed forces vast and deep in the drive of tide beneath us.

We were divided into watches of four for our overnight crossing of the Firth to Orkney. I was allocated the watch between 8pm and midnight as I had been on the previous trip, and enjoyed the camaraderie of a small group as light leached away to leave an aperture of apricot sky deepening between dark rolls of western cloud. Distant dolphins arced and sliced the sea to port, a display which had no need for an audience. The green hue of the sea turned inky as we steered towards Stromness, rolled by tide and swell.

A small thrill came as night properly descended and the flashed signature of Dunnet Head lighthouse on the mainland dimmed with distance, replaced by emergent lights from the islands. Crew member Becky and myself took turns at the helm, sitting close above the glow from the binnacle – the compass housing – our guide and tyrant. The radio murmured on from the open door of the chart room – Russian-accented English; the famous 'Stornoway-coastguard-lilt'. We'd been given a course but holding it demanded a certain muscularity; the body working against the wheel in pulses of pull and release. Sometimes our course registered on the GPS screen as a zig-zagging line of repeated deviation and over-correction.

As I left the helm for my bunk at midnight, the lights of the island of Hoy were becoming visible. However, we learned the next day that Nikki was still chugging towards our Stromness anchorage at 5am, making very few knots against the force of tide pouring from the deep-water enclosure of Scapa Flow between Hoy and South Ronaldsay.

The power of Orkney tides is legendary, funnelling torrents between islands, slamming against each other and driving complex forces in the water – currents, overfalls, eddies. Visible sea-features caused by a strong current in a restricted passage are known as 'roosts'. It clearly pays to know what you are doing in these waters.

When I woke, we were at anchor just east of the island of Inner Holm, in Cairston Roads. This naming of sea routes makes me think of well-travelled drovers' ways; rutted and visible in the minds of those who regularly ply them. A satellite image would score another 'road' sweeping the Atlantic between here and the south-west of England: to Lands' End and the Scilly Islands. To the north of Scilly, tides fill and empty the watery finger carrying vessels into and out of the Port of Bristol and its surrounding coasts. It was satisfying to think of the places of my quest connected by tide and water and by the ingenuity of people who have colluded with them for travel and trade.

The town of Stromness is named for a tidal race (*strom*) and the headland (*ness*) that pushes south into Hoy Sound. Low-lying land encircles Hamnavoe (Haven Bay) to the north and east of the town, creating a sheltered anchorage. We were anchored out beyond this, perhaps exactly at the spot where Orkney's infamous pirate, John Gow, also dropped his anchor without need of a pilot in 1725.

As a baby, in 1699, he had crossed the Pentland Firth with his father William Gow, a merchant from Wick who was making a home here. At that time Stromness was already a strategic port. John Gow grew up close to the water on the eastern shore of Hamnavoe, watching countless ships entering and leaving the Sound. Dreams of the origins and destinations of such vessels, that 'otherness', must have claimed him, and he ran away as a young lad to sea. When he returned in 1725 it was as master of a substantial merchant ship. He had a reputation already behind him and was in disguise.

Such an elaborate story is woven around John Gow's bloody escapades and impersonations that writers including Walter Scott, Tennyson, and George Mackay Brown have each 'retold' the story. Gilbert and Sullivan adapted elements of it and relocated it for *Pirates of Penzance*. It was Daniel Defoe, acting as a journalist, who wrote up the eventual trial and Ivan Dreever has a song, 'The Ballad of Pirate Gow'. But extracting fact from fiction is tricky.

In 1724 Gow had joined a restive crew as second mate of the *Caroline* in Amsterdam. When they got to Santa Cruz a bloody mutiny took place in which he seems to have played a key role. He was then elected as Captain and renamed the vessel *Revenge*. I wonder whether he had an earlier pirate in mind when he echoed the name of the flagship in which Francis Drake sailed to Cadiz in 1588 to undermine the Armada?

Attacking British ships as he went, Gow pirated around the coast of France, Spain and Portugal, turning for home when supplies ran low. The ship sailed into Hamnavoe with an apparently 'respectable' trader in charge, a Mr Smith, who told a story of being blown off course. In another rapid name change, the ship was now known as the *George*. The ploy soon wore thin when locals recognised crew, Master or ship, and prompted his quick getaway with a depleted and enforced crew, taking in a raid on the Hall of Clestrain at Orphir on the shore facing Stromness. A servant was forced to pipe the raiders, carrying the plunder, back to their ship.

Needing a quick getaway to the Baltic, they sailed on through Orkney's North Isles. His intention had been to attack, on the way, the lonely Carrick House at the southern end of the Sound of Eday. But word went ahead and he was betrayed by a pilot, caught out by the ferocious currents. They ran aground at the island, the Calf of Eday, and were then captured by his old schoolfriend James Fea of Carrick, taken to prison in Edinburgh and then for trial in London.

Gow's ship, known by the time of this escape-run as the 'George Galley', was abandoned on the shore, but the ballast of cannonball limestone was later retrieved. On a visit to Kirkwall I went to see it, roofing the spire of a summer-house in Tankerness Gardens known as the 'Groatie House' because it's covered in 'Groatie Buckies' (otherwise known as European cowrie-shells).

Gow was found guilty, with seven others, of murder and piracy and all were executed in June 1725 at the pirates' gallows in Wapping. The first attempt to hang Gow failed when the rope broke, forcing him to climb the ladder a second time. As a deterrent to others, the men's bodies were tarred and hung by chains on the bank of the Thames, remaining there for the pulse of three tides.

It seems to have been a relatively short piracy career, but a legendary one, still 'celebrated' in the John Gow Rum marketed with a Gothic image of a three-masted, ragged-sailed brig rising up the side of a huge black wave, and a strapline: 'Inspired by pirates, distilled beside the sea.' It's shipped world-wide from tiny Lamb Holm, famous for the Italian Chapel created by prisoners of war within a Nissen hut.

According to some versions of the story, on Mr Smith's return to Orkney he had courted a Helen Gordon of Stromness and a pagan handfasting took place; a pledge made as they joined hands through a hole in the Odin Stone, formerly at Loch of Harray near Stenness. To extricate herself from this bond after his death, she journeyed to London to touch the hand of his corpse. Without this, the pagan vow would extend even beyond the grave.

Our landfall by dinghy at Stromness separated us into small groups, passing and re-passing each other with ice creams to exchange excited accounts of our discoveries including local whisky in the Co-op; the charm of a harbour full of working and recreational vessels. The winding, narrow streets led me between handsome grey stone frontages, narrow vennels which sliced into cross-section the water of Hamnavoe, the Holm islands, sky. And sometimes in these slots I glimpsed the silhouette of *Bessie Ellen* at anchor, proud and prominent and waiting for us.

'Are you from the pirate ship?' I was asked by a shopkeeper.

Maritime history was recalled in landmarks, buildings and in plaques on walls. There was a carefully sealed-up well where the Hudson Bay Company's ships took in water from 1670 to 1891, as Captain Cook's vessels *Resolution* and *Discovery* did in 1780. This explained how, because Stromness was their first landfall after Cook's death in Hawaii, his own tea service and South Sea spears came to be kept in Orkney; they were sold by the 180-strong crew to pay for diversions ashore. Sir John Franklin's Arctic exploration ships *Erebus* and *Terror* also took on water here in 1845. This is not to mention the many merchant and whaling ships it served.

Geology and geography have long made Stromness a refuge for vessels limping in from all directions in a state of storm-torn disrepair to find shelter and expert help from shipbuilders and sailmakers. Nikki, in Stromness and Orkney for the first time, was excited by its strategic former location: for twentieth-century warships, when Scapa Flow hosted the naval fleet; transits for the Baltic trade; the nineteenth-century herring boom; whaling; and exploration of the 'north'. When Britain was at war with France, Orkney was on a highway that provided a means of avoiding the English Channel and offered a significant halt.

Orkney rose from the Atlantic as a significant staging post on many routes and at many times, meaning that islanders have always lived on a superhighway of world news. Stromness harbour must have facilitated maritime friendships between far-flung islands. Such connectivity, and its former status as a global cultural hub revealed by the neolithic archaeology, belies its sometimes-description as 'remote'.

The separate disciplines of map making and chart drawing have furthered such a divide in our perceptions. The former art, far more current in most of our imaginations than the latter, makes the case that it is now land, rather than water, that links communities to one another. Whilst today we concentrate our notion of culture and civilisation around cities, centres of population, it was the circuitry of the sea and its linked 'roads' and passages that once made coastal places so important. It struck me forcibly whilst here how few generations it's taken – two or three? – to turn our gaze inland so that most of us cease to recognise the power, history and associated endeavour invested in shorelines and shipping routes over centuries and millennia.

The poetry of the spoken Shipping Forecast whispers on, but can seem an obscure recollection of something once profound. I wonder how many of us, from our beds on *terra firma*, could identify at 00.48am or 5.20am when we stumble sleepily upon it on BBC Radio, where Sole or Dogger or Finisterre are on the maps of the British Isles? Mentions of North or South Utsira now carry our imaginations into the mythical. We hear: 'The General Synopsis at … There are warnings of gales in all areas except…,' and the bed covers cosy about us.

The naming of ships seems to have been quite distinct from the need for logic and precision in their building. Names pay tribute to family members or reflect superstition, custom and belief. Coastal families in Braunton often freighted their ketches and schooners with emotional resonance. *Emma Louise* for my great-great-grandmother; *Bessie Ellen* for John Chichester's two daughters. Allegiances to goddesses or female mythic figures were perhaps by then a thing of the past, although the idea of female nurture from the vessel seems to have remained.

Pirate was an uncommon name for a ship. I still puzzled over the Drakes' ketch, the one I'd invoked in the crafting of a paper boat to hang from the ceiling of Thurso Town Hall. How had the ship come to be registered in Barnstaple and work from Braunton's quay despite origins so far away on the Orkney mainland?

She was built in 1888, sixteen years before the building of *Bessie Ellen* in Plymouth, but the ketches were similar to each other in hull and rig as well as to other small ships the Drakes owned, mostly built locally to Braunton. In the command of two highly respected local master mariners related through marriage, my great-great-grandfather, Francis Drake, brought *Pirate* to join the Braunton fleet from 1900 and John Chichester brought *Bessie Ellen* there in 1907. They would have been sister ships.

To Granny and her mother Annie, Orkney must have sounded a foreign place, as remote as the Arctic. In the early twentieth century such women's households acted as 'North Stars', orbited by galaxies of ships, cargoes and men, and offering stability and a safe port when ships converged back in across the Bar. Annie herself became a majority owner of *Pirate* despite the ship's role in her brother-in-law's tragic loss, and the ship was honoured with a sketch in Granny's friendship album. She remained valued, it seemed, the name apparently not considered a dark omen.

The anomaly of *Pirate*'s geography with the family cargo-sailing business wakened me to the connectivity of the British coastal context and the sea as a medium of culture. A ship's master from the Scilly Isles could be eye-to-eye with one in Orkney or Shetland, sharing attitudes towards the continuity of sea and land, business realities, even life itself. Gossip rippled along Atlantic and east-coast shores, ship to ship, port to port, one sea captain to the next. Was that how my forebears heard about this fine ship *Pirate*, built with famed Orcadian strength?

On a visit to the archives in Kirkwall, I'd turned the pages of a leather-bound shipping register, equivalent to

Barnstaple's, and traced *Pirate*'s story. The builder, Peter Johnston Copland, had retained sixteen shares until 1898, after which she was owned jointly by a factor from the Orkney Isle of Sanday and the Master, David Smith, for the two years until the Drake purchase. I like to think of this ketch in the years before she sailed to the far south-west, trading between Orkney coasts, the mainland, the North Sea, the Baltic and even as far as Russia.

In an archived letter I found the signature of Francis Drake senior. With a lovely curl on the F and D, he accepted the transfer of ownership of all sixty-four of *Pirate*'s shares on October 17th 1900, less than a month after Granny's birth. It was extraordinary to think of his breath and mine close to this page, our fingertips brushing against each other, only separated by 120 or so years.

Turning the vast old pages, feeling the scratch of ink pen and chasing the scent of discovery, I was in my element. The archivist assisting my search that day was the one who had enthused on the library blog about a ship called *Pirate* being purchased by a Francis Drake. When I told her that I wasn't sure why he had purchased a ship from so far away, she shrugged: 'Maybe with a name like Francis Drake, he just wanted to own a ship called *Pirate*.'

I discussed with Nikki the possible logistics of a Braunton Master buying a ketch from an Orkney Master. Her thought was that it would have been opportunistic. Perhaps *Pirate* caught Francis' eye whilst in a port somewhere on some other business and an offer was made and accepted on the spot. Perhaps it was the result of bar-room chat. 'Your name's never Francis Drake? Best come and meet your namesake ship, then!' It probably approximates an explanation, in addition to the fact that shipbuilding in

Stromness and Orkney was legendary for its quality and robustness. In the nineteenth century customers from far beyond Orkney came here to purchase brigs, schooners, smacks and ketches.

I'd pictured my great-great-grandfather and his small crew chatting and drinking in the seafarers' bars of Stromness where people from diverse parts of the world must often have met like migratory birds. Their broad Devon accents echoed against soft Orcadian speech rhythms. I was disappointed to discover, then, that Francis *hadn't* travelled all the way to Stromness. The archives revealed a transfer of the ship at the Port of Grangemouth in the Firth of Forth. This transaction confirmed the eastern seaboard as *Pirate*'s route to her new home in the south-west of England, rather than the western route I'd imagined.

From Grangemouth they sailed the remainder of east-coast Britain and the English Channel, before rounding Lands' End for a new home within the Bristol Channel. I added to this the geometry of *Bessie Ellen*'s current route. Two months before our landfall here, she had rounded Lands' End from Fowey, making a six-week journey north up the west coast to Ullapool via tours of the Inner and Outer Hebrides. Then, with me on board, to Orkney. These journeys of two ships that I'm following through the years had scored in the sea a century-plus loop from the Orkney Islands around the majority of Great Britain. I was accomplice to a retracing of sea-routed history.

I was intrigued that Holly Berry, whose father Samuel had co-owned other ships with the Drakes, had maintained her investment right to the end of *Pirate*'s working life. In the 1911 Census she appears aged thirty-one as a 'spinster' in her father's house in Barnstaple, the only offspring, with a cook and servant resident. A newspaper report tells that she later married Sussex-based Lieutenant Hickson (engineer) in 1915 and a daughter, Mary, was born in North London. Despite marriage, Holly Berry not only retained her shares in *Pirate* but, unusually, used her maiden name for this. She never did follow the norm, which would have been to make these shares her husband's property.

This tenacious attachment made me curious, intrigued by the gaps in what was known. She'd acquired shares in *Pirate* aged twenty, and such financial independence may have removed any need to marry when she was young. She initially co-owned the ship with Francis Drake (junior). Could there have been a heartbreak at his loss at sea which both kept her single so long and fostered a sentimental attachment to their ship?

On a shore back home, another vessel had recently been given a name.

Just before leaving for the sailing trip, I'd been heartened by the delivery of some smart red and white cushions from a manufacturer in Cornwall – another pleasing connection to my mother's adopted homeland. They were sent with a cheery message from the maker, and 'Loch Tay' embroidered on their ends. These rowers' seats represented one of the final embellishments to the project mostly stalled by Covid since autumn 2020. According to the rules of the Scottish Coastal Rowing Association (SCRA), the livery of each boat must be distinct; we had painted our hull red with a white top strake and black second strake. She was the 198th skiff registered. A little more varnish, the completion of oars and seat fittings, and we would float her.

The Sea Road North

That summer we'd finally began to gather regularly again in the gloomy boatshed on Loch Tay's south-east shore where we'd moved her for final work. (Margaret was no doubt pleased to have her garage back only a couple of years later than intended). A summons would come from Adam on WhatsApp: 'Session at the boat shed Thursday 6pm sanding, varnishing and fettling.' Or, 'Sand and paint session for the oars at the workshop this evening from 7pm.' By now Angus had crafted the oars from Douglas fir.

One evening there were two people 'keying in' the surface of the gunwales and applying the last coat of varnish; two of us held lights for them. Angus had brought the seats and rudder he'd newly varnished. Six of us was too many for the tasks, but it seemed that even those without a job were simply happy to be there, to appreciate what seemed almost miraculous. In a slow process of accretion and the individual contributions of many people, we had built a boat.

Angus was in the darkest part of the shed crouching in a pool of torchlight to fit the rudder. Opposite him on the far side of the stern, Adam, Allan and Charlotte also huddled, kneeling, with another light shared between them. They leant in, assessing the gap between rudder and stern, heads angled in parallel concentration. They were so intent that they didn't notice me taking a photograph. With the red paint of the hull flaring under torchlight, the composition of four figures gathered in a pool of luminosity suggested the *Adoration of the Magi* – Velazquez, Boticelli, countless other artists – figures humbled by the presence of something that inspired deep feeling.

A baby; a newborn boat.

The skiff's name had now been painted on each white strake at the bow; on one it appeared in Gaelic, *Nighean*

Ruadh, and on the other in English: Red Haired Lass. Charlotte had suggested this name early on, drawing on the Loch Tay Boat Song in which unrequited love for his 'beauteous *Nighean Ruadh*' has the rower's heart 'full of woe'. Originally translated from a Gaelic song, the cadence encourages a rowing crew to keep time.

> *'For my heart's a boat in tow,*
> *and I'd give the world to know*
> *if she means to let me go,*
> *as I sing horee, horo.'*

There seems a rich seam of association in our cultures between vessels on water, affairs of the heart and heart-break. On that hot July night in the shed I also noted how Angus had cut the small tapering 'breastplate' that bridges the gunwales at the bow. He had not just made a functional triangle, but with two curves at its fullest point, a heart.

Later on that Stromness afternoon, the crew moved *Bessie Ellen* from the anchorage in Cairston Roads to tie her up against one of the piers in the harbour where the bustle of the town would surround us. Passers-by had only our chatter to listen to when they paused to gaze, but I'd read in a *Cornish Guardian* of 1926 that *Bessie Ellen*, lying in Padstow harbour awaiting a cargo, and having been recently fitted with a wire-less, had a loudspeaker on deck. Captain Chichester, being a public benefactor, charmed a 'considerable audience' with music and song as well as an evening service and sermon from St Martin's in the Fields, far away in London.

The faces of people pausing close to us in Stromness revealed a kind of longing for our vessel that seemed beyond rational explanation. I've been stilled myself by such a sight and wondered what it stirs. Perhaps it recalls us to inherited memory, stowed somewhere within us, when ordinary people either sailed such ships or watched them loading and unloading as a matter of course. It's as if a working sailing ship connects us in our deeps with a not-so-long-ago, half-known past. And in this location, it might also suggest the 'romance' of a voyage north.

The everyday needs of island and coastal dwellers used to depend on these ships and the men who travelled the sea roads; itinerants whose days were determined by the rhythms of landfall and departure, the rumble of anchor-chain paying out onto the seabed, the mercy of tides. Basil Greenhill calls such merchant vessels, whose builders and owners were often poor, 'the most beautiful tools of the human race.' Utilitarian art.

Our pier was on the west shore of Hamnavoe. Across the water on its east shore was the place where in 1878 George and Peter Copland established their boatbuilding yard. It had been equipped with Orkney's first steam-powered winch. This was where they built *Pirate* in 1888.

I crossed from one side of Hamnavoe to the other in the dinghy with Tom, a young Cornish crew member who had just left university. We landed at the remains of a walled enclosure and walked through a pillared entrance at the shore. This approach made the position of a prior slipway obvious. Perhaps wooden shutters had once stretched between the pillars to enclose the yard from the sea. The remains of a furnace on the inland boundary matched the position of a chimney in the photograph I'd seen in Bryce Wilson's book, presumably to power the winch. Noting these details, and in the supernatural evening light close to Midsummer, I felt the past brush my ankles along with grasses which disguised the lumpy surface of buried industry.

We stood in the place where the father of Pirate John Gow built his house and had dreamt of making a harbour for his own vessels; land that became known as 'Gow's Garden'. The Copland brothers demolished the house and used the stone to build the once-high enclosure walls of their yard. I pictured them raising their heads from sawing or hammering nails into a new hull, sawdust paling their eyebrows. They looked around, seeking a name for their first vessel and acknowledging the legacy of this place which had also launched a renowned pirate. Perhaps they discussed the bad luck such a name might bring before they agreed upon it anyway.

It seemed a good-enough explanation.

Tom and I returned to the shore, which oozed a salty scent of decay. From there we looked back across the water and admired the fine figure of *Bessie Ellen* resting against the quay opposite. The lines of her gracious hull and all the mysteries of her complex rigging echoed my mental image of *Pirate*. The sister ships, both of whom I felt moored to by family history, were now ghosting against each other in the same harbour.

Tom and I pushed the dinghy off the weed-covered rubble into the water, making the short crossing of 133 years between the building of *Pirate* and our voyage on *Bessie Ellen*.

A Boat-Shaped Future

Prior to my trip north on *Bessie Ellen* I'd reflected on the revival in small-scale cargo delivery through companies such as SailCargo and their flagship *Tres Hombres*. Named after the three friends who started a carbon-neutral 'clean shipping' movement in 2007, the engineless brigantine plies between the Americas and Europe, acting as an ambassador for sail-powered cargo shipping worldwide. She carries a maximum of 40 tons of organic and traditionally-crafted goods such as Rum, Cocoa, Coffee, Honey & Canned Fish.

It's an attractive, if rather niche, response to the climate crisis and the significant impact of cargo shipping. Arguably, the creak of timber and beat of canvas adds value to the products arriving in the hands of conscientious consumers. For owners of historic ships there must be satisfaction in returning vessels to such a purpose. And for consumers and bystanders, a ship arriving in port to unload brings all the thrill of an 'event', just as it did in my great-grandfather's time.

SailCargo have also been building a new timber container ship on the Pacific coast of Costa Rica. Ceiba will be the world's largest ocean-going 'clean' cargo ship. Three masts and $580m^2$ ($6,300ft^2$) of sail stand alongside solar panels, a uniquely designed electric engine, and batteries. She will easily reach 12 knots, 16 at her fastest, and carry up to 250 tonnes, which is roughly equivalent to nine standard shipping containers. Conventional ships typically carry 15,000 containers and travel at between 16 and 22 knots. Due for launch in 2025, she will begin by transporting products such as green coffee, cacao, organic cotton and turmeric oil north to Canada. Bio-packaging, electric bicycles, premium barley and hops will go south for Costa Rica's burgeoning craft beer market.

At the heart of the project is confidence in harnessing the elements, rather than fossil fuels, to cross oceans for trade, and a refusal to discard technology that's been trusted for at least seven thousand years. It demonstrates an alternative approach, making a point and adding value rather than being economically viable in current circumstances.

The same timber slope of hull against which I lay down at night aboard *Bessie Ellen* would previously have held a cargo of coal or slate or manure. As part of my voyage north and in the spirit of her former days, I wanted to deliver something, and hatched a plan with Charlotte of the skiff build. Since 2007 she's been growing a small business on the shores of Loch Tay, making chocolate from fairly-sourced cocoa which she flavours with seasonally-foraged plants. Spring might include wild garlic or sloe blossom; in winter fresh rosemary or sea buckthorn. For my voyage, she made up a package to stow in *Bessie Ellen's* hold. These were summer flavours: dark chocolate with Scots Pine and white chocolate infused with elderflower.

Charlotte grasped my urge to do this, also motivated by a seafaring ancestry. She had learned that her mother's great-grandfather John William Pyman was a nineteenth-century sea captain based in the north of England. Tragically, he was lost at sea in June 1879. He did not own the ship, nor the official cargo, but sea captains at the time were allowed to run a small business on board, selling goods to the crew. Presumably these were luxuries such as tobacco, and this practice allowed captains to earn a little more than their pay. The stock they brought aboard might amount to their life savings and as all Pyman's wealth went down with him in that ship, his widow and three children were left destitute.

If I found no recipient for the cargo ashore, perhaps I'd still be following a tradition if I sold the bars of chocolate onboard. But I had an idea – the delicatessen Kirkness & Gorie. Winkled into a narrow vennel in Kirkwall, it opens up a world of wine and a display of tinned sardines too bright and beautiful to ever open and eat. It's run by writer Duncan McLean, also a publisher (and the first to publish Irvine Welsh). He has lived in Orkney for many years and when I approached him, the idea of a cargo ship delivering to his shores under sail appealed to him.

By a strange geographical symmetry, he was actually in Perthshire at the time we were in Scapa Flow. In his absence he suggested I deliver to Stromness Books and Prints, a tiny but well-stocked bookshop tucked into the town's mesh of narrow streets and alleys. It has a rich chain of legacy since its foundation in 1970 by Glasgow poet Charles Senior, passing then into the hands of John L Broom, the author of *John Maclean*, and after him to Tam MacPhail, the husband of landscape photographer Gunnie Moberg. Duncan himself had once worked there. The bookshop would have been a certain destination for me anyway when we went ashore.

I took a photo of skipper Nikki holding the package of goods on the foredeck and later of the bookshop's Freyja, to further represent all the hands the package passed through. A week later the chocolate reached Duncan and he sent a photo of it displayed in his Kirkwall shop. It was a tiny symbolic gesture, yet it pleased me to connect this triangle of passionate endeavours – chocolate maker, historic ship captain, artisan shopkeeper – each one representing a business put together with care, personal investment and ethical thought and each tangibly moored to its watery location.

Perhaps the future can be changed by the accumulation of small efforts.

When I hear the first simple piano notes of Peter Maxwell Davies'‘Farewell to Stromness’, a prickle of foreboding always tiptoes up my spine. Then the melody comes in, announcing it as a melancholy folk song. He wrote it in response to an external threat to the Orkney mainland in 1977: uranium extraction proposed by the South of Scotland Electricity Board, which would intrude a mining corridor for 6 miles between Stromness and Yesnaby. The whole population rose in resistance and marched in a silent procession through Stromness; it was said to be too serious for noise.

They overcame.

As we left Stromness for waters further north, the southwest corner of the Orkney Mainland at Breakness lay on *Bessie Ellen*'s starboard side. Some large, brilliant yellow buoys were marking an exclusion zone in the water at Billia Croo. In 2003 this site in the mouth of Hoy Sound became the world's first wave-energy test centre. Exposed to the full power of the North Atlantic, the average wave height here is 2–3m, but the highest recorded has been 18m. The installation is now connected to the grid.

Orkney's *tidal* energy is also being exploited. Just after our sail around these islands, the largest tidal turbine ever to be connected to the European Marine Energy Centre, Orbital O2, was anchored in the fast-flowing Fall of Warness, just west of Orkney's Isle of Eday. It would generate enough energy for 2000 local homes for eleven years.

A Boat-Shaped Future

Orkney, as a former power house of traditional ship-building, is now lending its muscle to high-tech sustainable energy solutions that harness wave and tide. These islands may have lost their strategic position on a long-standing sail-trading route since the rise of steam and combustion engines, but powerful waves and tide, combined with the benign, deep shelter of Scapa Flow in which to safely organise and build, make it an apt energy pioneer.

On the same day that Orbital O2's generation began, an eighth-to-tenth-century Pictish stone was discovered in Sanday. Here together was deep past and the cutting edge; the ancient and the futuristic. I wonder if a place that nurtures its cultural roots might also cultivate greater attention to what future generations will inherit.

On leaving the ship in Ullapool at the end of our voyage, I found the mainland sizzling, as if to reassure tourists on their enforced UK holidays that there was no need to travel to the Mediterranean. The Highlands seemed more frantic with cars than I had ever known.

As news began to clatter in, I learnt that the capsule of my sailing journey north had protected me from a worldwide disaster movie. A climate aberration on the western coast of Canada had generated a period of such intense and unprecedented heat that mussels in the intertidal zone had popped open and cooked, pungent on approach. Air temperatures in Lytton, British Columbia, had topped 121°F and the town was all but destroyed by wildfire. It was agreed that the cause was global heating; the burning of fossil fuels was driving up temperatures faster than models had predicted.

Next came catastrophic floods in the north-east of Germany. Then it was China's turn and the provincial capital of Henan province, Zhengzhou, had a year's average rainfall in three days. A dam was breached. Railway tunnels flooded and passengers on underground trains were driven to standing on their seats as they watched water leak through the doors, rising slowly to their ankles, knees, and up to their necks. As I read I found it hard to breathe. There had apparently been plenty of warning that widespread dam construction was worsening climate-related problems in China's flood zone, severing natural connections between rivers, lakes and absorbent floodplains. Fifty died and four hundred thousand were evacuated.

The terrifying onslaught didn't stop. During one day in late July, a significant surge in Greenland's ice-melt was recorded, expected to change the island's topography and trigger an irreversible process of worldwide consequence. The water would be enough in itself to inundate the entire state of Florida. In further news verging on the fantastical, super-rich players had escaped into space, travelling to other planets. Perhaps they were 'house hunting' for safer terrain to begin the process of planetary destruction all over again, or identifying a dumping ground in order to continue living with careless regard on Earth.

A balance had tipped. For the first time since the beginning of the Covid pandemic, and in over forty years in which I've tried to limit my own impact on the natural order, I registered in myself not just a generalised anxiety about the effect of human life on the planet and our collective fate, but something that smelt like actual fear. What had always seemed a *future* threat was now very starkly present. I wondered how new parents would be feeling. I thought of my mother's horror at the scale of change within her lifetime.

She would shake her head. 'Idiots,' she'd mutter.

As the summer went on, a drastic shortage of HGV drivers in the UK led to empty shelves and the closure of outlets. At Royal Portbury Dock outside Bristol, a sign at the entrance to a depot urged people to 'drive for us,' offering £5000 for signup and retention bonuses. Reliability was critical. This was, after all, the main reason road haulage became preferred over sea and sail in the first place.

My male forebears in Braunton worked their way up as boys and young men, from crewing on local ketches and schooners, becoming mate, Master and finally, if they were fortunate, owner of a vessel; their passport to possible affluence. They delivered essential goods but took a risk on loss, not always insuring their vessels. It struck me that in their heyday my great-grandfather Robert, his brother and their father were not unlike today's HGV drivers. They were simply elevated by the chance of ownership.

The impact of cargo shipping today is hidden to many of us, but in spring 2021 land-based consumers had woken up to their dependence for goods on ships and fluid routes. The *Ever Given*, 400m long and capable of carrying 20,000 containers, ran aground in high winds and lay for a week wedged across the 300m-wide Suez Canal. This didn't only delay the delivery of its own cargo, but that of all the ships forced to wait for the narrow but essential channel to be cleared. There were complaints from consumers about delayed computers, training shoes, scooters, but also about massive commercial losses.

Rose George, writing in the *Guardian* of the 'ditch in the desert' built with forced labour, noted that although the wind had been blamed for the accident, generally in maritime accidents human error is to blame. This isn't surprising, as crews of commercial ships have massively reduced in size and sleep is short.

In a historically male industry and with only 2% of the world's seafarers female, it was also 'interesting' when a twenty-nine-year-old Egyptian woman was blamed for the *Ever Given* incident through rapid circulation of a fake Arab news headline on English-language social media. At the time of grounding, the accused woman, Marwa Elselehdar, had been hundreds of miles away acting as first mate on another ship. As Egypt's first female ship captain and, in 2015, the first and youngest female to captain a ship through the newly-expanded Suez Canal, she commented, 'People in our society still don't accept the idea of girls working in the sea away from their families for a long time'. But she hopes to become a role model, encouraging other women to fight for what they love, including the sea.

With 450 ships waiting at either end of the canal, which can carry 12% of global trade including oil and gas, it was estimated that the hold-up could cost £7bn a day. And yet until this televised spectacle, many of us in the rich countries of the world had been unaware of the 'invisible' industry that underpins our lifestyles, with 90% of everything we consume arriving by sea. An ironic outcome of our climate crisis is that, with melting ice caps in the Arctic, an east-west sea route may open up year-round off the northern coast of Russia; a much shorter journey than the 'ditch in the desert' provides. This trading passage may see Orkney once again becoming an important staging post.

Once we rushed toward fossil fuels in the face of post-World War pressures, sail power from fickle wind was mostly relegated to recreation. But things are now changing. In anticipation of greater regulation, research is focusing on large-scale commercial cargo vessels once again designed to capture wind power. The first Swedish-designed *Oceanbird Wing* will have four 80m rigid 'wings' and carry 7000 cars on a North Atlantic crossing at an average speed of 10 knots. The wings, vertical tongues of metal and composite, can be retracted as required in stormy conditions or for low bridges and are adjustable to wind direction. Additional engines provide manoeuvrability and backup. It's slower than a conventional ship but will reduce emissions by as much as 90%. A life-cycle analysis suggests that after less than one year's work, the *Oceanbird Wing* will have saved enough emissions to make up for the carbon footprint of its construction.

This vessel, the world's largest at 200 x 40m, is expected to be sailing in 2027 and the wing technology can be retrofitted to existing vessels to back up engine power. With pressure on shipping companies and stricter regulations on emissions, wind-driven vessels – a slower but cleaner means of travel – could once again become viable.

In late August 2021 we were gathered again at the boat shed on Loch Tay. We wheeled the skiff into dappled light on the leaf-mould floor outside, then down the slope towards a long jetty and the evening's brilliance. Andy, Adam, Allan, Angus, Charlotte, Paul, Robin and myself. Out of oak, Angus had also now made pegs to secure the seats, and thole pins from which the oars would lever.

There were some last-minute jobs to do – fitting oak pads to each oar and to the gunwales at the point where the two meet. But suddenly it seemed we were ready and all hands helped to take the long and unwieldy oars, brand-new fenders and life jackets so far unused, down to the jetty.

Beyond the trees' shade, sunlight danced on the Loch at the end of a hot day. We began pushing the boat on the trailer out of the shed and into the shallows. At first the water reached only to our knees, seeming to resist deepening. But eventually came a moment when the trolley became stationary and the hull was supported by water.

'She's floating!' Charlotte called out.

We were all grinning, guiding her out until the trolley could be pulled away. The whole length of her met water for the first time. Sunlight sprang against clean, curving lines and the red of the hull was doubled in a warm sheen of reflection. We were no longer using any strength; on water she danced, responsive to a slight nudge, the pull of the painter on the bow, as we brought her alongside the jetty.

We stood, looking down at her in admiration until the realisation came – there was nothing left to do but get in. Andy, with a little more experience than the rest of us, offered to cox, taking up the perch in the stern with the tiller in his hand. The end of it had recently been finished by Angus with a sphere of oak, turned on a lathe to display concentric grain lines four times over.

At first the rest of us looked at each other with polite reticence (or uncertainty about our ability).

'Right, I'll go,' said Angus, climbing onto the first bench and taking up the stroke position.

Adam and I climbed onto the next two benches and Allan sat in the bow. The oars seemed impossibly long, heavy and unwieldy until fitted to their pins, and immediately easier to handle once water buoyed the blades.

A gentle push away from the jetty and we were heading out away from the shade, awkward and uncoordinated. But then Andy had us turn the bow to point towards the northern shore where a conifer plantation climbed steeply. Below it lay the beach where, in the dark turn of the previous year's winter solstice, I'd launched a different kind of glowing vessel onto these waters in memory of my mother.

How she would have enjoyed watching this moment. She'd compare our 'beauty' to the Scilly gigs, tell us of the times she'd watched them racing, spread her hands wide in appreciation and say, 'What a fantastic achievement!'. And her mother – Granny – or Emma Louise herself, what would they have had to say? They'd be reminded of the rowing boat which ferried them across the estuary from Crow Point to Appledore. 'But we never had to row ourselves, mind!'

Our first strokes clashed, at odds with each other.

Andy imposed order. 'Oars up. Come forward to row … Follow Angus' stroke! And row … and … row.'

And then we were moving. The oars and the oak pads made purchase against each other. She whispered out into direct sunlight and the blades lifted and fell, pulled through the languid water and lifted again. A blue evening sky arced over us. We were making way through light itself. Transported. Grinning. Concentrating. It may not have been salty, but I was making a pact with the water itself; I promised to make it part of my regular life from now on.

From the centre of the Loch, our familiar landscape was rejigged into a different pattern, distinct from the way we see it from the roads that link shoreside villages. A new community was being gathered by this shared body of bright water. We were coming out of the gloom.

Caught in photos taken from the shore, the skiff and her team are luminous, with drips golden between oar tip and surface, the red of her hull glowing. Was she art or a boat?

We knew the answer.

A synchronised machine of human muscle, coordinated spirit, timber, epoxy glue and pure love.

A month later we had rowed our 'lass' across the Loch to her permanent home on the shore at Kenmore and soon afterwards held an official launch event. Cloud billowed over the hills to our west as a crowd of well-wishers, dignitaries and potential rowers gathered. We sang a version of the 'Loch Tay Boat Song' with lyrics I'd doctored to reflect love for our boat rather than for a lassie.

A moving moment, of stillness, came when poet Jon Plunkett blessed the boat. Although he hadn't been involved with the building, his poet's intuition had tapped the project's spirit and graft:

> *Let her sit light in the water*
> *as though held by the hands and hope*
> *of all who sanded and shaped,*
> *painted and learned*
> *the deep grain of her.*

And he reflected back to us her wider value to the world:

> *May she stay strong, a symbol*
> *of what can be done*
> *when we work with nature,*
> *and pull together. Row*
> *in unity. Row, for unity*
> *and let those ripples spread*
> *far beyond this loch.*

A Boat-Shaped Future

Our MSP, John Swinney, who had visited to show interest during the building process, officiated, tying one of the red ribbons into a bow on the gunwale and trickling a libation of Aberfeldy malt whisky over her hull, before proposing a toast for everyone's 'nip'. Then he climbed from a pontoon into position on stroke oar for her first public encounter with the waters of Loch Tay.

The cox was Charli, a warm and confident young woman who'd come to support our launch with a party from the St Andrews coastal rowing club. They had also brought their own boat to ensure everyone who wished could try rowing that day. She commanded with un-bossy clarity and the *Red Haired Lass* slipped neatly backwards from the shore with the rowers' faces turned towards us – Charlotte and Angus lit up with smiles. Margaret, of course, had been quick to exchange her walking stick for an oar.

Charli rallied her crew to turn the bow towards open water.

'I'm going to ask port rowers to turn us around.'

The way she drew out the word 'ask' made me wonder.

Later, she pointed to our red and white cushions from Cornwall. 'My Dad made those,' she told me.

As a Cornishwoman she had grown up racing pilot gigs with her family and had now adapted her skills to the gig's Scottish cousin. I was thrilled by this confirmation of lines still thrown between here and my mother's south-western shores.

St Andrews' *Sandbay Century* skiff – powder blue and white – followed the *Red Haired Lass* onto the water.

We were not yet sure of ourselves and glad of the other club's support. And soon we'd benefit again when Cornish Charli would return to give us training sessions, bringing others with her. Later still, on many further shores at coastal rowing gatherings, she'd greet us with her wide smile and powerful hugs.

For the time being, though, that September day in 2021, we had launched.

Re-treading Motherlands

In *The Sea Around Us* American marine biologist Rachel Carson (1907–1964) notes that we each begin life in a miniature ocean within our mother's womb. Obvious though this is, such marine intimacy – my early, planktonic life *within* my mother's oceanic body – feels like some absurd magic. But there's more. Warm blood pumps through our veins in a combined stream of sodium, potassium and calcium salts in similar proportions to sea water. I inherited this body, it seems, both from my parents and the sea. Is it any wonder then, that when I stand on a shore something blindly elemental tugs me towards it with what Carson refers to as 'an unconscious recognition of … lineage'?

I exist on Earth with this salt-sea affinity and the once-umbilical connection to my mother before I was 'wrecked' by birth, cast up on a separate bodily island. Nevertheless, her sea longings and sea loss seem animate in my own heart. Maybe I have even engineered it. By making physical distance from loved ones, I've fashioned a lifestyle similar to all my seafaring foremothers, widowed or not. As each intimate relationship has ended, I've experienced catastrophic and sometimes disproportionate loss.

Towards the end of 2021, I teetered on the first anniversary of my mother's death. Sodden auburn leaves banked up on the ground in a slow transformation to future humus; death and renewal. It struck me for the first time that she had died on the 'Day of the Dead' at the turn of the Celtic year known as *Samhain*, later solemnised into the Christian calendar as All Saints. Had it been easier for her to slip away then into her own briny chasm? Seen in some cultures as a joyful opportunity for reunion with the dead, it's a time when traditionally the veil between this world and the next is thin. We might visualise it as the surface tension between air and water. Depth and detail are revealed on the far side when the reflection falters.

My mother duly prowled through my daytime thoughts and starred in my dreams around the time of this annual summons. Ancestor worship, a normal practice in many cultures, was at its most prosaic for me: her birthday, close to Remembrance Sunday, flashed up, as it will do year on year, in my electronic diary, reminding me how narrowly she missed her eighty-ninth.

The dark felt particularly animated: laden with memory, shadowed by those dark days in West Cornwall just after her death when we started the initial sorting of her house and stayed under the dependable pulse of Pendeen Watch. That compassionate blaze in the dark brought to mind Robert Louis Stevenson's poem 'Skerryvore' honouring his uncle and other men toiling 'to plant a star for seamen' on an isolated reef off Tiree.

Just before this anniversary, I'd spent three weeks in the south-west of England. Kate – the irreverent Reverend – and I had a final section of Cornwall's coast path to complete. By a pleasing coincidence, it was the six days west from Perranporth. Once at Hayle on the north side of West Cornwall's narrow isthmus, we would walk the northern shore of the peninsula, passing Pendeen Watch, then circle around Land's End to arrive on the south coast at Penzance. My mother had more or less made this Celtic outlier, West Penwith, into her 'island'. Since our earliest holidays here in the 1970s, this has been our well-trodden coast and there was no stretch of it that I had not covered at least once, some of it numerous times. The prospect of this familiarity and the joined-up journey we would make around the peninsula was comforting.

The week began with searing winds that whisked the sea into breakers pulsing white stripes to the shore, and brought kitesurfers out in numbers to speed across this occasional terrain, sometimes soaring into the sky itself. The long miles of expansive beach at Hayle gave way to wrinkled cliffs and shorelines onto which the Atlantic continued to pound long after the wind dropped. Then it became end-of-summer warm, and we had days of walking with thrill and dazzle and steep-cliffed coves; the curved horizon to our right a constant reminder of 'the offing' that had summoned my forebears.

There were so many places on our way that my mother had walked and painted into her bones in a 'language' of saturated colour; this rugged place of violent cliffs, small ancient-boundaried fields marked by scribbles of stone, vertiginous mine shafts and Neolithic monuments. As we progressed around the peninsula, the Runnel Stone bell buoy sang out the swell from a mile offshore. Aware of its mournful moan as we approached Gwennap Head, once rounded and on the south coast, its music changed to something sharper and tinnier.

We were keen to swim on at least one point of the week's walk, but on the evening we reached the white beach at Porthcurno – a day's walk short of our final destination – it was still too rough to consider. My mother had continued to swim here into her seventies, secure in a bay embraced by golden granite, and with the watch of a lifeguard in the summer months. To the east of her was the long, blocky peninsula on which the Logan Rock balances, and on the other side, the cliff into which the Minack Theatre was carved in the 1930s by Rowena Kade and her gardener.

We hoped that, if the wind dropped overnight, we would have a good chance of calmer conditions at low tide the next morning. So before breakfast, already in our costumes, we walked down to meet the sunrise. The sea rolled gently, the sky over the land hung with veils of deep pink cloud, darkening the sand. The sun rose between two pinnacles on the Logan Rock headland as we stood assessing the sea and partially undressing, the soles of our feet massaged by coarse shell sand.

I remembered that as teenagers we were always cautious about a steep slope, a 'shelf' that crossed this cove, especially when concealed underwater. Because of the state of tide, the waves were now breaking just at its top lip, crashing on impact, and subsequently hissing an apron of water onto the higher beach before making a pebble-rattling retreat. Although calm beyond that, we would quickly be out of our depth. We were reduced to dithering.

Another woman appeared on the beach, an Irish actress from the current Minack production, also keen to swim.

'I will if you will,' I promised.

'I'm not coming in to rescue you,' Kate said, just as my Mum would have done.

But then I was wading through surf in newly-broken sunlight and swimming into the gentle swell beyond, parallel to the beach as she had always insisted. I was stretching my body, supported by a salt cradle and euphoric. It was not cold.

I must have turned towards the shore, treading water, to look to where Kate waited. Perhaps I moved in too close to the beach or perhaps it was a super-sized seventh wave that I didn't see coming. But after the briefest roar from behind, I was underwater. Rather than surfacing as it passed overhead, I seemed to be caught inside its muscular curl, my eyes open to fizz, bubble, greenish light. My ears were full of water, my hands scrabbling to propel myself towards the medium of air, whichever way was 'up'. Between abrasive depth and sky, all churning together, impossible to separate, I was succumbing to the sea.

It seemed to take forever to puncture the surface. And then I was high on the back of a breaking wave above the beach, arms stroking wildly towards land. But rather than getting closer to the shore, I was apparently leaving it. Sucked and carried backwards. There was no ground to touch under my feet and I was aware of the danger of going under again if I reached my toes towards it. I had time to think of the irony. Heard my overcautious mother warning not to swim after eating, not to swim if there was no lifeguard, not to swim out of my depth. As long as she articulated the worst, she must have thought it couldn't happen. But she wasn't there to say it. Was I about to drown on her favourite beach?

I threw arms and hands at the water to force myself forward and finally found my feet grazing sand and pebbles that were fast being dragged away from under them. I pushed up the steep slope, scrabbling like an animal on feet and hands. Desperate to be free of water, I finally stood up on beloved land. Squeak-eared and deaf, swimming costume dragged down by a gusset full of dredged shell sand, I was grateful and frightened in a way that I couldn't recall from playing in such seas through my teenage years.

I remained shaken for several hours, betrayed by a place so connected to our family history.

Sea Marked

The gathering organised at the Morrab Library in memory of my mother a few days after the end of our walk had a celebratory feel. My sister and I stood in a circle of people in a large book-lined room with a view through palm trees and giant ferns down to the sea. Cakes and snacks were carried in. Tea was made. We knew a few of her co-volunteers and some of the friends made during her long stint as Honorary Librarian and other roles that had put this library at the centre of her life.

'She was never flappable,' they said of her.

One of her roles had been to recruit and organise monthly speakers. They were often eccentric individuals pursuing niche fascinations. She was proud of finding them, noting their names down on a corner of the *Guardian* when they turned up on the TV or radio, especially if they lived not too far away.

'I don't know how she got them to come without any payment. How did she do it?' her friends asked.

My sister and I read out some small pieces of a 'Morrab Memoir' she'd written for a Library anniversary, demonstrating the diversity of speakers she'd coaxed 'down-country' along the long narrow peninsula of Cornwall. There was a kora player from Mali who enchanted his audience; a Japanese professor from a museum of fairies; a lecture on 'Flanders and Swann' – a hugely popular comic singing duo in the 1960s. On that particular bitter January day, she wrote that the entire audience joined in, singing uproariously 'Mud, Mud, Glorious Mud' just as we had done with her as children in our Surrey sitting room. It had always felt like 'my song'. I was the one who returned from long days playing in the garden covered in the stuff. Its stickiness also evoked the dark banks of the Basingstoke Canal where we played as children while she painted rotting wharfs and barges. These days I picture the acres of mud that seem to rise and expand across the Taw-Torridge estuary at low tide, diminishing the watercourse itself to a minor player every twelve and a half hours.

My mother was not a solemn person; she was known in this community for her mischievous vivacity and ready smile. It was a happy event and there was much laughter as well as shared memories.

'She lives on in you both,' someone told us. 'She was proud of you.'

I allowed myself to believe this now, despite feeling during her lifetime that with her 1950s parental reserve, I had fought for her recognition and failed. Now, after time for reflection, I was discovering my feet firm on our common ground.

On one of the last occasions I'd tempted her out of Penzance with me, unbroken blue sky and light winds soared over us. We took a picnic to Botallack on the north coast. The cliffs here, as all around the coast at St Just, were mined for tin, arsenic and copper from at least the 1500s, and the last Cornish tin mine didn't close until 1998. The clifftop area memorialises this past in tall buildings with ecclesiastical-looking arched windows – tumbling now – slag heaps and overgrown tunnel entrances, a vast infrastructure created under and over-ground and sinking incrementally. But from this elevated point, the eye always plummets to the base of the cliffs where on Crown Rocks, two ruined engine houses cling to a granite headland only just above the sea's thrashing. They pumped out the lodes which stretch half a mile out under the sea.

The place has always excited me. In addition to my

endless drawings and photographs, it had been a kind of playground, especially when as a young adult I returned here with friends and climbing partners. It was less visited in those days before *Poldark* popularised it on TV, and the two-hundred-year-old buildings had not been stabilised or fenced off. We used to scramble all over them, thrilled by our exposure above the waves, by this meeting place of human history with the elemental.

My mother and I sat on the clifftop in deckchairs that day amongst the old mine workings, watching gannets fly over the Crown Rocks on a migratory path. I have a photo of her leaning on her stick with a broad smile, white hair gleaming against clear sky, wearing white trousers and a powder-blue fleece. She is a picture of contentment in her own small patch where she could name all the engine houses, and locate herself directionally by the timbre of the Runnel Stone bell buoy.

As Kate and I had walked towards Penzance on the coast path, I'd collected into a notebook observations such as my mother might have made – her familiar touchstones. Later, I compressed these images into lines for a poem. Her home played its part in it too. The house just within storm-slapping distance of the promenade, from where it was an easy walk to the library, a place rowdy with ideas and laughter, where her friendships flourished. I read the poem at the celebration, stumbling with emotion only on the final line.

I imagined her there, joining in the singing of 'Mud', rocking as she sang, even raising her hands as a conductor would, and afterwards collapsing forward into laughter. She had loved Elizabeth David, Madhur Jaffrey, anything to do with the Scilly Islands. Contemporary poetry, squill flowers, Glen Lyon close to my home, Belted Galloway cattle.

Once upon a time she had tailored her own suits, and more recently hatched plants from exotic seeds, some of which have ended up in the Morrab Gardens.

It seemed I had stepped my way into a new appreciation of her as a person and a mother as well as enjoying again her 'island' where the sea governs with ancient and unforgiving force.

Once home, I reread some of her letters, the ones I'd kept. I have to look for clues in the text to approximate the year and month – a reference to the solar eclipse in 1999, events in my own life and her visits to me, or mine to her; our 'jaunts'. I was sorry we never reached Orkney together.

I found a beautiful letter which I can date to early 2001 because it refers to the final decision to separate from my long-term partner after a few years of limbo. She addresses me as 'Darling Linda' and the letter is full of love and kindness and support. I have no memory of receiving it, and am very glad I kept it.

In another letter she writes: 'One does tend to gravitate in later life back to one's roots – Cornwall feels like the Devon of my childhood – and the people, too, fiercely independent, manic-depressive, nonconformist and so on. Maybe that's why the Scots don't feel particularly strange or different to me. The extremities of the country seem to breed the same characteristics.'

And into this period of re-reading letters on winter evenings landed a new short story by Margaret Atwood. It took the form of a letter in which a woman, apparently elderly and recently widowed, is replying to a younger relative who has enquired how she is. The letter reveals all the feeling and circumstance, the indignities and loneliness of getting used to widowhood; the sense of the husband's remaining presence still acute. I gasped when I came to the final brief paragraph of the story which was the *actual* letter she sent; what was possible to say. Cheery, matter-of-fact, projecting the message: 'no need to worry overly about me', along with details of the season and growth in the garden.

The story, 'Widows', was so beautifully wrought that it tripped me emotionally, but more than that, the letter *actually* sent was so similar to the ones I received from my mother over the years since her second widowhood. The details of tourists being annoying or caught out without understanding of tides; the datura she was growing, threatened by weather too dry or wet or cold; the seagulls calling down her chimney or antics of neighbourhood squirrels. And did I ever think beyond this, try to imagine her loneliness or how she might still feel my stepfather alongside her? Her pain was never mentioned.

I imagine her mother was the same sort of widow, and her mother too. They fade back through time in a series of straight-backed women, pinned down by photographers like dead moths.

After the 'motherland' visit and the event at the library, I went to reconnect, after a long absence, with 'Granny-land'. The train journey between Cornwall and Devon raised memories. Passing Dawlish, the railway line teeters on the edge of red cliffs with glimpses of Exmouth across the estuary. The poignancy of the Morrab memorial party for my mother seemed to re-open the wound of Granny's loss so many years earlier. These were the seaside haunts that we visited with her as children.

I associated Granny with cream teas, the scent of Germylene hand cream, a paper tube of blackcurrant pastels always in her handbag. But now I could picture her before I knew her. A devoted mother baking cake and parcelling it up with fresh eggs, pats of butter and a newly sewn winter coat for her brilliant daughter at Oxford. I saw the marvellous long black hair and flashing teeth of her youth; the young woman diligent at the piano or hiking or cycling or making for the beach; the version of her in the newly-married photographs, wearing stout walking-shoes on the Pilgrim's Way, handsome in a solid, Devonshire kind of way.

Different versions of my mother rose up too: the pretty girl dressed up by her mother who grew up to be elegant and clever, tall and creative. The young widow cartwheeling across our Surrey garden and the one who carried a wicker picnic basket onto the Cornish cliffs containing sliced bread, boiled eggs, McVitie's Jamaica Ginger Cake; and for herself, a sketchbook. Who mostly weathered trouble in her life with quiet dignity, and didn't lose her access to joy.

The sun was dropping towards Appledore as the bus rumbled through the industrial and commercial buildings on the outskirts of Barnstaple. Round hills rose in green cushions inland to my right, while a stand of trees blocked the view to my left.

Suddenly the treeline broke, revealing the whole glittering mosaic of mud and water. The Taw River, narrow and luminous, arced serpentine away from me towards Fremington on the far side, the mud around it stretching rich and brown and shiny. As I watched, an arrow of silhouetted geese rose up alongside the bus and my heart performed an unexpected leap. Joy of the changing season; joy of a return.

When I got off the bus at Georgeham Cross in the north of the village, the short walk to my accommodation took me past St Brannock's Church with its thatched lychgate and a row of now-familiar gravestones where I might trace with a finger the name 'DRAKE' over and over.

I took a narrow lane climbing into the hills and paused at the white wall that enclosed Sylvester House. I couldn't see much from this back view. I was pleased, though, to feel cold harling under my hand and hear voices trilling up from a garden which I knew would slope down to the pretty rill of the Caen river. All this in the knowledge it had been owned at one time by Mary Hacche Drake – a spinster who passed it down to her nephew (and Granny's Grandfather) Francis Drake, owner of *Pirate* and *Emma Louise*.

Mary had been born in 1824, one of the children of mariner Francis Hacche Drake. He was the one rumoured in family history to have had a duel at sea with the ship's captain and had left a sword and an earring to family members. Perhaps that was all he had following his disinheritance (except for one shilling). This was as punishment for failing to keep away, as instructed (and whilst married to Sarah Huxtable), from Mary Gould of Georgeham, a 'red-haired cook' in the Drake household. Before they were able to marry in 1820, he and Mary had two illegitimate sons, one of whom was our antecedent Francis Gould Drake who became a master mariner. I wondered if this lineage could explain the red hair of one of my nieces.

As I walked further up the lane to where I would stay, I gathered into myself the history I'd excavated over the last years. At the beginning of the search Peter Pay had explained this Gould–Drake diversion in the family tree to me, but it had taken all this time and concrete evidence to embed it in my personal archaeology. There was quite a lot else he'd discovered that had now become pleasingly palpable.

I'd reached one of these physical touchstones on a visit I'd finally made to Musbury near Axminster in South Devon. At the top of the small village on a sunny September day, with the burbling primary school to my left, a lovely symmetry presented itself ahead. The square, fifteenth-century church tower of St Michaels rose behind a pillared gateway, doors lying open to frame darkness within. But as I came closer I saw, at the centre of this darkness, a stained-glass window flaring above the altar.

Up close, ammonites studded the pale stone of the arched doorway, bestowing the church with the heft of a medieval cathedral as I stepped through into the gloom. Chiffon scarves and bunches of roses and white chrysanthemums decorated each of the pew ends. I remembered then that when I'd contacted the church warden to make sure it would be open, they told me there was to be a renewal of marriage vows that afternoon.

It took no time to find the name Drake rhyming across stone slabs on floors and walls. Johns and Dorothys and Williams. Red wyverns, with a spitting tongue and clamped claws, appeared here and there, on walls and in plaster. And then in a transept, a huge tomblike plinth on which three sixteenth-century Drake couples knelt in a line, separated by pilastered screens. First John, then 'our' Sir Bernard, then another John. Swords were slung on their hips, red sashes across their chests, golden trims decorating their armour. With white ruffs around their necks, they were pointy-bearded and wore long boots, each the same yet subtly varied. Each scabbard was differentiated in design. Their wives were hidden behind them but also wore neck ruffs, brocaded bodices, pale caps on their heads, and had differently-shaped chins.

Pigeon coos echoed through the calm stone columns. With its imprint of centuries of prayer and community, the building carried a sense of calm kindness; a beacon of humanism. From the porch I picked up a sheet of paper and a fat green crayon left there for children and took a rubbing from the floor – the letters D R A K E appeared boldly in negative. Something to take away.

When I'd told Peter Pay I would make this visit, he'd encouraged me to take up my ancestral 'right' and venture to Ash House (the 'Ash' an echo of 'Hacche'). It was just outside the village, and defended by a busy A-road, a long private drive and high trees, and the repeated mantra in the church that the new owners 'value their privacy'. Judging from all the Drake descendants who had entered their names in the visitors' book, many from the US, they may have had regular callers. Instead, I climbed a nearby hill drifted across by charms of goldfinches and, through heavy heads of black-berry, looked down on Ash House. Through the day's haze I made out some high chimneys, farm buildings, not much else. It didn't matter; the church had satisfied me.

At the end of that day of ancestral iteration I slept at a guest house, alone in a wide bed. Instead of sprawling across it, I allowed spare pillows, bedding, clothes and books to pile up alongside me just as I'd seen my mother doing as she aged. Had I learnt this habit or inherited it?

Prompted by glorious weather in Braunton, and wanting to beat the bounds of places not visited for some time, I hired a bike for two days. The first was spent on a circuit of the coast from the quay at Velator. I followed the flood defence bank to the estuary and then turned west towards the Bar.

Before going on to the beach at the White House, I climbed over the flood defence bank to look across at Horsey Island. The sea wall had been breached since I'd last been here, possibly irreparably. The whole area was now in the ownership of the Devon Wildlife Trust. Divorced from the Marshes, this floated-off triangle of land looked a different place – stained to a battlefield palette following numerous tidal inundations. Any residual green of the old lands and scrubby trees was gone in a transformation from freshwater marsh to saltmarsh. The river Caen was reasserting its old route to the sea.

This mud would be rich with residual memory. Although Conrad speaks of the ocean having 'no compassion, no face, no law, no memory,' Rachel Carson points to the depths of sea-memory when we consider sediments that fall and build up on the sea *floor*. They convert, she says, into 'a sort of epic poem of the Earth.' Such layered 'writings' tell of events in the waters above and on surrounding lands – the advance and retreat of ice, floods, volcanic eruptions. Way beneath the Atlantic waters that were crossed by my seafaring forebears carrying salt to Newfoundland, such sediments accumulate to a depth of 2 miles.

In shallow, tide-pulsed waters such as here on the Taw-Torridge estuary, the sea floor still bears up fragments of wrecks, the scent of prowling wolves. As I left the bike to walk out to Crow Point, Northam Burrows was just in sight on the far side of the Bideford Bar. Nineteenth-century fishermen discovered here, under the surface of mud and sand, a submerged forest, bones of red deer, horse, hog, and long-fronted ox, a mammoth tooth, and a piercing-tool fashioned from a red deer antler.

Sea Marked

I walked to the site of the former lighthouse and coast-guard station whose brick and cement base had long ago shattered and scattered. Once-stout pillars of timber had been gnawed by the sea back to stumps of grain and knot. Sometimes the sea had exfoliated so deeply into the original tree grain that just a few 'fingers' now waved above the sand.

The place that day was scraped wide open in swathes of sky and mud. Yet I was not the only person here, attracted by this half-colonised, half-wild place that isn't quite sea or land, but tells of an ancient argument between the two. I looked out towards the Bideford Bar buoy and to the mussel bank where we had stopped for a sandwich on the kayak trip several years earlier, and observed the rush inwards of the tide. All the wrecked vessels, drowned and mud-roofed now, speak of a long history of attempts to co-operate with this capricious place.

I had no specific agenda for this visit, but intuitively it felt important to trace the outline of the Taw-Torridge estuary, meeting myself there once again to revise the local knowledge I'd gathered. My limbs felt energised by this the next day as I cycled the 'Tarka Trail', following the 13-mile route of a Victorian railway which edges the bipartite estuary from Braunton to Instow.

I was light-drunk on this clear morning. At Foxhole near Chivenor I paused to look across stripes of low-tide sheen and matt in the estuary channel, lozenge-shaped islands with feathered edges; a visual intricacy, mysterious and teeming with lives both visible and invisible – snails and mud shrimps and lugworms. About six hundred Canada geese were gathered into the great north-pushing loop made here by the serpent Taw, converging like columns of marching soldiers to travel upstream together on some mission obscure to me.

After Barnstaple's bridge I doubled back west on the opposite bank for South Yelland. Such are the limits of the landbound. Although I had learnt the main landmarks and more or less internalised the map, their relationship to each other still shifted and surprised me. From the turn at Yelland towards the confluence with the Torridge river, the white hulk of the Saunton Sands Hotel loomed, apparently close, across the flats. Yet it had always seemed distant even from Braunton – properly on the coast rather than within the Bar. The contemporary Crow Point Lighthouse also seemed ludicrously near across the gulf. A very short ferry crossing from there once connected travellers to Instow or Appledore, thus avoiding the 20-mile diversion inland to find a bridge.

Estuarine tides once determined so much here, telling geese when and where to assemble, fishermen where and when they may fish. I arrived at Instow to cross the Torridge on what is now the only remaining ferry within the Bar. In the summer season it still carries foot passengers between the facing seafront villages, but at low tide the crossing point is mostly mud. In the past a small rowing/sailing boat was run by a series of men in the John family going back to 1870. One of them, known as 'Low Water Dick', was famous for making the crossing viable at all states of tide, mooring his boat strategically close to an inlet or pool and finding the safest landing place for his passengers.

On this particular day it was possible to cross between 1.20pm and 4.20pm. A crew of volunteers were on board the small open motor boat, each wearing matching 'Appledore Instow Ferry' sweatshirts. In the covered wheelhouse at the bow, the skipper was training others. He had the manner (and cap) of a yachtsman. The ticket seller, using a card reader for the first time, introduced a little hilarity: 'Should there be unforeseen circumstances such as icebergs, there are life jackets under your seats'.

As well as the simple pleasure of being out on the water, there was a sense that we were upholding an important tradition. Passengers faced each other on two short benches, smiling, cameras at the ready. The journey took only five minutes, yet sitting close to the sparkle altered my perspective – powering blue into the back of my eyes and heartening me. At both ends of the crossing a grey-haired woman attended at the quay, each capable and strong-looking, taking the line and casting off every ten or fifteen minutes; the only boat swinging on and off the facing quays.

A ferry such as this makes a bridge where there is none, links communities which might yearn for each other across a half-mile gap. Everyone else drives around it, looking inland for opportunities.

The weather changed later in the week and became damp and murky. I returned to Braunton Museum, reminding myself of the records available here of births, deaths and marriages. I was struck again by the frequency in the late nineteenth and early twentieth century of child deaths, and the violent ends of adults to gales, guns and runaway horses.

The accounts of deaths at sea, taken from inquest reports, showed how often they were caused prosaically. For example, in 1882 when sixteen-year-old Henry Incledon was on a vessel in the estuary, his partner William Chichester lost his hat overboard in high winds. When the boy tried to use the anchor to catch the hat both were thrown into the water, clambering onto the upturned boat which then began to sink. They were only twenty yards from the shore but Henry could not swim. Two days later his body was found by mariners at Appledore.

The Museum also reminded me that Granny's mother, Annie Lock Roach, came from the nearby village of Georgeham, high on those green, round hills behind the coast. Although I'd gone there some years before with Peter Pay, my enquiry had been too new and uncertain – I didn't know what or who to look for.

I caught a bus there one morning when wind drove parallel bands of surf onto Saunton and Croyde beaches, going first to the graveyard. Amongst the names that rhymed through the generations of this area – the Roaches and Perrymans and Badcocks and Hows – I found, carved on the same headstone, Annie's grandparents on her mother's side. It showed that they belonged to a farm called South Hole. I knew that Annie's mother Agnes, of the square jaw and ringlets, appeared at this address in the census record for 1871.

I had planned to walk from Georgeham across the hills and down to Broadlands Farm to see the Hartnoll family, and it happened that the old holloway I followed took me past South Hole Farm. Presumably Agnes had lived there with her newly married husband, Josiah, but something must have gone wrong because by the time of the 1881 census she was living with her brother William in Chapel Street, Braunton. Whatever happened to Josiah, which is unclear, it appears that Agnes lived mostly as a widow would.

A sense of long tradition remains woven amongst the hedges around Georgeham. South Hole was well-named, tucked into a hollow between deeply folding hills, with tinkling streams and clattering magpies. A renovation was underway at the farmhouse: an extensive ornamental lawn and pond being laid at the front, ancient barns being converted at the back. I imagined the forthcoming adverts for luxury holiday accommodation. It made me sad to see an original set of Devon agricultural buildings and a workable field gentrified in this way. What would Agnes have thought?

When I arrived at the Hartnoll's farm down on the flat land bordering the estuary, a young man was manoeuvring a tractor in the yard, the same Will – David's son – I'd met on my first visit, now working here full time. Then, pottering in the farmhouse garden, and wheezing, I found his grandfather John.

He was charming and affable, still maintaining his role as Marsh Inspector, but he seemed deafer and less sure of himself as he led me into the large kitchen-diner decorated with his late wife's paintings. I felt a little sad thinking of his confident joviality at our first meeting four years earlier. Soon afterwards we were joined by David for tea.

My purpose was unclear and I wondered at my claim on these people's time. Although our connection was extraordinary to me – our Hartnoll lineage through Granny's mother; the shared ownership of vessels – it was all quite tenuous and too thicketed to easily explain. I've always wished to feel a sense of belonging somewhere, but compared to their long continuity, the threads fastening me here were frail. The Hartnolls had inherited the *actual* soil that still ingrained their hands. The sea's veins practically ran through their long-occupied land. Nevertheless, they shared news with me of the family, mostly still clustered in the West Country except for one of John's daughters, working in California.

After tea David took me out in his pickup truck. We first drove around a vast field of pumpkins which Will and his girlfriend had grown. Bulbous, orange and prolific, they were ready for Halloween when people would come from the local area to pick them at a special event. Such abundance reminded me how I'd once read that, 'A Bra'nton man has only got to plant a sixpence for it to come up a half crown!' It was also said that Braunton's coasting sailors 'takes their bikes to sea with 'em.' When windbound in Ilfracombe or Appledore, rather than passing time by knotting sennit mats from recycled rope, a sailor with a bicycle on board could cycle home to work his garden or plot on the Great Field.

The field John Drake owned a little further towards the estuary in 'the Marshes' is accessed by Gallowell Road – one of the long, straight, Dutch-engineered private tracks with a ditch either side. The previous week his ashes had been scattered here. The cows hooted at us when we arrived but continued grazing the tufty mixed grass encouraged by an Environmental Stewardship Scheme.

The field is known as Pyke's Big.

'It's not that it's big,' David said, 'but to differentiate it from Pyke's Small.

David pointed out to me that the farming system in Braunton has remained largely medieval in that one farm might have a bit of land on the hill at Georgeham, another on the Marshes or Great Field, so that their working land was owned or leased in a great number of small parcels with varied qualities and uses.

From John Drake's field we drove out onto the road again, at a point close to the Great Sluice. It takes the form of three tunnels under the road. A gate controls the meshing of tidal water from the pill on one side and on the other the freshwater that flows through the Marshes. In a film at the museum I'd seen some vast, antique-looking, wooden doors here that would shut towards high tide simply with the pressure of incoming seawater. These days this essential gateway between the worlds of fresh and salt is governed by a substantial metal sluice gate.

It was 5pm by this time and not long before the peak of high tide. As it was a spring tide, it would be especially high. A wide channel of churning water was now rushing towards the White House along the inland edge of Horsey Island, delineating the former boundary of the drained marshes. This was the original river route and it was obvious that it would soon leave a much smaller island. There had apparently been anger locally when the wall was breached. This might be taken for exaggerated self-belief, a foolish human challenge to the sea in a place of monstrous tides and a time of universal sea-level rise. But they also blamed human negligence and poor maintenance. Both David and John assured me that they'd be looking after their own banks around the Marshes for as long as possible.

As David needed to drive up to Georgeham to look at one of their crops in a field there, he offered to drop me off in the village on the way. A sense of loss and uncertainty I'd been carrying around with me now felt balanced with hopefulness.

'See you next time,' I said, as I got out. And I meant it.

I felt determined to remain connected to these kind and welcoming people and their country to which I carried some allegiance in my genes as well as through my interest. By coming here as a related stranger perhaps I'd fastened myself back to the chain of generations latterly scattered by fractured relationships and geographies.

The journey I'd made this time between the 'homelands' of my mother 'Jill' (or Jenny) and her mother, Dorothy, had spliced together their special places: where Dorothy began her life and where my mother lived out hers. Tracing their geographies felt like a memorial to them and the chain of women before them who I'd begun to know – Annie, Agnes, Emma Louise. My curiosity had 'commissioned' this exploration in person and through words, writing to seek pattern, connection and meaning. It began as a quest for maritime legacy but had taken me well beyond. I'd found several new sea-rooms in my own mythology.

Despite their estrangement, my mother and her mother shared the same salt saturation of water in their wombs, in their blood, and rolling along their coasts. Each bore, and passed on, a legacy from seafaring days. They withstood absences, lost fathers and husbands. I could now envisage them closer in death than they had been in life, returning into each other's ambit in mutual regard for the sea, the south-western coasts, the family ships and their offspring.

As I walked the lanes and fields and the well-worn treads of my boots shed Cornish sand onto Braunton earth, I was laying a family palimpsest.

From Keel to Keel

It seemed I had learnt relatively little that was personal to the men of my Drake family – mostly it was dates and places and ships. But perhaps I understood more about their 'type'. I felt sure they would share the gentle manner of the Hartnolls and the older men in Braunton's Black Horse Inn who I'd witnessed ribbing each other. And they would have been notable for their pulses of absence and return.

Thinking of these past seafarers as glorified HGV drivers had clarified them. Yet I still fancied that their special relationship with their ship and the sea might set them at a slant from home, family and community. Is it wishful thinking to imagine that they experienced a sense of wonder at the world when they were at sea, would hear in a storm the 'wild and exalting voice of the world's soul' as well as the 'invisible orchestra' of the ship itself, as Joseph Conrad did?

Conrad saw mariners, men of many different temperaments, as practising a true art and not just earning a living, even though they might lack imagination and be taciturn and tough. Being at sea was 'an outlet for the peculiarities of their temperament', and the sea itself the 'accomplice of human restlessness'. To Conrad the ship was a live creature, demanding respect and tenderness.

Some of my notions were deflated when I met again with Michael Guegan, Chairman of the Appledore Maritime Museum and ex-shipyard foreman. When I suggested that, considering our current circumstances on Earth, it was a shame we had ditched the use of sail in such a wholesale way, he shook his head and said: 'Don't think it was romantic. Don't think it was nice.'

He told me that his grandfather had worked the Newfoundland trade and when his own son, Michael's father, spoke of joining the Navy, he told him not to.

'It's a dog's life,' his grandfather had said.

Michael agreed: 'It was hard work, it was dangerous, and you lived like pigs even on the steamships. It was only in the '70s and '80s when conditions started getting better.'

He did admit that a sailing ship was one of the best things that man has ever produced for a utilitarian purpose, and the best *looking*. 'But,' he added, 'it wasn't easy, wasn't romantic. I'd love to see them back but not with me on 'em!'

He recalled a miner standing up to challenge a group of folk singers lamenting coal pit closures: 'Do any of you want your sons to go down the mines? I bloody well don't.'

The end of the coastal sailing trade was often referred to with such romanticism, he thought, despite it being a trade in which up to 70% of the ships were wrecked and at least 25% of sailors drowned in the course of their work.

He was also sceptical about future sail-powered cargo shipping.

'Let's wait and see,' he said. 'Let's wait and see.'

If you scan the list of wrecks around the most north-westerly headland in Devon, it's clear that Morte Point lives up to its name, and also makes plain the sheer scale of past traffic on these seas. An RNLI station was built at Morte Bay in 1871 but was not an easy place from which to launch.

When Kate and I approached this part of the coast path from the east in the midst of Storm Ophelia in 2017, we had to abort before Morte Point after Kate was blown from her feet. We took refuge in the village post office in Mortehoe so we didn't see the lighthouse built in 1974 after cliffs collapsed under the original of 1879. A mortuary had been lobbied for and built in the village because of the frequent deliverance there of the dead from the sea.

Following my return visit to the Hartnolls, I took a bus to Woolacombe to walk around Morte Point from the south. There was a strong north-easterly which made conditions somewhat similar to that last attempt. But walking towards Morte Point with the lashing sea on my left rather than the right and the wind behind was a good call. I passed Grunta Bay, so-called because of the wreck of a shipload of live pigs, some of whom lived on happily for a while there, eating seaweed.

Fearsome wreckers had practised from here, deliberately luring or hastening shipwrecks in order to plunder cargo – legally so, once all lives had been lost. The wreckers included a notorious woman, Elizabeth Berry (and I ponder her surname and any relationship to the Holly Berry who'd been a co-owner of *Pirate*). She was said to assist the death of survivors with a pitchfork. She plundered the *William and Jane* in 1850 and served twenty-one days of hard labour when caught struggling home with her gains.

Volunteer 'Coast-watchers' also operated here, including a John Dyer (1852-1941) who responded to a sneering dismissal by a member of the gentry who called them 'farm labourers', implying an inferior class. Dyer wrote of the rockets fired to warn off ships, the men 'nimble as rabbits' on their local cliffs. 'Even farm labourers,' he wrote, 'have the souls of men and the heroism of Britishness', and 'know every rock and creek between Baggy and the Bull on a dark winter's night.' Later the coast-watchers were awarded medals.

A rainbow arced ahead of me, framing a stretch of horizon and the Point. I reached it easily and, unstable in the gusts and deafened by wind, I squatted on a jagged spear of elevated slate, with squally seas lashing below me on both sides. Half a mile out from where I sat, a black rock rose from wide, white skirts. I knew it was infamous for wreckings, a fixed point amidst treacherous currents: the Morte Stone.

I looked west, out over it, and was surprised to see a ship out there. The Marine Traffic app showed it as an Armenian vessel, 'Aastun', heading from Fowey on Cornwall's south coast towards Avonmouth. The white crane tower stood high at the stern, appearing separated by sea from its bow. The ship was travelling at 7.5 knots against the tide which was nearly at its lowest around now at 12.20pm Another ship in its wake was French, on a course from Dunkirk to Swansea and already four hours later than its ETA. This one was carrying a 'general cargo'. Both these ships must have circuited Land's End via the English Channel earlier that morning and it was strange to see how still and stable they looked from this distance against the heaving sea immediately below me.

When I scaled up the Marine Traffic map on my phone, it revealed a dense shoal of ships coursing in both directions through the English Channel. Some veered south-west around Brittany, others heading toward the Atlantic coast of Spain and into the bottleneck at Gibraltar. It was busy out there, despite the rough weather and the apparent emptiness of the sea seen from my slatey seat.

Morte Point, together with Bull Point further east along the peninsula, marks a decisive turning point, a right angle in the land. After this the Bristol Channel begins to close its gates and narrows eastwards towards Avonmouth where Aastun was heading. As I walked between the two points, the vertical cliffs of slate sang and glittered in the day's damp-filtered sunlight. There was an exhilarating sense of open sea here in contrast to the way that everything within the Bideford Bar feels enclosed by land, despite its other dangers.

In January 1910, *Bessie Ellen* hit the Morte Stone, sustaining serious damage to her keel. After limping to Ilfracombe for temporary repairs she was then towed to Appledore for more permanent ones. But she continued to leak afterwards and had to be further restored at Appledore some years later. Michael Guegan spoke of the endless maintenance involved in wooden ships, and how in commercial times, as they worked all year around, this could only be done as and when possible.

These days, *Bessie Ellen* has the winters off. As I watched this turbulent place that had threatened her over a century before, she was undergoing a major refit on the Truro river at the Rhoda Mary Shipyard, established to promote traditional boat building skills in Cornwall. I'd watched on video the main mast being hoisted up by crane from the depths of the hull. A new one was being fashioned from a Douglas fir tree procured from Gunnislake, near Plymouth. These are tall trees producing timber which can withstand high loads, and grow to a great age (and are not fir at all). The Latin name, *Pseudotsuga menziesii*, pays homage to Archibald Menzies, an adventurer from my hometown of Aberfeldy who brought Douglas fir to Scotland in 1791. He spent many years at sea serving both in the Royal Navy and for private merchants, and also introduced the monkey puzzle tree to Britain. It's presumably because of this link that there are a number of Douglas firs close to my home. One of them was among the tallest trees in Britain at over sixty-one metres until felled by a storm in January 2017.

Video footage showed *Bessie Ellen*'s old and new masts laid along the quay on trestles. The new mainsail boom lay alongside them, made of white cedar which Nikki described as smelling like Turkish Delight, and there were other spars – booms and gaffs – which were being rubbed down and revarnished. Whilst the old mast showed worrying cracks and rot caused by compression from the rigging, the orange wood of the new one, slightly wider in diameter, revealed in profile the original rings of the tree's life spanning concentrically out. A picture of natural health at over a century in age.

The scale of repairs shocked me; the ship looked naked without a main mast, almost as if it was being returned to a 'hulk' at the end of a sailing career. A tent was rigged up over the wheel box that was being taken right back to the deck in places due to small areas of rot. Five or six people seemed to be immediately involved in the renovation plus other shipyard people in the background. With this scale of intrusive repair to the ship, it struck me once again what a leap of faith must be taken, in addition to financial investment and the harvest of fresh trees from the forest, to keep such a ship sailing.

At home on Loch Tay, despite autumn saturation both of colour and moisture, we scheduled rowing with our oars of Douglas fir twice a week. We began to gain confidence. Coxes became evident, Angus in particular, who in his own gentle way seemed to have a spark in his eye for speed, and got us doing racing turns in which rowers on one side dig their oars into the peat-dark water to brake, whilst the other side rows on, revolving the boat, helped by Angus on the tiller.

Some days were squally and we learnt to launch more smartly to avoid being blown onto the jetty alongside our small beach. When we encountered choppiness out in the centre, the oars sometimes sliced unexpectedly through air or stalled, catching a peak of water, but we felt confidence in the vessel. St Ayle's skiffs, designed for northern waters, have been tested extensively for capsize, which has proved hard to provoke.

A day came in late November of low temperatures; short, bright daylight; some scuttering north-westerlies that funnelled down the southern edge of the Loch towards small, white Kenmore church, harboured in a copse of dark pines. We were still getting to know these waters. How the topography of high hills and low-lying water might bend winds. How waves could be ruffled up by gusts, and mysterious currents in the abyss beneath might move us as if the moon was working with it in some freshwater version of tides. Ten of us gathered, and extra excitement came in the form of Susan Nicholson, who was making a short piece about the first *inland* rowing club for the news on STV.

Soon we were prepared. A crew and cox were in the boat and Susan stowed in the bow with her camera equipment. Under Angus's command we were back-rowing away from the beach and into deeper water. Then we turned the boat, and set off with rowers travelling backwards, cox facing down the Loch. From a static boat, the first strokes are heavy with inertia, but soon there was a growing ease as we picked up rhythm and pace; we were slipping across water that stretched between dark hills, sky vaulting over us.

In several layers of clothing, hat and gloves, I was soon warm with effort as we coursed along on a synchronised stroke. Far from any shore surprisingly soon, beyond the tawny-treed 'Spry Island', we paused, turned the bow back towards Kenmore as we rowers, always facing the stern, now looked west towards the bend in the Loch at Fearnan. It is above here that the grandest local hills loom.

A catch in my breath.

'Look at Ben Lawers!' I couldn't help calling out.

The highest peak in Perthshire rose to our north into wintry muscularity. Cloud hung over its head, snow caped it down to about 2500 feet, highlighting the scoop of its steep, carved corrie. The sky was blue, the sun shone and the landscape I had known intimately for so many years rearranged itself around this expanse of deep water which takes one year to travel between the end of one river and the beginning of another.

To be out on the water, making effort, moving forward in breathy union with others in a humble wooden craft that we had built ourselves, felt exhilaratingly like joy.

'Row,' Angus called.

Pause.

'Row.'

Pause.

'Row.'

We concentrated again on our coordinated lean forward, then back, the pull of blade through water and the recovery, the sense of air rushing against our faces as we balanced miraculously on a skin of light.

Susan Nicholson interviewed some of us afterwards, giddy with it all even before we'd begun to join in with regattas, races, longer social rows with other clubs along the length of the Tay estuary from Perth. We were growing a cheery membership as people came forward a little nervously to 'have a go' and went away excited.

Angus, jacketed up, hatted, bearded, couldn't help commenting on the good looks of the skiff.

'It's quite a nicely built boat, I have to say.' Realising as he said it both his understatement and a trace of immodesty, he and the presenter broke into laughter. 'Even if I do say it myself.'

We all seemed to agree that quite apart from the satisfaction of the boat itself, and the being outdoors and physical effort, what we appreciated above all was the teamwork, the friendship and camaraderie.

I felt so in love with what we had created that it occurred to me that the three ships I had focused on in my family exploration had now become four: *Bessie Ellen*, *Pirate*, *Emma Louise* and now the *Red-haired Lass* (*Nighean Ruadh*). My heart felt full of all of them. The dichotomies that pull at me – of safety and danger, land and sea, home and away – felt in some way appeased.

I've enjoyed thinking of our own lines across Loch Tay as re-scoring the routes of past rowing boats; small ferries which cut miles off land journeys, delivering materials to Lochside villages, carrying cattle to connect a drove road from northern to southern shores and so to the markets of Crieff or Falkirk.

Rachel Carson alerted me to much earlier rowers. In Mezosoic times, some reptiles, despite fifty million years of life on land, once again became sea creatures in a sort of evolutionary return. Huge and formidable, some of these had oar-like limbs and 'rowed' through the water. Carson's was a properly ancient vision. Of these new sea creatures she said, some had serpentine necks and webbed feet. Although humans were still a long way off then in evolutionary terms, I can't help wondering whether the idea of the Loch Ness monster is some ghosted memory of such creatures.

Discussion of the human impact on planetary health and the climate crisis rumbles on as indigenous groups continue to challenge political intransigence on the issue. These are people whose lives are most directly and imminently threatened. Emigration from the Marshall Islands, one of the countries considered most at risk of disappearing due to sea-level rise, is already underway. It's not surprising that we begin to imagine the Earth continuing without us, and other forms of life emerging or renewing.

Poet Kathleen Jamie has been tugging at our sleeves over the last ten years, showing us the importance of simply paying attention as a first step towards political resistance: 'A "serious noticing" of the natural world might … save it from slow death … the noticing itself, prior to any transformation into art, can be a political act we are all capable of.' The Dalai Lama tells us that joy is an act of resistance, too. And I think again of the beauty of Maxwell Davies' 'Farewell to Stromness', capturing the poignant, ultimately triumphant struggle of the small against the giant.

If attention, creating joy, laughter and fostering connection can be acts of resistance, how articulate is the building (or repair) of a wooden vessel, a shared conveyance demanding mutual human effort: a thing of beauty, a tool, a symbol of hope.

In spring 2022 I pursued the Pirate Gow story to the northern Orkney Isle of Eday, arriving by ferry as a foot passenger.

I wanted to map out the geography of a story with my body and senses. Surrounded by curlews, eiders gurgling, shrieking Arctic terns, I seemed to be the only human visitor. Very few cars passed me on the road but the few people I met as I walked the length of the island from the ferry towards the hamlet of Calfsound were all keen to chat.

I came to a tiny airstrip, 'London Airport', and then left the road and marvelled past a number of Neolithic stones and chambered cairns as human habitation thinned further towards the north of the island. A path followed the spine of a hill to the high headland that urges northwards, Red Head, punctuated dramatically with an OS trig point.

Below to the right lay the whole map of Pirate Gow's demise. The sweep of the Sound passed the tall, pale Carrick House and its tamed grounds, then turned north, between me and the rise of the 'Calf' opposite. It was easy to imagine how a combination of dramatic tides and lack of local knowledge could betray even a highly experienced seafarer. I wasn't just lacing together geography now, but legend and history and centuries; an impulse generated by scratches of ink on a Shipping Register page relating to the Drake ship *Pirate*.

The long, fine, May evening was windy and suffused with luminosity. Although the view from here was wide, there was no further sign of human activity. Initially I was euphoric, self-contained on my look-out with oatcakes and tea. To the west lenticular islands lay as low, grey silhouettes, misty and featureless in the sheet-metal brilliance that surrounded them. Westray was somewhere in that mesh, where we had sailed on *Bessie Ellen* after leaving Stromness.

But then a sudden feeling – something like vertigo – dizzied me. The sea stretched away to the north into haze.

From Keel to Keel

Separated from humanity, I was alienated from my known places on this elevated edge of sheer red rock. It was as if I had floated so far from the coast of mainland Scotland on this fragmented land that I might never find my way back.

My own discomfort surprised me. An apocalyptic sense that I had drifted in open water, alone, on a small piece of floating land at the fifty-ninth degree, bringing me parallel to Nunavut and Alaska, Labrador and Newfoundland. With no land between me and the North Pole, I felt exposed to an overly watery world.

On a visit to the Royal Maritime Museum in Greenwich, I'd stopped for coffee within an airy atrium. A 'Great Map' of the world covered the courtyard floor. Sweeping archipelagos and continents were delicately marked; clusters parting for the breadth of Pacific and Atlantic. What struck me about this inviting space, and perhaps the point of it, is the dominance of the colour blue. I wouldn't be the first to question the accuracy of the name 'Earth' for our planet.

A class of six-year-olds arrived with lunch boxes. I don't know what instruction was given but I watched as the space giddied them into running, sliding, lying on their stomachs as if to swim, whooping into the echoing heavens. But when they settled with their lunch, each of them chose to sit or lie on a piece of marked land, often not risking the tiny islands such as Great Britain.

From Red Head's trig point marking a 70m contour on the map, I now threw an imaginary line 273 miles back home to the summit of Schiehallion where contours were invented, and from there a further 632 miles to Newlyn harbour and my mother's home, officially at zero metres. Mooring myself back to these places soon soothed the alienation.

Orkney is at the southern boundary of an idea of north. Sub-polar yearnings within our southern bodies are perhaps as biological and magnetic as they are for migrating geese. On the *Bessie Ellen* trip, it was as if crew and ship collectively slipped onto some former Sea Road, a different geography which promised adventure and smelt of ice. The two phalaropes, which my fellow sailor Annette and I had seen sailing close to Westray, long-necked and mysterious, marked the edge of this new territory. Seasonally long light in the north impelled us, and perhaps our helmsman. For a while, when we should have turned south-west back towards Cape Wrath, he had been misreading the compass and had added 100°, thus heading us towards Iceland.

As I sat alone and high on that headland, my mother took shape beside me. In her active days she would have embraced this elemental adventure, this staying out into a long evening while the weather is good, not rushing home for the press of mealtime convention. And she might have brought a Ginger Cake with her and spoken of one of the female explorers who she liked to read: Isabella Bird or Christiane Ritter living out in those exposed Arctic plains. It was a strange collision of joy, fear and melancholy that filled me on Red Head. Despite its discomfort I was glad that the place prompted hefty feeling.

My mother stayed with me as I walked south. Then I travelled back alone through the smaller islands to the Orkney mainland. With a bit of distance since her death, regret and even shame had risen. Against her perceived lack of interest in me, her failure to nurture a personal memory of my father, I'd recalled more positive aspects of her mothering. There was my regularly-met plea at childhood bedtimes for her to 'come and tuck me in'. I remembered examples of her kindness in my teenage years – her offer to make Spaghetti Bolognese for a group of my friends on my eighteenth birthday, and how she walked from the house to meet me one afternoon as I returned from school in my sixth-year, eager to tell me that I had won the local arts prize. Much later, she shared my celebration at the ceremony in 1998 at which we learned I had won the *Macallan / Scotland on Sunday* short story competition, which launched my writing career. I couldn't really claim she was disinterested.

Perhaps I had simply been too prickly. A vessel battered by its own waves.

I hope that this journey of discovery I've been taking since 2016, with or for my mother, will mean stories pass on into the future. The new generation, my nieces and nephew, are out in the world and taking paths that pick up some of the byways of their forebears: creativity, justice, travel and communication, each of them reflecting back to me something recognisable. They fill me with hope and pride.

Looking back through photos of the skiff-building process, I was struck by the apparent simplicity, even slightness, of the most fundamental part. The keel lay on the floor of the workshop, nothing but a straight line of 2¾ x 2-inch larch on solid earth, clamped into a statement of intent by Angus and Adam on February 26th 2019.

The essential skeleton of larger vessels was created in the same way by fixing arcing timbers from the keel and topping the line of the keel with the wider, bulkier 'keelson'. Then came the planks of the hull, the deck and so on. Such a ship is gradually dismantled, in the reverse sequence, by human abandonment and the elements. In sheltered places on the coastal margins of Britain, such weed-wrapped, seed-shaped carcasses still lie. Trees harvested from the earth now returning to it. These are the informal monuments to a heritage we will soon lose completely. They'll continue to rot, collapse, until just the keel remains: a bald statement mirroring that initial expression of hope. Perhaps such relics are already meaningless to people younger than I am.

Basil Greenhill notes that in West Country places like the Taw-Torridge estuary, such rotting carcasses are often from ships abandoned between the wars. He describes the relics of the working ship spreading across the mud in a display of 'broken lamps and dead-eyes, belaying pins, pots, pans, shattered plates, and with it the indications of the lives on board ... Then at last the mud entered it and, with its growing weight, achieving slowly what the violence of the sea had never achieved'. Greenhill articulates a heartbreak as the deck beams ruptured, the curved frames split, and the fore and aft of the vessel cracked apart.

Keel to keel.

Ashes to ashes.

The Mother Ship I had built remained in dry dock in my sitting room, unlikely to go anywhere. But something else still remained to be released and it needed more than one generation to make it feel like a succession rather than an ending.

For the funeral, we'd hoped to send my mother off in a white wool cocoon felted and embroidered by my old friend Yuli Somme from Devon. But the undertaker had reservations, so we'd chosen instead a simple pine coffin and decorated it with a felted throw which Yuli embroidered with my mother's favourite wild flowers, in particular the lilac shoots of squill that pierce Cornish cliff-top turf in springtime. This thing of brightness and light did not go into the fire with her, but was retained as a family heirloom.

I was aware that her ashes would be as much made up of the wooden vessel in which she departed as from her own dust, when we gathered with them nearly two years after her death. My sister and I, our partners, our brother and two of his (adult) children left cars at Pendeen Watch. Bold, white and monumental, we all loved this lighthouse as a far-western landmark in our mother's memory, a place from where she gazed at the waves below and out to the horizon.

Together with bottles of Cava and the heavy black carton of ashes, we carried the sandwiches and cake Robin had carefully made for us north along the coast path on a blustery but brightening day of blackberry-heavy hedges. We scrambled down craggy slopes to Portheras Bay where coarse granite slabs sang red against the sand and the sea crashed white and navy. Erratic rocks strewn across the bay make it less obvious as a swimming beach and there were only one or two other groups of picnickers there.

Since my turbulent 'swim', I'd been back to Porthcurno to make my peace with the place and the sea, slinking through a delicious blue calm on a hot summer's day, the beach crowded and watched by lifeguards. But here I had no thought of swimming.

Skies cleared. We played on rocks, dug diversions for the descending freshwater stream, ate the sandwiches, caught up with each other's news.

Then a ceremony began, without any spoken plan or choreography, as is characteristic of my family. In increasing sunshine at the time of lowest tide, we carried the carton sea-wards to the bare, wet sand. Taking turns, we shook out the contents at the meeting point of land and sea, just inland of the frill of surf. An orchestra of gulls played.

The incoming tide soon carried her off and we spontaneously gathered into a wet-faced group hug, standing in a small arc to face the horizon, acknowledging our inheritance – the ocean.

A further part of the jigsaw called me 120 miles 'up country' along this south-western peninsula. Finally, my discussions with Michael Guegan in Appledore had a clear focus in the form of assembled paperwork from him and a little more informed questioning from me. Despite his great practicality and my greater romanticism about this history, he was willing to meet me even on a day when the Museum would normally be closed.

The story of *Emma Louise* started with a very brief handwritten 'plan' on a small piece of paper. The intention for the build by William Westacott included: 'frame, beams, keelson, from upper strakes outside and covering braid to be of English oak. Keel and flat of bottom outside, English elm. Remainder of plank pitch pine'. The 'outside' refers to the outer hull of a double-hulled vessel. It was illustrated on this scrap of paper by a midship cross-section drawing, showing the differentiation of elm and oak parts. The copperplate writing is framed prettily by these double layers of hull. This briefest of documents was signed off on December 27th 1882, after which work presumably began.

Thus a handsome ship came to sail off, trusted for many years, taking the name of a poetry-loving woman who had been born into, and married into, the seafaring life. Emma's husband Francis and their sons owned the ship *Pirate* as well as many others, and her brother's son, John, became owner and master of *Bessie Ellen*, still sailing as I write.

Michael also brought along a pile of black-and-white photographs which illustrated periods of the ship's life journey. In 1935 she lay against Minehead quay, presumably delivering coal close to where she's commemorated through a painting in the tiny quayside church. She looks workish, robust, sitting out the low tide. A photo of her at a yard in 1952 shows her deck crowded with a small rowing boat, bundled sails, and with a housing of some sort now behind the mizzen mast.

After Peter Herbert of Appledore acquired *Emma Louise* in 1953, she became redundant. A further photograph shows her as a de-masted hulk. Stripped to her deck, her name remains visible on the bow, the bow sprit and union flag fiddlehead still in place. In the next she's abandoned on a slope of mud, apparently resting on her old elm keel with a slight list to port where the tidal current has pushed her. Whilst her hull remains sturdy-looking, the ghost-ribs of other hulls arc upward from keels lying beneath her. It appears to be a place of palimpsest, layered with the partially decayed carcasses of past ships. She'd now been 'broken up' and dismissed to her graveyard.

Although she's been 'up Snuffy' since 1954, Michael told me he could take me there to see what remained. I pictured a thin line of darkened keel.

We walked out of the village up-river towards Bideford, passing the shipyard where Michael had worked, still operating in some small way. I felt we were accomplices now, approaching historical evidence in which we were both invested. I was incredibly grateful for his memory store of detailed facts, which this time I felt able to fully engage with.

We joined the coastal path with the high concrete arc of the Bideford bypass in occasional sight when the oak woods parted to give a view east. The path undulated above the shore. Then on the descent to a particular inlet, Michael said, 'this is it'. After slipping across rock and weed, we turned around a small headland, mud sucking and squelching under our feet. Michael walked cautiously. He had put on his old coat in case he fell.

As we rounded the rocks, a small bay opened out under a cliff where the mud was scattered with a shingly layer of stones and patches of seaweed. The graveyard now became apparent. Although there was no looming hull as shown in the photograph, the skeletal shapes of four timber ships were marked out like plans in darkened, gnarled timber, some submerged in seaweed, others bare, revealing pointing timbers and beams. There was something dinosauric in the texture and jagged, bone-like structures that remained. And what they revealed in their decay was the first essentials of structure and architecture of the ships: keel, keelson, arcing ribs.

Michael pointed to a bare, timber skeleton: 'Somebody's life savings went into that. But at least they had their money's worth.'

He had until now found *Emma Louise* easily by the huge engine casing lying nearby. It was no longer there.

'Someone must have had it,' he said.

He told me the names and history of each of the hulks. The largest was the *M A James*, closest to the water and looking like she would soon be received by it. She'd traded to Newfoundland and back with the cod trade and was used for barrage balloon service during World War II. One of her ribs rose up further than the others, indicating the original curve of the great hull, now raising one finger to the new world who no longer wished to work with wood. The *Hobah,* mostly buried under mud and nudging up against our *Emma Louise*, traded until 1939–40 when her engine 'packed up'. *Bessie Clarke* traded until 1942 and then was part of the degaussing experiments of World War II, which eliminated the magnetic field from ships' hulls to make them undetectable by mines. I liked the way that Michael referred to the ships, as he pointed them out, as 'he' or ''e', in the Devon way: 'that one' or 'this one'. He still referred to the ships beyond our current view as 'she'.

There was nothing frail about these remnant beams and timbers; they suggested heft and strength. I touched the gnarled wood of *Emma Louise*, eroded by so many tides. Porous to history, scarred yet beautiful as an aged face in which wrinkles have deepened, revealing character. The wood was warm to the touch and friable like bone that no longer holds marrow, lightly bearded by lichen on its sheltered side. It was as if her timbers were reverting to the bark-covered trees from which they came. Still firmly embedded in some of these timbers were a few two-finger-wide bolts of galvanised iron to which the planking of the hull had once been fixed. Underneath, the slippery mud would be preserving anaerobically the lowest point of the ship: the keel.

We noted that the restless tide was still ebbing on the immediate shore, moving gently out towards the Bar. And yet in the centre of the estuary, Michael pointed out, the water had now turned and was moving powerfully up-river. He spoke about all the people who had got into rescue situations recently, oblivious to the dangers of standing far out on a sandbank, even with small children, with the tide coming in. The lifeboat had been well used that summer.

The place seemed to hold old and new, the ancient tide, and in the background the traffic noise and visual sweep of the concrete flyover. Weed-draped timbers were the survivors around our feet. On the opposite shore, four tugboats had been jauntily run up on marsh and mud to become homes for people in a place where there is little low-cost housing. Meanwhile the wildlife carried on its rhythms, swirls marking fish in the water, a buzzard mewing overhead, a gurgle of curlew. The constants.

Some invisible geometry of time and place correlated with this transformation at 'Snuffy' where timber skeletons revert to keels, back to carbon, back to mud. On another estuary 80 miles away on the opposite coast, *Bessie Ellen* was being re-caulked, and that new, mighty mast fitted. One vessel decays whilst a sister-ship is revived: an audacious act of hope with her newly-varnished blocks and dead-eyes, serviced shrouds and sails enabling another generation to learn of this lost way of life. A duty perhaps to a vessel that is more than inert, that is a creature of sorts; that is loved.

'If you hear me screaming, you'll know I've fallen over'.

Michael prepared to walk back to Appledore but I wanted to sit there a while longer, eat my sandwich and contemplate as fingers of water edged further up the shore.

'Us won't get cut off here,' Michael had said.

I continued to sit amidst mud-tang whilst the tide measured out my remaining stay. Alone in this conclusive place, the sediments of learning from my last years' exploration were layering like estuary mud. Our generational strata were captured too in seams of love, loss and endurance. I had sketched out a family tree, a geography, and found that our unambiguous relationship with the sea and ships still gripped us. Unearthing these previously-hidden things located me more securely in a generational pattern.

With distance I understand my mother as a child always longing, like myself, to retrieve her lost-so-young father. And then as a widow in pain without clear means of expression despite her creative urges. She produced children and gained grandchildren, took on responsibilities, wrote poems at a slant from buried emotion and painted the colours of West Cornwall's coast. I have produced words and books; taken adventures. Together we contribute to a legacy.

From the vantage point of my seventh decade I now recognised my own expertise at creating emotional or geographical oceans, distancing myself from my mother and from successive partners. A means of shoring myself up against further heartbreak, as if I was rehearsing again the absence of seafarers to their wives or the loss of my father so young. It struck me that I now faced a special challenge. A kind of bravery would be called for to close the distance in my current relationship.

I looked to Emma Louise, the woman four generations before me, and her namesake ship whose bones I sat alongside – dry but soon to be submerged again. Woman and ship had parallel longevity. I sensed an heirloom of kindness and nurture from both.

Across the water was the village of Instow, and perched in the hills above I could see the stately home of Tapeley Park. Peter Pay had told me that the parents of Francis Hacche-Drake, from whom we descend illegitimately, made social calls at all the country houses locally, including this one. Such landmarks now anchor me here. I have touchstones to return to: West Penwith, Exeter, the Taw-Torridge estuary.

Despite Michael's assurances, the tide turned me unsentimental with its scallop edges of foam edging up the shore. It might soon close the gateway through which I could return to the path. It meant there was no time to sit and sketch the shapely remains of my great-great-grandmother's namesake. But knowing now the location of her slippery graveyard meant I could return to chart the next stages of her journey.

Finally, I stood up and stepped between foam and rock, crossing fields of mud, famed for preserving memory. The door of the tide allowed me out.

Notes

1. Sea Summons

Page 5:   On the fortieth anniversary of the 'Penlee Disaster' (20/12/21) a drama-documentary *Solomon Browne* by Callum Mitchell was broadcast on BBC Radio 4 using authentic voices from the village and fragments of the radio communications of that night. It was a moving and beautifully realised piece of memorialisation concluding that the village died that night, but it also speaks powerfully of communities who work with the sea. More can be read of it here: www.telegraph.co.uk/radio/what-to-listen-to/mousehole-died-night-penlee-lifeboat-disaster-unfolded

Page 6:   Tom Bawcock's Eve, Mousehole. It's said that Tom Bawcock braved a storm on 23rd December after many days in which local fishermen couldn't get to sea. He caught enough fish to make a pie that fed the whole village.

Page 7:   Information about *Bessie Ellen* can be found on the website of the National Historic Ships Register and on her current voyaging website: bessie-ellen.com

Skipper-owner Nikki Alford's 'Ship's (B)log' on the latter site is a rich source of insight into the challenges and joys of running and maintaining such a ship today.

2. Getting My Bearings

Page 24: The word 'pill' is common within the shores of the Bristol Channel, meaning a tidal inlet. Cultural geographer Owain Jones (Bath Spa University) writes a very interesting blog *Tidal Cultures* which includes a glossary of such terms.

Page 27:   For coastal flooding projections, see coastal.climatecentral.org

Page 28: The schooner *Result* continued trading until 1967, after which her hull made its way back to her original home in Northern Ireland. There is currently a campaign to return this 'workhorse, warrior and film star' to the place of her building in Carrickfergus where she will become a historic attraction, education hub and event venue. www.carrickfergustallship.com.

Page 28:   Maritime historian Basil Greenhill was former Director of the National Maritime Museum, Greenwich. His comments on *Result* and other attributed references in later chapters are drawn from his book *The Merchant Schooners,* now out of print but most recently published by Conway Maritime (1988).

Page 32: Iain Oughtred died in March 2024 and was much fêted, including in a fine obituary available online in *Classic Boat* magazine.

Page 33:   More on Angus Ross's bespoke furniture can be found at website www.angusross.co.uk/

3. Crossing the Bar

Page 48:   Joseph Conrad's words about the pilot come from the first paragraphs of *Heart of Darkness.* The full quotation is: 'The Director of Companies was our captain and our host. We four affectionately watched his back as he stood in the bows looking to seaward. On the whole river there was nothing that looked half so nautical. He resembled a pilot, which to a seaman is trustworthiness personified.'

Page 56:   The full account of Terry Winsborough's trip aboard *Emma Louise* as a boy, 'Very First Trip', can be found on the website of the Southampton Master Mariners' Club: www.cachalots.org.uk/wp-content/uploads/2011/01/Very-First-trip.pdf

4. How to Throw a Line

Page 64:   Conflicting accounts of the ship Juba can be found at the *Discovering Bristol* website ('The Fortunes of Four Ships') and *Heritage Gateway* (Historic England Research Records).

Page 65:   In 2022 the Royal Albert Memorial Museum in Exeter put on an exhibition 'In Plain Sight: Transatlantic slavery and Devon'. The website provides some very useful resources for exploring this history.

Page 70:   The website of the Henry Williamson Society includes interesting background to *The Pathway* and Williamson's intentions for the novel.

5. The Cargo We Carry

Page 98:   Joseph Conrad wrote of men's love of their ship as 'nearly as great as that of man for woman'. This (and Conrad quotes in subsequent chapters) come from his 1906 memoir of seafaring on 19th century vessels, *The Mirror of The Sea, Memories and Impressions*, available as a free e-book from the Gutenburg project.

Page 100: The Scottish Coastal Rowing Association (scottishcoastalrowing.org/) acts as an umbrella organisation, facilitating events, sharing information, offering training, and guidance on building and registering new St Ayles skiffs.

6. An Inland Soul at Sea

Page 111: More on the evolution and advantage of gaff-rig sailing can be found in an article on the *Classic Sailing* website called "'Hold on the Peak, up on the Throat!" Let's explore the Gaff Rig.'

Page 118: The MarineTraffic app is a wonderful resource which displays near real-time positions of ships and yachts worldwide.

7. Holdfast Women

Page 136: The book referenced is *The Newlyn Tidal Observatory*, various contributors (Newlyn Archive, 2018), ISBN 978-0-9567528-4-0. It is sometimes possible to visit the observatory. Contact the Newlyn Archive.

Page 136: The story of Neville Maskelyne, fifth Astronomer Royal at Greenwich (1765 -1811), and his experiment to 'weigh the Earth' over two years on Schiehallion is fascinating. At the final celebration, whisky was taken, the ghillie produced a fiddle, and the bothy (and reputedly the fiddle) caught fire.

Page 142: For anyone interested in more about the St Ayles skiff including full building instructions, see www.staylesinternational.org/.

8. A Blaze in the Dark

Page 167: 'Song to the Siren' was written by Tim Buckley and Larry Beckett. First performed by Buckley in 1968, there have been numerous versions by other artists, most memorably for me by This

Mortal Coil in a debut single in 1983. The deep meaning of this song to many people was explored in an episode of the BBC Radio 4 programme *Soul Music* in December 2021 and remains available.

9. Ancestral Anchor Chains

Page 172: 'Celebrated Writers on the Culturally Controversial Choice Not to Have Children' by Maria Popova, is online at *The Marginalian*.

Page 175: *Stay With Me* by Nigerian writer Ayòbámi Adébàyò was published by Canongate in 2017.

Page 176: Details of Roman Krznaric's publications, resources on being a good ancestor and thinking in long-term ways are available at this site: www.romankrznaric.com/good-ancestor.

Page 186: Robert Louis Stevenson's essay 'The English Admirals' was collected in *Virginibus Puerisque and Other Essays in Belles Lettres*, (William Heinemann 1924).

Page 188: *HMS Weazle 1782-1799*, by Bob and Ann Brock, (North Devon Museum Trust 1998) is a fascinating collation of all that is known, and can be conjectured, about the causes and outcomes of the loss of this sloop off the North Devon coast.

Page 191: My essay about the barnacle-encrusted shores of the Rosneath peninsula, 'Lunar Cycling', was first published in anthology *Antlers of Water*, ed Kathleen Jamie, (Canongate 2020/2021) and later in my essay collection *Writing Landscape*, (Saraband 2023).

10. The Sea Road North

Two books helped inform this chapter. *Stromness: A History* by Bryce Wilson, (The Orcadian/Kirkwall Press, 2013) and *The History of Orkney Literature* by Simon W Hall, (Birlinn, 2010).

11. A Boat-shaped Future

Page 211: A tragic incident for the sail-cargo community saw the loss of Blue Schooner's 36.2m ship *De Gallant* (built 1916) on May 11th 2024. Bound for Europe from Colombia and loaded with coffee, cocoa, and cane sugar, they met sudden violent weather south of the Bahamas and sank with the loss of two crew.

Page 218: Rose George wrote about the *Evergiven* incident in the *Guardian* in both March and April 2021. Marwa Elselehdar's story was reported on the BBC News website on 4th April 2021.

Page 222: Poet Jon Plunkett is also the founder of the Corbenic Poetry Path close to Dunkeld in Perthshire, described as 'a magical and inspiring place where people, poetry and landscape meet' (Andy Jackson). www.corbenicpoetrypath.com.

12. Re-treading Motherlands

Page 225: The two quotes by Rachel Carson in this chapter are from *The Sea Around Us*, first published in 1951 and reissued by Canongate Books in 2021. She has been credited with advancing the global environmental movement and writes with poetic as well as scientific authority.

Page 226: Robert Louis Stevenson's poem 'Skerryvore' can be found in his *Underwoods* collection. There is a terrifying account of the building of this lighthouse in Bella Bathurst's *The Lighthouse Stevensons*.

Page 230: Michael Flanders (1922–1975) and Donald Swann (1923–1994) were British musicians who wrote and performed comic songs together.

Page 233: Margaret Atwood's short story 'Widows' appeared in the *Guardian* on 25th February 2023 and can still be accessed online.

13. From Keel to Keel

Page 250: Information about Mortehoe's coastwatchers and John Dyer, including his passionate letter in defence of the volunteers can be found at the website woolacombemortehoevoice.co.uk

Page 257: The Kathleen Jamie essay referred to, 'Lissen Every Thing Back', was published in Little Toller's online magazine, *The Clearing*, in 2019 and subsequently in their anthology of nature and place, *Going to Ground*, editor Jon Woolcott, 2024.

Acknowledgements

Over the years of my exploration, discovery process and writing, many people have been involved in reading drafts and/or offering information, research or experiences. It has taken a long time and I apologise to those I have forgotten to include.

Thanks go to Peter Pay for detailed family research on my behalf and a tour of the geography; Michael Guegan of the North Devon Maritime Museum, Appledore, for the sharpness of his memory and guidance on local seafaring history; David & John Hartnoll and family for their welcome to a related stranger. Peter Thorn and other members of the Bideford Kayak Club gave me a wonderful, spray-filled experience of the Taw-Torridge estuary; Nikki Alford and her crew provided priceless sailing experiences aboard the beautiful *Bessie Ellen*. My rowing colleagues both at home and across Scotland continue to inspire and be the best of outdoor friendship networks.

For offering information and for feedback on drafts, thanks to: Neil Trevithick, Richard Cockram, Bryce Wilson, Martine Robinson, Kate Whyman, Sue Bailey, Julia Masson, Mark Shiner. John Whitlock shared his time and historical knowledge as well as his book *Pilots and Pilotage on the Rivers Taw and Torridge*. The staff of record offices in both Kirkwall and Barnstaple were enthusiastic supporters of my archival searches.

I was fortunate to be awarded a Robert Louis Stevenson Fellowship which offered time at Hotel Chevillon, Grez sur Loing in 2019. The Society of Authors awarded me an

Acknowledgements

Authors' Foundation grant for work-in-progress in 2021 and the Creative Scotland Open Fund enabled writing time in October 2022. Each of these was invaluable to the long development of this project.

Thanks go to Stephanie Cross for a very useful manuscript appraisal at an earlier stage, and to Mark Smalley and Helen Mark of BBC Radio 4 *Open Country* for their interest in my research and for involving me in an episode which was broadcast on 23/12/2017.

A version of Chapter 3, 'Crossing the Bar', was first published in Issue 11 (Summer 2022) of *Hinterland* magazine, a place-writing special edition.

Through her book *The Lighthouse Stevensons* Bella Bathurst introduced me to the term 'sea-marked' which she applied to Robert Louis Stevenson, and I have adopted as the book's title (*The Lighthouse Stevensons*, HarperCollins Ltd, 1999).

The book which set off this entire exploration was *Braunton: Home of the Last Sailing Coasters* by Robert d'Arcy Andrew and other authors (Braunton & District Museum, 2007). The museum's staff and volunteers were also very helpful on my visits. I'm particularly grateful to Christine Skinner for permission to quote from the Corney family postcards held there (Chapter 5).

My editor at Saraband, Rosie Hilton, has been a joy to work with and a patient and creative midwife for the book. I'm also grateful for the support of my agent Jenny Brown, my siblings, and Robin for endless cups of tea, moral support and his tolerance of my absences.

Sea Marked

Over the course of the project, a number of other books were good companions. These included:

Tide by Hugh Aldersley-Williams (Penguin, 2016)

The Long Way by Bernard Moitessier (Granada, 1977)

Down to the Sea in Ships by Horatio Clare (Vintage, 2015)

The Levelling Sea (HarperPress, 2011) and *The Summer Isles* (Granta, 2019), both by Philip Marsden.

The Foghorn's Lament by Jennifer Lucy Allan (White Rabbit, 2021)

Dark, Salt, Clear by Lamorna Ash (Bloomsbury 2020)

The Frayed Atlantic Edge by David Gange (William Collins, 2019)

The Log from the Sea of Cortez by John Steinbeck (Viking Penguin, 1941)

Boatlines by Ian Stephen (Birlinn, 2023)

For permission to quote extracts, thanks to:

John Whitlock for *Pilots and Pilotage on the Rivers Taw and Torridge* (Edward Gaskell 2012).

Terry Clark, editor of *The Cachalot,* newsletter of the Southampton Master Mariners for Terry Winsborough's 'The Very First Trip'.

Maria Popova for her article in *The Marginalian*, 'Celebrated Writers on the Culturally Controversial Choice Not to Have Children', www.themarginalian.org/2015/05/11/selfish-shallow-and-self-absorbed-meghan-daum/

Kathleen Jamie and Little Toller for 'Lissen Every Thing Back'.

David Higham Associates Ltd for lines from Water Music by Elizabeth Jennings published in *The Collected Poems* (Carcanet, 2012).